**PENGUIN
VITAE**

WHAT CLASSIC BOOKS would you place together on a shelf to represent the course of your life? This is the question that sparks our hardcover series, Penguin Vitae, or, loosely translated, "Penguin of one's life." A diverse world of storytellers from the past speak to us at pivotal chapters of our lives and connect a community of readers across time and generations. Penguin Vitae invites readers to curate their own personal Penguin Classics canon from this series and to discover other seminal works of timeless inspiration, intellectual engagement and creative originality. To enrich the reader's experience of these gift editions, Paul Buckley designs bold typographic covers inspired by each work, with vibrant foil-stamping and colored endpapers, contributing to Penguin's acclaimed history of innovative book design.

We hope you find yourself within Penguin Vitae, discover something new, and share these classic books with others.

ELDA ROTOR
Publisher
Penguin Classics

When first published in 1930, *Not Without Laughter* established Langston Hughes as not only a brilliant poet and leading light of the Harlem Renaissance but also a gifted novelist. In telling the story of Sandy Rogers, a young African American boy in small-town Kansas, and of his family—his mother, Annjee, a housekeeper for a wealthy white family; his irresponsible father, Jimboy, who plays the guitar and travels the country in search of employment; his strong-willed grandmother Hager, who clings to her faith; his Aunt Tempy, who marries a rich man; and his Aunt Harriet, who struggles to make it as a blues singer—Hughes gives the longings and lineaments of Black life in the early twentieth century an important place in the history of racially divided America.

PENGUIN CLASSICS

NOT WITHOUT LAUGHTER

LANGSTON HUGHES (1902–1967), a central figure of the Harlem Renaissance and one of the most influential and esteemed writers of the twentieth century, was born in Joplin, Missouri, and spent much of his childhood in Kansas before moving to Harlem. His first book of poetry, *The Weary Blues,* was published in 1926; its success helped him to win a scholarship to Lincoln University, in Pennsylvania, from which he received his BA in 1929 and an honorary LittD in 1943. Among his other awards and honors were a Guggenheim Fellowship, a Rosenwald Fellowship, and a grant from the American Academy of Arts and Letters. Hughes published more than thirty-five books, including works of poetry, short stories, novels, an autobiography, musicals, essays, and plays.

ANGELA FLOURNOY was a finalist for the National Book Award for her debut novel, *The Turner House.* Her fiction has appeared in *The Paris Review*, and she has written nonfiction for many publications, including *The New York Times*, *The Nation*, and the *Los Angeles Times*. A graduate of the Iowa Writers' Workshop, Flournoy was raised in Southern California by a mother from Los Angeles and a father from Detroit.

LANGSTON HUGHES

NOT WITHOUT LAUGHTER

INTRODUCTION BY
Angela Flournoy

PENGUIN BOOKS

PENGUIN BOOKS

An imprint of Penguin Random House LLC
penguinrandomhouse.com

First published in the United States of America by Alfred A. Knopf, Inc., 1930
Previously published with an introduction by Angela Flournoy in Penguin Books 2018
This edition published in Penguin Books 2021

Introduction copyright © 2018 by Angela Flournoy
Penguin supports copyright. Copyright fuels creativity, encourages diverse voices,
promotes free speech, and creates a vibrant culture. Thank you for buying
an authorized edition of this book and for complying with copyright laws
by not reproducing, scanning, or distributing any part of it in any form
without permission. You are supporting writers and allowing
Penguin to continue to publish books for every reader.

ISBN 9780143134428 (hardcover)

THE LIBRARY OF CONGRESS HAS CATALOGED THE PAPERBACK EDITION AS FOLLOWS:
Names: Hughes, Langston, 1902–1967, author. | Flournoy, Angela, author.
Title: Not without laughter / Langston Hughes ; introduction by Angela Flournoy.
Description: New York, New York : Penguin Books, 2018. | "First published in
the United States of America by Alfred A. Knopf, Inc. 1930"—Title page verso.
Identifiers: LCCN 2017031692 | ISBN 9780143131861
Subjects: LCSH: City and town life—Fiction. | Kansas—Fiction. |
Domestic fiction. | Bildungsromans.
Classification: LCC PS3515.U274 N6 2018 | DDC 813/.52—dc23
LC record available at https://lccn.loc.gov/2017031692

Printed in the United States of America
1 3 5 7 9 10 8 6 4 2

Set in Sabon LT Std

To J. E. and Amy Spingarn

CONTENTS

INTRODUCTION

For a writer like Langston Hughes, who made a name for himself as a poet before the age of twenty-one, his debut novel, *Not Without Laughter*, feels like an effort to stake out a bigger claim on his abilities, to create artistic and thematic breathing room. Arna Bontemps, celebrated poet and friend to Hughes, described *Not Without Laughter* as the novel that both Hughes and his readers knew he had to write, coming as it did on the heels of Hughes's two well-received poetry collections, *The Weary Blues* (1926) and *Fine Clothes to the Jew* (1927). Hughes published these collections while a student at Lincoln University, and he released *Not Without Laughter* in 1930, shortly after graduating. "By the date of his first book of prose Hughes had become for many a symbol of the black renaissance," Bontemps writes. The stakes were high, then, for the young man born in Joplin, Missouri. He had to deliver.

Not Without Laughter crystallizes some of the themes introduced in Hughes's first two poetry collections and examines in detail subjects he would return to throughout his decades-long career, among them the experiences of working-class and poor blacks, the importance of black music to black life, the beauty of black language, and the trap of respectability. It begins as a tale of family life, following the Williamses—the matriarch, Aunt Hager; her daughters, Harriet, Annjee (Annjelica), and Tempy; and Annjee's husband, Jimboy—in the small Kansas town of Stanton. After establishing the conflicts and desires of the adults, the narrative morphs into bildungsroman. Here it finds its true purpose: chronicling the upbringing of Sandy, the son of Jimboy and Annjee, as he struggles to forge an identity outside of the boxes the white and black worlds have put him in, and tries to find stability within his increasingly unstable home. Each family member provides an example of how Sandy might navigate his world. Sandy's father is a blues man, a guitar picker with an itch for traveling, who leaves his son and his wife for months on end. Sandy's mother works long hours as a cook for an exacting white woman and comes home so exhausted and lovesick that she doesn't have much attention to spare for her young son. Soon enough she leaves Stanton for good, determined to stay by Jimboy's side and find happiness in their reunion.

Aunt Hager is Sandy's primary caretaker, and it is her grandson in whom she invests all her hopes for her family line. "I's gwine raise one chile right yet, if de Lawd lets me live—just one chile right!" In an unkind light Hager can be read as a Mammy, a former slave who chose to stay by her mistress's side for several years after emancipation rather than "scatter like buckshot," as most freed people did, and who now washes the clothes of white people and tends to their illnesses when called. Hughes takes care to flesh out Hager's motivations, which prove to be more complicated than unblinking servitude. Hager finds sanity and solace in forgiveness, in assuming the best in people who are too ignorant to reciprocate that courtesy. Her benevolence is her own existential armor. Hate "closes up de sweet door to life an' makes ever'thing small an' mean an' dirty," Hager insists. Her beliefs stand in stark contrast to those of many other negroes, including her own children.

Hager's youngest daughter, Harriet, is beautiful, and has a voice made to sing the blues. She gives her mother and Annjee's way of life a chance—working at a country club where old white men make passes at her—but ultimately opts out, hoping to escape Stanton altogether. She runs away with the circus, then returns to town and dabbles in sex work before finally getting a break as a singer. Her story begins as one of classic teenage rebellion but ends as an example of fierce determination.

In his famous essay "The Negro Artist and the Racial Mountain," Hughes expresses fondness for "the low-down folks, the so-called common element." Poor African Americans made up a majority of the black population but were rarely depicted as fully realized characters in the serious literature of the day. "They furnish a wealth of colorful, distinctive material for any artist because they still hold their own individuality in the face of American standardizations," Hughes writes. A writer who extols the virtues of a group of people based on any demographic denominator runs the risk of flattening or essentializing his characters, but in the face of popular novels centered on middle- and upper-class black experiences, such as those by his contemporary Jessie Redmon Fauset, Hughes's call for nuanced consideration of working-class (and even out-of-work) black people was noteworthy. The early decades of the twentieth century were also a period when "color mania" was part of day-to-day black social and professional life, with lighter skin seen as correlating with increased romantic prospects and more opportunities for upward mobility. Hughes's focus on main characters with darker skin tones—something we are reminded of throughout the novel—seems like a conscious statement against racial assimilation and conformity.

In reviewing Hughes's first autobiography, *The Big Sea* (1940), Richard Wright recalls Hughes's first two poetry collections being greeted with shock by the black reading public. "Since then the realistic position assumed by Hughes has become the dominant outlook of all those Negro writers who have something to say," Wright observes. Indeed what stays with the reader longer than the overall narrative arc of *Not Without Laughter* is the frequent, unexpected uses of imagery and language that make the characters and their lives feel real. Sandy recalls Aunt Hager, a woman who frowns on secular dancing—even if that dancing takes place in her own yard—whirling round and round at a revival in religious ecstasy. With the same amount of fondness he recalls his aunt Harriet "balling the jack" to Jimboy's guitar music in the yard. Both Aunt Hager and Sister Johnson tend to pronounce the word "idea" as "idee," a subtle nod to what the historian Henry Louis Gates Jr. calls "the linguistic legacy of slavery." During conversations between black characters, the word "nigger" rolls off their tongues often—sometimes pejoratively, sometimes humorously, but more often as a general descriptor—and it's a testament to Hughes's ear for black language that we are never in doubt about the intended tone. This focus on rendering realistically *how* black folks behave among themselves, whether or not such behavior would be considered proper in other contexts, is one of the novel's greatest achievements.

Like his one-time collaborator and contemporary Zora Neale Hurston, Hughes takes an anthropological approach to setting and character development. The town of Stanton where *Not Without Laughter* is set is similar to Lawrence, the small Kansas town where Hughes grew up with his maternal grandmother while his father worked in Mexico and his mother lived in Topeka. It was the sort of place where blacks and whites might live in close proximity to one another, but where a black boy would avoid walking by his white neighbor's front lawn for fear of having insults and slurs—or worse—hurled at him. Like the novel's hero, Sandy, Hughes grew up with a largely absent father and an interest in books. Already a budding public figure by the time of the novel's release, Hughes likely saw his own life pulling him farther and farther away from the small-town Midwestern world that raised him. Reading *Not Without Laughter*, one can't help but feel as if Hughes had a desperate need to get all of his early cultural memories down on paper, from the "sooty grey-green light" that turns to blackness before a tornado touches down, to the possum, peach preserves, and yams that make up a humble Thanksgiving dinner.

Sandy is an ideal protagonist for a novel so interested in place and culture—an observant boy with a penchant for finding the extraordinary in the ordinary. He listens intently during warm nights spent on the porch with Aunt Hager, with an occasional visit from Sister Johnson or the speechifying Madam de Carter. He overhears grown black folks parsing out the psychology of whites who want to keep blacks close to them—nursing their children, preparing their meals—but always beneath them, and withholds his own judgment, already wise enough to know he doesn't yet know enough. As a teen Sandy sweeps up at a neighborhood barbershop, a place "filled with loud man-talk and smoke and laughter," and gets a crude sexual education from the conversations of the shop's day laborer customers and barbers, as well as plenty of lessons in playing the dozens—"the protective art of turning back a joke." He inhabits this new space the same way he inhabits every other one, simultaneously attuned to its peculiarities and somewhat set apart.

In "The Negro Artist and the Racial Mountain," Hughes addresses the issue of respectability, the belief that promoting only the best, brightest, and most palatable forms of blackness might somehow temper white bigotry. "'Oh, be respectable, write about nice people, show how good we are,' say the Negroes," he laments. The respectability argument is so attractive to some that nearly eight decades later it still rears its head with regard to black art and representation. For Sandy, the pressure to be respectable comes from Aunt Tempy, Aunt Hager's oldest child, who avoids visiting her washerwoman mother in an effort to preserve the illusion of her middle-class upbringing. After Hager's death, Sandy moves in with Tempy, and with his usual levelheadedness is able to see the futility of her and her husband's way of thinking: They look down on the Baptist church for its "nigger music" but are still made to use the servant's entrance at some of the town's finer white establishments. Sandy is nobody's fool, though: He sees the benefits their lifestyle affords him, like his own room and the freedom to read as much as he wants.

Not Without Laughter is an early Great Migration novel. Many blacks in Kansas arrived from the South after emancipation,

and with the advent of automation and the decline of agricultural work, blacks kept traveling north and west in search of opportunities. A migration narrative is necessarily a story of change. The author's task is to replicate the nostalgia and hope his characters feel as they set out for new futures, or the fear, resentment, and loneliness of those left behind. Jimboy, the novel's most frequent migrant, sings a song that encapsulates both sides of the experience:
He begins:

> I got a mule to ride.
> I got a mule to ride.
> Down in the South somewhere.
> I got a mule to ride.

His sister-in-law, Harriet, responds:

> O, don't you leave me here.
> Babe, don't you leave me here.
> Dog-gone yo' comin' back!
> Said don't you leave me here.

As a depiction of a period of transition, the migration novel often makes a priority of capturing life as it is led in its very moment, since there's no telling what might change when characters find themselves in new landscapes. The changing way of life between one generation and the next is a persistent point of tension in *Not Without Laughter*. Aunt Hager pumps water for her laundry washing, as well as for the cooking and cleaning, yet a few miles away Tempy lives with electric lights and indoor plumbing. Hager sees hotels as breeding grounds for vice and sin, but both Harriet and Sandy jump at the chance to work at one, motivated by a paycheck. Hughes uses the songs and dances of Jimboy and Harriet as well as the church revival culture of Hager and Annjee—in scenes taking place on the same night, less than a half mile apart—to depict the crossroads between the traditions that have given expression to the community in the past and those that might fill that role in the future.

Sandy's father, Jimboy, is caught in a cycle of desiring to be on the road to find better work (and freedom from responsibility) and of nostalgia for the culture and familiarity of the South. Jimboy's wanderlust is offensive to Hager, but Sandy idolizes his father, begging him to teach him how to box and fish and play guitar. The scene of Jimboy about to cut out for the road once again—this time for good—is one of the most poignant in the book. Sandy discovers his father "sitting dejectedly on the well-stoop in the sunshine, with his head in his hands," his posture conveying the sort of defeat only a man intending to abandon his family feels. The father takes his son in his arms and kisses him awkwardly. He does not say goodbye. Later that afternoon Sandy discovers Jimboy has left town.

What prevents Hughes's characters from being mere archetypes of working-class black folks, or of the Great Migration, is their ability to change and respond to one another. *Not Without Laughter* is a novel not without forgiveness. Its characters ultimately prize family over their own ideological resolve, though it takes some longer than others to get there. After hearing news of Harriet's arrest for streetwalking, Hager doesn't speak her daughter's name for some time, but she does not disown her; Hager's dying wish is for Harriet to be happy. Even Tempy's taking in of Sandy can be seen as an attempt to pull her family close again after keeping her distance for so long. The one exception is Jimboy, who remains elusive throughout the novel, a father figure always out of reach.

A poet who writes fiction can imbue his prose with a considerable amount of magic. For Hughes, his magic is an appreciation for the lyrics and rhythms of jazz and blues. It's one thing to appreciate the cultural aspects of these musical forms, yet another to home in on the lyrics, the power of the repetition employed therein, the subtle turns of phrase and uses of wit.

Not Without Laughter includes lyrics to songs that are mournful, bawdy, vengeful, and downright silly. They underscore the importance Hughes felt they played in black life and consciousness. One gets the sense that Sandy's upbringing has been shaped just as much by overhearing these songs as by Aunt Hager's teachings. As the novel progresses, Sandy's thoughts are rendered in musical streams of consciousness, quickly turning from anticipation to curiosity to anger to desire. The result is a realistic portrayal of the rhythms of a young man's inner life: Sandy lays in bed at night and riffs on his own past and future.

In perhaps the most peculiar scene of the novel, Sandy is pursued by a solicitous older man, a "yellow man with a womanish kind of voice," on the streets of Chicago. Sandy quickly ascertains that the man is one of the "queer fellows" who try to convince boys to come up to their rooms. The scene ends with Sandy running away, but Hughes writes that Sandy wondered what such men did with the boys they seduced. "Curious, he'd like to find out—but he was afraid." For the time period, to acknowledge homosexual activity, and to allow that it might pique one's interest, was quite rare. The scene would remain one of Hughes's more direct engagements with the topic of homosexuality in his prose until the 1961 short story "Blessed Assurance."

The tragedy and senselessness of racism is felt throughout *Not Without Laughter*, and Hughes takes care to show how it manifests itself in ways small and large. Sandy cries after he overhears Annjee's boss, Mrs. Rice, berate his mother as she packs up leftovers for him. When Sandy and his friends are turned away from the Children's Day Party at the theme park, the other kids talk loudly about the injustice of it, and Sandy just keeps muttering, "I suppose they didn't mean colored kids," a feeble attempt to make sense of a surprising and hurtful situation. His friend Buster plans to pass as white and tells the gang that if one day they should run into him in a big city, to act like they don't know him. Colorism seeps down to every aspect of life, even those moments made for pleasure, like at Benbow's dance: "'High yallers, draw nigh! Brown-skins, come near!' somebody squalled. 'But black gals, stay where you are!'"

Hughes would not write another novel for nearly thirty years, until 1958, but four years after the publication of *Not Without Laughter* he released the short story collection *The Ways of White Folks*, a series of vignettes about the interaction between white and black people, often with grim, moralistic endings. By this time he had parted ways with his white benefactor Charlotte Mason; his resentment over the split might explain why these stories reach for concrete conclusions that do not similarly burden his novel.

Not Without Laughter is a debut in the best of ways: It covers uncharted territory, it compels its readers to see part of the world anew, and it prizes exploration over pat conclusion. Hughes accesses the universal—how all of us love and dream and laugh and cry—by staying faithful to the particulars of his characters and their way of life. With this book the young poet from Joplin, Missouri, manages to deliver something more valuable than simply an admirable debut—he gives his readers and contemporaries a guide for careful consideration of the lives of everyday black people. Such a guide is still useful to readers and writers today. Perhaps now more than ever.

ANGELA FLOURNOY

NOT WITHOUT LAUGHTER

I.

STORM

Aunt Hager Williams stood in her doorway and looked out at the sun. The western sky was a sulphurous yellow and the sun a red ball dropping slowly behind the trees and house-tops. Its setting left the rest of the heavens grey with clouds.

"Huh! A storm's coming'," said Aunt Hager aloud.

A pullet ran across the back yard and into a square-cut hole in an unpainted piano-box which served as the roosting-house. An old hen clucked her brood together and, with the tiny chicks, went into a small box beside the large one. The air was very still. Not a leaf stirred on the green apple-tree. Not a single closed flower of the morning-glories trembled on the back fence. The air was very still and yellow. Something sultry and oppressive made a small boy in the doorway stand closer to his grandmother, clutching her apron with his brown hands.

"Sho is a storm comin'," said Aunt Hager.

"I hope mama gets home 'fore it rains," remarked the brown child holding to the old woman's apron. "Hope she gets home."

"I does, too," said Aunt Hager. "But I's skeared she won't."

Just then great drops of water began to fall heavily into the back yard, pounding up little clouds of dust where each drop struck the earth. For a few moments they pattered violently on the roof like a series of hammer-strokes; then suddenly they ceased.

"Come in, chile," said Aunt Hager.

She closed the door as the green apple-tree began to sway in the wind and a small hard apple fell, rolling rapidly down the top of the piano-box that sheltered the chickens. Inside the kitchen it was almost dark. While Aunt Hager lighted an oil-lamp, the child climbed to a chair and peered through the square window into the yard. The leaves and flowers of the morning-glory vines on the back fence were bending with the rising wind. And across the alley at the big house, Mrs. Kennedy's rear screen-door banged to and fro, and Sandy saw her garbage-pail suddenly tip over and roll down into the yard, scattering potato-peelings on the white steps.

"Sho gwine be a terrible storm," said Hager as she turned up the wick of the light and put the chimney on. Then, glancing through the window, she saw a black cloud twisting like a ribbon in the western sky, and the old woman screamed aloud in sudden terror: "It's a cyclone! It's gwine be a cyclone! Sandy, let's get over to Mis' Carter's quick, 'cause we ain't got no cellar here. Come on, chile, let's get! Come on, chile! . . . Come on, chile!"

Hurriedly she blew out the light, grabbed the boy's hand; and together they rushed through the little house towards the front. It was quite dark in the inner rooms, but through the parlor windows came a sort of sooty grey-green light that was rapidly turning to blackness.

"Lawd help us, Jesus!"

Aunt Hager opened the front door, but before she or the child could move, a great roaring sound suddenly shook the world, and, with a deafening division of wood from wood, they saw their front porch rise into the air and go hurtling off into space. Sailing high in the gathering darkness, the porch was soon lost to sight. And the black wind blew with terrific force, numbing the ear-drums.

For a moment the little house trembled and swayed and creaked as though it were about to fall.

"Help me to shut this do'," Aunt Hager screamed; "help me to shut it, Lawd!" as with all her might she struggled against the open door, which the wind held back, but finally it closed and the lock caught. Then she sank to the floor with her back against the wall, while her small grandson trembled like a leaf as she took him in her lap, mumbling: "What a storm! . . . O, Lawdy! . . . O, ma chile, what a storm!"

They could hear the crackling of timbers and the rolling limbs of trees that the wind swept across the roof. Her arms tightened about the boy.

"Dear Jesus!" she said. "I wonder where is yo' mama? S'pose she started out fo' home 'fore this storm come up!" Then in a scream: "Have mercy on ma Annjee! O, Lawd, have mercy on this chile's mama! Have mercy on all ma chillens! Ma Harriett, an' ma Tempy, an' ma Annjee, what's maybe all of 'em out in de storm! O, Lawd!"

A dry crack of lightning split the darkness, and the boy began to wail. Then the rain broke. The old woman could not see the crying child she held, nor could the boy hear the broken voice of his grandmother, who had begun to pray as the rain crashed through the inky blackness. For a long while it roared on the roof of the house and pounded at the windows, until finally the two within became silent, hushing their cries. Then only the lashing noise of the water, coupled with the feeling that something terrible was happening, or had already happened, filled the evening air.

After the rain the moon rose clear and bright and the clouds disappeared from the lately troubled sky. The stars sparkled calmly above the havoc of the storm, and it was still early evening as people emerged from their houses and began to investigate the damage brought by the twisting cyclone that had come with the sunset. Through the rubbish-filled streets men drove slowly with horse and buggy or automobile. The fire-engine was out, banging away, and the soft tang-tang-tang of the motor ambulance could be heard in the distance carrying off the injured.

Black Aunt Hager and her brown grandson put their rubbers on and stood in the water-soaked front yard looking at the porchless house where they lived. Platform, steps, pillars, roof, and all had been blown away. Not a semblance of a porch was left and the front door opened bare into the yard. It was grotesque and funny. Hager laughed.

"Cyclone sho did a good job," she said. "Looks like I ain't never had no porch."

Madam de Carter, from next door, came across the grass, her large mouth full of chattering sympathy for her neighbor.

"But praise God for sparing our lives! It might've been worse, Sister Williams! It might've been much more calamitouser! As it is, I lost nothin' more'n a chimney and two washtubs which was settin' in the back yard. A few trees broke down don't 'mount to nothin'. We's livin', ain't we? And we's more importanter than trees is any day!" Her gold teeth sparkled in the moonlight.

"'Deed so," agreed Hager emphatically. "Let's move on down de block, Sister, an' see what mo' de Lawd has 'stroyed or spared this evenin'. He's gin us plenty moonlight after de storm so we po' humans can see this lesson o' His'n to a sinful world."

The two elderly colored women picked their way about on the wet walk, littered with twigs and branches of broken foliage. The little brown boy followed, with his eyes wide at the sight of baby-carriages, window-sashes, shingles, and tree-limbs scattered about in the roadway. Large numbers of people were out, some standing on porches, some carrying lanterns, picking up useful articles from the streets, some wringing their hands in a daze.

Near the corner a small crowd had gathered quietly.

"Mis' Gavitt's killed," somebody said.

"Lawd help!" burst from Aunt Hager and Madam de Carter simultaneously.

"Mister and Mis' Gavitt's both dead," added a nervous young white man, bursting with the news. "We live next door to 'em, and their house turned clean over! Came near hitting us and breaking our side-wall in."

"Have mercy!" said the two women, but Sandy slipped away from his grandmother and pushed through the crowd. He ran

round the corner to where he could see the overturned house of
the unfortunate Gavitts.

Good white folks, the Gavitts, Aunt Hager had often said,
and now their large frame dwelling lay on its side like a doll's
mansion, with broken furniture strewn carelessly on the wet
lawn—and they were dead. Sandy saw a piano flat on its back
in the grass. Its ivory keys gleamed in the moonlight like grinning teeth, and the strange sight made his little body shiver, so
he hurried back through the crowd looking for his grandmother. As he passed the corner, he heard a woman sobbing
hysterically within the wide house there.

His grandmother was no longer standing where he had left
her, but he found Madam de Carter and took hold of her hand.
She was in the midst of a group of excited white and colored
women. One frail old lady was saying in a high determined
voice that she had never seen a cyclone like this in her whole
life, and she had lived here in Kansas, if you please, going on
seventy-three years. Madam de Carter, chattering nervously,
began to tell them how she had recognized its coming and had
rushed to the cellar the minute she saw the sky turn green. She
had not come up until the rain stopped, so frightened had she
been. She was extravagantly enjoying the telling of her fears as
Sandy kept tugging at her hand.

"Where's my grandma?" he demanded. Madam de Carter,
however, did not cease talking to answer his question.

"What do you want, sonny?" finally one of the white women
asked, bending down when he looked as if he were about to
cry. "Aunt Hager? . . . Why, she's inside helping them calm
poor Mrs. Gavitt's niece. Your grandmother's good to have
around when folks are sick or grieving, you know. Run and set
on the steps like a nice boy and wait until she comes out." So
Sandy left the women and went to sit in the dark on the steps
of the big corner house where the niece of the dead Mrs. Gavitt
lived. There were some people on the porch, but they soon
passed through the screen-door into the house or went away
down the street. The moonlight cast weird shadows across the

damp steps where Sandy sat, and it was dark there under the
trees in spite of the moon, for the old house was built far back
from the street in a yard full of oaks and maples, and Sandy
could see the light from an upstairs window reflecting on the
wet leaves of their nearest boughs. He heard a girl screaming,
too, up there where the light was burning, and he knew that
Aunt Hager was putting cold cloths on her head, or rubbing
her hands, or driving folks out of the room, and talking kind
to her so that she would soon be better.

All the neighborhood, white or colored, called his grandmother when something happened. She was a good nurse, they
said, and sick folks liked her around. Aunt Hager always came
when they called, too, bringing maybe a little soup that she
had made or a jelly. Sometimes they paid her and sometimes
they didn't. But Sandy had never had to sit outdoors in the
darkness waiting for her before. He leaned his small back
against the top step and rested his elbows on the porch behind
him. It was growing late and the people in the streets had all
disappeared.

There, in the dark, the little fellow began to think about his
mother, who worked on the other side of town for a rich white
lady named Mrs. J. J. Rice. And suddenly frightful thoughts
came into his mind. Suppose she had left for home just as the
storm came up! Almost always his mother was home before
dark—but she wasn't there tonight when the storm came—
and she should have been home! This thought appalled him.
She should have been there! But maybe she had been caught by
the storm and blown away as she walked down Main Street!
Maybe Annjee had been carried off by the great black wind
that had overturned the Gavitts' house and taken his grandma's porch flying through the air! Maybe the cyclone had gotten his mother, Sandy thought. He wanted her! Where was
she? Had something terrible happened to her? Where was
she now?

The big tears began to roll down his cheeks—but the little
fellow held back the sobs that wanted to come. He decided he
wasn't going to cry and make a racket there by himself on the

strange steps of these white folks' house. He wasn't going to cry like a big baby in the dark. So he wiped his eyes, kicked his heels against the cement walk, lay down on the top step, and, by and by, sniffled himself to sleep.

"Wake up, son!" Someone was shaking him. "You'll catch your death o' cold sleeping on the wet steps like this. We're going home now. Don't want me to have to carry a big man like you, do you, boy? . . . Wake up, Sandy!" His mother stooped to lift his long little body from the wide steps. She held him against her soft heavy breasts and let his head rest on one of her shoulders while his feet, in their muddy rubbers, hung down against her dress.

"Where you been, mama?" the boy asked drowsily, tightening his arms about her neck. "I been waiting for you."

"Oh, I been home a long time, worried to death about you and ma till I heard from Madam Carter that you-all was down here nursing the sick. I stopped at your Aunt Tempy's house when I seen the storm coming."

"I was afraid you got blowed away, mama," murmured Sandy sleepily. "Let's go home, mama. I'm glad you ain't got blowed away."

On the porch Aunt Hager was talking to a pale white man and two thin white women standing at the door of the lighted hallway. "Just let Mis' Agnes sleep," she was saying. "She'll be all right now, an' I'll come back in de mawnin' to see 'bout her. . . . Good-night, you-all."

The old colored woman joined her daughter and they started home, walking through the streets filled with debris and puddles of muddy water reflecting the moon.

"You're certainly heavy, boy," remarked Sandy's mother to the child she held, but he didn't answer.

"I'm right glad you come for me, Annjee," Hager said. "I wonder is yo' sister all right out yonder at de country club. . . . An' I was so worried 'bout you I didn't know what to do— skeared you might a got caught in this twister, 'cause it were cert'ly awful!"

"I was at Tempy's!" Annjee replied. "And I was nearly crazy, but I just left everything in the hands o' God. That's all." In silence they walked on, a piece; then hesitantly, to her mother: "There wasn't any mail for me today, was there, ma?"

"Not a speck!" the old woman replied shortly. "Mail-man passed on by."

For a few minutes there was silence again as they walked. Then, "It's goin' on three weeks he's been gone, and he ain't written a line," the younger woman complained, shifting the child to her right arm. "Seems like Jimboy would let a body know where he is, ma, wouldn't it?"

"Huh! That ain't nothin'! He's been gone before this an' he ain't wrote, ain't he? Here you is worryin' 'bout a letter from that good-for-nothing husband o' your'n—an' there's ma house settin' up without a porch to its name! . . . Ain't you seed what de devil's done done on earth this evenin', chile? . . . An' yet de first thing you ask me 'bout is de mail-man! . . . Lawd! Lawd! . . . You an' that Jimboy!"

Aunt Hager lifted her heavy body over fallen tree-trunks and across puddles, but between puffs she managed to voice her indignation, so Annjee said no more concerning letters from her husband. Instead they went back to the subject of the cyclone. "I'm just thankful, ma, it didn't blow the whole house down and you with it, that's all! I was certainly worried! . . . And then you-all was gone when I got home! Gone on out—nursing that white woman. . . . It's too bad 'bout poor Mis' Gavitt, though, and old man Gavitt, ain't it?"

"Yes, indeedy!" said Aunt Hager. "It's sho too bad. They was certainly good old white folks! An' her married niece is takin' it mighty hard, po' little soul. I was nigh two hours, her husband an' me, tryin' to bring her out o' de hysterics. Tremblin' like a lamb all over, she was." They were turning into the yard. "Be careful with that chile, Annjee, you don't trip on none o' them boards nor branches an' fall with him."

"Put me down, 'cause I'm awake," said Sandy.

The old house looked queer without a porch. In the moonlight he could see the long nails that had held the porch roof to the weather-boarding. His grandmother climbed slowly over the door-sill, and his mother lifted him to the floor level as Aunt Hager lit the large oil-lamp on the parlor table. Then they went back to the bedroom, where the youngster took off his clothes, said his prayers, and climbed into the high feather bed where he slept with Annjee. Aunt Hager went to the next room, but for a long time she talked back and forth through the doorway to her daughter about the storm.

"We was just startin' out fo' Mis' Carter's cellar, me an' Sandy," she said several times. "But de Lawd was with us! He held us back! Praise His name! We ain't harmed, none of us—'ceptin' I don't know 'bout ma Harriett at de club. But you's all right. An' you say Tempy's all right, too. An' I prays that Harriett ain't been touched out there in de country where she's workin'. Maybe de storm ain't passed that way."

Then they spoke about the white people where Annjee worked . . . and about the elder sister Tempy's prosperity. Then Sandy heard his grandmother climb into bed, and a few minutes after the springs screaked under her, she had begun to snore. Annjee closed the door between their rooms and slowly began to unlace her wet shoes.

"Sandy," she whispered, "we ain't had no word yet from your father since he left. I know he goes away and stays away like this and don't write, but I'm sure worried. Hope the cyclone ain't passed nowhere near wherever he is, and I hope ain't nothin' hurt him. . . . I'm gonna pray for him, Sandy. I'm gonna ask God right now to take care o' Jimboy. . . . The Lawd knows, I wants him to come back! . . . I loves him. . . . We both loves him, don't we, child? And we want him to come on back!"

She knelt down beside the bed in her night-dress and kept her head bowed for a long time. Before she got up, Sandy had gone to sleep.

II.

CONVERSATION

It was broad daylight in the town of Stanton and had been for a long time.

"Get out o' that bed, boy!" Aunt Hager yelled. "Here's Buster waitin' out in de yard to play with you, an' you still sleepin'!"

"Aw, tell him to cut off his curls," retorted Sandy, but his grandmother was in no mood for fooling.

"Stop talkin' 'bout that chile's haid and put yo' clothes on. Nine o'clock an' you ain't up yet! Shame on you!" She shouted from the kitchen, where Sandy could hear the fire crackling and smell coffee boiling.

He kicked the sheet off with his bare feet and rolled over and over on the soft feather tick. There was plenty of room to roll now, because his mother had long since got up and gone to Mrs. J. J. Rice's to work.

"Tell Bus I'm coming," Sandy yelled, jumping into his trousers and running with bare feet towards the door. "Is he got his marbles?"

"Come back here, sir, an' put them shoes on," cried Hager, stopping him on his way out. "Yo' feet'll get long as yardsticks and flat as pancakes runnin' round barefooted all de time. An' wash yo' face, sir. Buster ain't got a thing to do but wait. An' eat yo' breakfast."

The air was warm with sunlight, and hundreds of purple and white morning-glories laughed on the back fence. Earth and sky were fresh and clean after the heavy night-rain, and the young corn-shoots stood straight in the garden, and green pea-vines wound themselves around their crooked sticks. There was the mingled scent of wet soil and golden pollen on the breeze that blew carelessly through the clear air.

Buster sat under the green apple-tree with a pile of black mud from the alley in front of him.

"Hey, Sandy, gonna make marbles and put 'em in the sun to dry," he said.

"All right," agreed Sandy, and they began to roll mud balls in the palms of their hands. But instead of putting them in the sun to dry they threw them against the back of the house, where they flattened and stuck beautifully. Then they began to throw them at each other.

Sandy's playmate was a small ivory-white Negro child with straight golden hair, which his mother made him wear in curls. His eyes were blue and doll-like and he in no way resembled a colored youngster; but he was colored. Sandy himself was the shade of a nicely browned piece of toast, with dark, brown-black eyes and a head of rather kinky, sandy hair that would lie smooth only after a rigorous application of vaseline and water. That was why folks called him Annjee's sandy-headed child, and then just—Sandy.

"He takes after his father," Sister Lowry said, " 'cept he's not so light. But he's gonna be a mighty good-lookin' boy when he grows up, that's sho!"

"Well, I hopes he does," Aunt Hager said. "But I'd rather he'd be ugly 'fore he turns out anything like that good-for-nothing Jimboy what comes here an' stays a month, goes away an' stays six, an' don't hit a tap o' work 'cept when he feels like it. If it wasn't for Annjee, don't know how we'd eat, 'cause Sandy's father sho don't do nothin' to support him."

All the colored people in Stanton knew that Hager bore no love for Jimboy Rogers, the tall good-looking yellow fellow whom her second daughter had married.

"First place, I don't like his name," she would say in private. "Who ever heard of a nigger named Jimboy, anyhow? Next place, I ain't never seen a yaller dude yet that meant a dark woman no good—an' Annjee is dark!" Aunt Hager had other objections, too, although she didn't like to talk evil about folks. But what she probably referred to in her mind was the question of his ancestry, for nobody knew who Jimboy's parents were.

"Sandy, look out for the house while I run down an' see how is Mis' Gavitt's niece. An' you-all play outdoors. Don't bring no chillen in, litterin' up de place." About eleven o'clock Aunt Hager pulled a dustcap over her head and put on a clean white apron. "Here, tie it for me, chile," she said, turning her broad back. "An' mind you don't hurt yo'self on no rusty nails and rotten boards left from de storm. I'll be back atter while." And she disappeared around the house, walking proudly, her black face shining in the sunlight.

Presently the two boys under the apple-tree were joined by a coal-colored little girl who lived next door, one Willie-Mae Johnson, and the mud balls under her hands became mud pies carefully rounded and patted and placed in the sun on the small box where the little chickens lived. Willie-Mae was the mama, Sandy the papa, and Buster the baby as the old game of "playing house" began anew.

By and by the mail-man's whistle blew and the three children scampered towards the sidewalk to meet him. The carrier handed Sandy a letter. "Take it in the house," he said. But instead the youngsters sat on the front-door-sill, their feet dangling where the porch had been, and began to examine the envelope.

"I bet that's Lincoln's picture," said Buster.

"No, 'taint," declared Willie-Mae. "It's Rossie felt!"

"Aw, it's Washington," said Sandy. "And don't you-all touch my mama's letter with your hands all muddy. It might be from my papa, you can't tell, and she wants it kept clean."

" 'Tis from Jimboy," Aunt Hager declared when she returned, accompanied by her old friend, Sister Whiteside, who peddled on foot fresh garden-truck she raised herself. Aunt Hager had met her at the corner.

"I knows his writin'," went on Hager. "An' it's got a postmark, K-A-N-, Kansas City! That's what 'tis! Niggers sho do love Kansas City! . . . Huh! . . . So that's where he's at. Well, yo' mama'll be glad to get it. If she knowed it was here, she'd quit work an' come home now. . . . Sit down, Whiteside. We gwine eat in a few minutes. You better have a bite with us an' stay an' rest yo'self awhile, 'cause I knows you been walkin' this mawnin'!"

" 'Deed I is," the old sister declared, dropping her basket of lettuce and peas on the floor and taking a chair next to the table in the kitchen. "An' I ain't sold much neither. Seems like folks ain't got no buyin' appetite after all that storm an' wind last night—but de Lawd will provide! I ain't worried."

"That's right," agreed Hager. "Might o' been me blowed away maself, 'stead o' just ma porch, if Jesus hadn't been with us. . . . You Sandy! Make haste and wash yo' hands, sir. Rest o' you chillens go on home, 'cause I know yo' ma's lookin' for you. . . . Huh! This wood fire's mighty low!"

Hager uncovered a pot that had been simmering on the stove all morning and dished up a great bowlful of black-eyed peas and salt pork. There was biscuit bread left from breakfast. A plate of young onions and a pitcher of lemonade stood on the white oilcloth-covered table. Heads were automatically bowed.

"Lawd, make us thankful for this food. For Christ's sake, amen," said Hager; then the two old women and the child began to eat.

"That's Elvira's boy, ain't it—that yaller-headed young-one was here playin' with Sandy?" Sister Whiteside had her mouth full of onions and beans as she asked the question.

"Shsss! . . . That's her child!" said Hager. "But it ain't Eddie's!" She gave her guest a meaning glance across the table, then lowered her voice, pretending all the while that Sandy's ears were too young to hear. "They say she had that chile 'fore she married Eddie. An' black as Eddie is, you knows an' I knows ain't due to be no golden hair in de family!"

"I knowed there must be something funny," whispered the old sister, screwing up her face. "That's some white man's chile!"

"Sho it is!" agreed Hager. . . . "I knowed it all de time. . . . Have some mo' meat, Whiteside. Help yo'self! We ain't got

much, but such as 'tis, you're welcome. . . . Yes, sir, Buster's
some white man's chile. . . . Stop reachin' cross de table for
bread, Sandy. Where's yo' manners, sir? I declare, chillens do
try you sometimes. . . . Pass me de onions."

"Truth, they tries you, yit I gits right lonesome since all ma
young-ones is gone." Sister Whiteside worked her few good
teeth vigorously, took a long swallow of lemonade, and smacked
her lips. "Chillen an' grandchillen all in Chicago an' St. Louis
an' Wichita, an' nary chick nor child left with me in de
house. . . . Pass me de bread, thank yuh. . . . I feels kinder sad
an' sorry at times, po' widder-woman that I is. I has ma garden
an' ma hens, but all ma chillens done grown and married. . . .
Where's yo' daughter Harriett at now, Hager? Is she married,
too? I ain't seen her lately."

Hager pulled a meat skin through her teeth; then she answered: "No, chile, she too young to marry yet! Ain't but sixteen, but she's been workin out this summer, waitin' table at
de Stanton County Country Club. Been in de country three
weeks now, since school closed, but she comes in town on
Thursdays, though. It's nigh six miles from here, so de women-
help sleeps there at night. I's glad she's out there, Sister. Course
Harriett's a good girl, but she likes to be frisky—wants to run
de streets 'tendin' parties an' dances, an' I can't do much with
her no mo', though I hates to say it."

"But she's a songster, Hager! An' I hears she's sho one smart
chile, besides. They say she's up with them white folks when it
comes to books. An' de high school where she's goin' ain't
easy. . . . All ma young ones quit 'fore they got through with
it—wouldn't go—ruther have a good time runnin' to Kansas
City an' galavantin' round."

"De Lawd knows it's a hard job, keepin' colored chillens in
school, Sister Whiteside, a mighty hard job. De niggers don't
help 'em, an' de white folks don't care if they stay or not. An'
when they gets along sixteen an' seventeen, they wants this,
an' they wants that, an' t'other—an' when you ain't got it to
give to 'em, they quits school an' goes to work. . . . Harriett
say she ain't goin' back next fall. I feels right hurt over it, but

she 'clares she ain't goin' back to school. Says there ain't no use in learnin' books fo' nothin' but to work in white folks' kitchens when she's graduated."

"Do she, Hager? I's sho sorry! I's gwine to talk to that gal. Get Reverend Berry to talk to her, too.

". . . You's struggled to bring up yo' chillens, an' all we Christians in de church ought to help you! I gwine see Reverend Berry, see can't he 'suade her to stay in school." The old woman reached for the onions. "But you ain't never raised no boys, though, has you, Hager?"

"No, I ain't. My two boy-chillens both died 'fore they was ten. Just these three girls—Tempy, an' Annjee, an' Harriett— that's all I got. An' this here grandchile, Sandy. . . . Take yo' hands off that meat, sir! You had 'nough!"

"Lawd, you's been lucky! I done raised seven grandchillen 'sides eight o' ma own. An' they don't thank me. No, sir! Go off and kick up they heels an' git married an' don't thank me a bit! Don't even write, some of 'em. . . . Waitin' fo' me to die, I reckon, so's they can squabble over de little house I owns an' ma garden." The old visitor pushed back her chair. "Huh! Yo' dinner was sho good! . . . Waitin' fo' me to die."

"Unhuh! . . . That's de way with 'em, Sister Whiteside. Chillens don't care—but I reckon we old ones can't kick much. They's got to get off fo' themselves. It's natural, that's what 'tis. Now, my Tempy, she's married and doin' well. Got a fine house, an' her husband's a mail-clerk in de civil service makin' good money. They don't 'sociate no mo' with none but de high-toned colored folks, like Dr. Mitchell, an' Mis' Ada Walls, an' Madam C. Frances Smith. Course Tempy don't come to see me much 'cause I still earns ma livin' with ma arms in de tub. But Annjee run in their house out o' the storm last night an' she say Tempy's just bought a new pianer, an' de house looks fine. . . . I's glad fo' de chile."

"Sho, sho you is, Sister Williams, you's a good mother an' I knows you's glad. But I hears from Reverend Berry that Tempy's done withdrawed from our church an' joined de Episcopals!"

"That's right! She is. Last time I seed Tempy, she told me she couldn't stand de Baptist no mo'—too many low niggers belonging, she say, so she's gonna join Father Hill's church, where de best people go. . . . I told her I didn't think much o' joinin' a church so far away from God that they didn't want nothin' but yaller niggers for members, an' so full o' forms an' fashions that a good Christian couldn't shout—but she went on an' joined. It's de stylish temple, that's why, so I ain't said no mo'. Tempy's goin' on thirty-five now, she's ma oldest chile, an' I reckon she knows how she wants to act."

"Yes, I reckon she do. . . . But there ain't no church like de Baptist, praise God! Is there, Sister? If you ain't been dipped in that water an' half drowned, you ain't saved. Tempy don't know like we do. No, sir, she don't know!"

There was no fruit or dessert, and the soiled plates were not removed from the table for a long time, for the two old women, talking about their children, had forgotten the dishes. Young flies crawled over the biscuit bread and hummed above the bowl of peas, while the wood fire died in the stove, and Sandy went out into the sunshine to play.

"Now, ma girl, Maggie," said Sister Whiteside; "de man she married done got to be a big lawyer in St. Louis. He's in de politics there, an' Maggie's got a fine job herself—social servin', they calls it. But I don't hear from her once a year. An' she don't send me a dime. Ma boys looks out for me, though, sometimes, round Christmas. There's Lucius, what runs on de railroad, an' then Andrew, what rides de horses, an' John, in Omaha, sends me a little change now an' then—all but Charlie, an' he never was thoughtful 'bout his mother. He ain't never sent me nothin'."

"Well, you sho is lucky," said Hager, " 'cause they ain't no money comes in this house, Christmas nor no other time, less'n me an' Annjee brings it here. Jimboy ain't no good, an' what Harriett makes goes for clothes and parties an' powderin'-rags. Course, I takes some from her every week, but I gives it right back for her school things. An' I ain't taken nothin' from her these three weeks she's been workin' at de club. She say she's savin' her money herself. She's past sixteen now, so I lets her have it. . . . Po' little thing! . . . She does need to look purty." Hager's voice softened and her dark old face was half abashed, kind and smiling. "You know, last month I bought her a gold watch—surprise fo' her birthday, de kind you hangs on a little pin on yo' waist. Lawd knows, I couldn't 'ford it—took all de money from three week's o' washin', but I knowed she'd been wantin' a watch. An' this front room—I moved ma bed out last year an' bought that new rug at de second-hand store an' them lace curtains so's she could have a nice place to entertain her comp'ny. . . . But de chile goes with such a kinder wild crowd o' young folks, Sister Whiteside! It worries me! The boys, they cusses, an' the girls, they paints, an' some of 'em live in de Bottoms. I been tried to get her out of it right along, but seems like I can't. That's why I's glad she's in de country fo' de summer an' comes in but only once a week, an' then she's home with me. It's too far to come in town at night, she say, so she gets her rest now, goin' to bed early an' all, with de country air round her. I hopes she calms down from runnin' round when she comes back here to stay in de fall. . . . She's a good chile. She don't lie to me 'bout where she goes, nor nothin' like that, but she's just wild, that's all, just wild."

"Is she a Christian, Sister Williams?"

"No, she ain't. I's sorry to say it of a chile o' mine, but she ain't. She's been on de moaner's bench time after time, Sunday mawnins' an' prayer-meetin' evenin's, but she never would rise. I prays for her."

"Well, when she takes Jesus, she'll see de light! That's what de matter with her, Sister Williams, she ain't felt Him yit. Make her go to church when she comes back here. . . . I reckon you heard 'bout when de big revival's due to come off this year, ain't you?"

"No, I ain't, not yet."

"Great colored tent-meetin' with de Battle-Ax of de Lawd, Reverend Braswell preachin'! Yes, sir! Gwine start August eighteenth in de Hickory Woods yonder by de edge o' town."

"Good news," cried Hager. "Mo' sinners than enough's in

need o' savin'. I's gwine to take Sandy an' get him started right
with de Lawd. An' if that onery Jimboy's back here, I gwine
make him go, too, an' look Jesus in de face. Annjee an' me's
saved, chile! . . . You Sandy, bring us some drinkin'-water from
de pump." Aunt Hager rapped on the window with her knuck-
les to the boy playing outside! "An' stop wrastlin' with that gal."

Sandy rose triumphant from the prone body of black little
Willie-Mae, lying squalling on the cinder-path near the back
gate. "She started it," he yelled, running towards the pump.
The girl began a reply, but at that moment a rickety wagon
drawn by a white mule and driven by a grey-haired, leather-
colored old man came rattling down the alley.

"Hy, there, Hager!" called the old Negro, tightening his
reins on the mule, which immediately began to eat corn-tops
over the back fence. "How you been treatin' yo'self?"

"Right tolable," cried Hager, for she and Sister Whiteside
had both emerged from the kitchen and were approaching the
driver. "How you doin', Brother Logan?"

"Why, if here ain't Sis' Whiteside, too!" said the old beau,
sitting up straight on his wagon-seat and showing a row of
ivory teeth in a wide grin. "I's doin' purty well for a po' wid-
ower what ain't got nobody to bake his bread. Doin' purty
well. Hee! Hee! None o' you all ain't sorry for me, is you?
How de storm treat you, Hager? . . . Says it carried off yo'
porch? . . . That's certainly too bad! Well, it did some o' these
white folks worse'n that. I got 'nough work to do to last me de
next fo' weeks, cleanin' up yards an' haulin' off trash, me an'
dis mule here. . . . How's yo' chillen, Sis' Williams?"

"Oh, they all right, thank yuh. Annjee's still at Mis' Rice's,
an' Harriet's in de country at de club."

"Is she?" said Brother Logan. "I seed her in town night 'fore
last down on Pearl Street 'bout ten o'clock."

"You ain't seed Harriett no night 'fore last," disputed Hager
vigorously. "She don't come in town 'ceptin' Thursday afternoons, an' that's tomorrow."

"Sister, I ain't blind," said the old man, hurt that his truth
should be doubted. "I—seen—Harriett Williams on Pearl

Street . . . with Maudel Smothers an' two boys 'bout ten o'clock day before yestidy night! An' they was gwine to de Waiters' Ball, 'cause I asked Maudel where they was gwine, an' she say so. Then I says to Harrictt: 'Does yo' mammy know you's out this late?' an' she laughed an' say: 'Oh, that's all right!' . . . Don't tell me I ain't seen Harriett, Hager."

"Well, Lawd help!" Aunt Hager cried, her mouth open. "You done seed my chile in town an' she ain't come anear home! Stayed all night at Maudel's, I reckon. . . . I tells her 'bout runnin' with that gal from de Bottoms. That's what makes her lie to me—tellin' me she don't come in town o' nights. Maudel's folks don't keep no kind o' house, and mens goes there, an' they sells licker, an' they gambles an' fights. . . . Is you sho that's right, Brother Logan, ma chile done been in town an' ain't come home?"

"It ain't wrong!" said old man Logan, cracking his long whip on the white mule's haunches. "Gittiyap! You ole jinny!" and he drove off.

"Um-uh!" said Sister Whiteside to Hager as the two toil-worn old women walked toward the house. "That's de way they does you!" The peddler gathered up her things. "I better be movin', 'cause I got these greens to sell yit, an' it's gittin' 'long towards evenin'. . . . That's de way chillens does you, Sister Williams! I knows! That's de way they does!"

III.

JIMBOY'S LETTER

KANSAS CITY, MO.
13 June 1912

Dear Annjelica,

I been laying off to written you ever since I left home but you
know how it is. Work has not been so good here. Am with a section gang of coloreds and greeks and somehow strained my back
on the Union Pacific laying ties so I will be home on Saturday.
Will do my best to try and finish out weak here. Love my darling
wife also kiss my son Sandy for me. Am dying to see you,

> affectionately as ever
> and allways
> till the judgment day,
> JIMBOY ROGERS

"Strained his back, has he? Unhuh! An' then comes writin' 'bout till de judgment day!" Hager muttered when she
heard it. "Always something wrong with that nigger! He'll be
back here now, layin' 'round, doin' nothin' fo' de rest o' de
summer, turnin' ma house into a theatre with him an' Harriett
singin' their rag-time, an' that guitar o' his'n wangin' ever'
evenin'! 'Tween him an' Harriett both it's a wonder I ain't
plumb crazy. But Harriett do work fo' her livin'. She ain't no
loafer.... Huh!... Annjee, you was sho a fool when you married that boy, an' you still is!... I's gwine next do' to Sister

Johnson's!" Aunt Hager went out the back and across the yard, where, next door, Tom and Sarah Johnson, Willie-Mae's grandparents, sat on a bench against the side-wall of an unpainted shanty. They were both quietly smoking their corn-cob pipes in the evening dusk.

Sandy, looking at the back of the letter that his mother held, stood at the kitchen-table rapidly devouring a large piece of fresh lemon pie, which she had brought from Mrs. J. J. Rice's. Annjee had said to save the two cold fried lamb chops until tomorrow, or Sandy would have eaten those, too.

"Wish you'd brought home some more pie," the boy declared, his lips white with meringue, but Annjee, who had just got in from work, paid no attention to her son's appreciative remarks on her cookery.

Instead she said: "Ma certainly ain't got no time for Jimboy, has she?" and then sat down with the open letter still in her hand—a single sheet of white paper pencilled in large awkward letters. She put it on the table, rested her dark face in her hands, and began to read it again. . . . She knew how it was, of course, that her husband hadn't written before. That was all right now. Working all day in the hot sun with a gang of Greeks, a man was tired at night, besides living in a box-car, where there was no place to write a letter anyway. He was a great big kid, that's what Jimboy was, cut out for playing. But when he did work, he tried to outdo everybody else. Annjee could see him in her mind, tall and well-built, his legs apart, muscles bulging as he swung the big hammer above his head, driving steel. No wonder he hurt his back, trying to lay more ties a day than anybody else on the railroad. That was just like Jimboy. But she was kind of pleased he had hurt it, since it would bring him home.

"Ain't you glad he's comin', Sandy?"

"Sure," answered the child, swallowing his last mouthful of pie. "I hope he brings me that gun he promised to buy last Easter." The boy wiped his sticky hands on the dish-cloth and ran out into the back yard, calling: "Willie-Mae! Willie-Mae!"

"Stay right over yonder!" answered his grandmother through the dusk. "Willie-Mae's in de bed, sir, an' we old folks settin' out here tryin' to have a little peace." From the tone of Hager's voice he knew he wasn't wanted in the Johnson's yard, so he went back into the house, looked at his mother reading her letter again, and then lay down on the kitchen-floor. "Affectionately as ever and allways till the judgment day," she read, "Jimboy Rogers."

He loved her, Annjee was sure of that, and it wasn't another woman that made him go away so often. Eight years they'd been married. No, nine—because Sandy was nine, and he was ready to be born when they had had the wedding. And Jimboy left the week after they were married, to go to Omaha, where he worked all winter. When he came back, Sandy was in the world, sitting up sucking meat skins. It was springtime and they bought a piano for the house—but later the instalment man came and took it back to the store. All that summer her husband stayed home and worked a little, but mostly he fished, played pool, taught Harriett to buck-dance, and quarrelled with Aunt Hager. Then in the winter he went to Jefferson City and got a job at the Capitol.

Jimboy was always going, but Aunt Hager was wrong about his never working. It was just that he couldn't stay in one place all the time. He'd been born running, he said, and had run ever since. Besides, what was there in Stanton anyhow for a young colored fellow to do except dig sewer ditches for a few cents an hour or maybe porter around a store for seven dollars a week. Colored men couldn't get many jobs in Stanton, and foreigners were coming in, taking away what little work they did have. No wonder he didn't stay home. Hadn't Annjee's father been in Stanton forty years and hadn't he died with Aunt Hager still taking in washings to help keep up the house?

There was no well-paid work for Negro men, so Annjee didn't blame Jimboy for going away looking for something better. She'd go with him if it wasn't for her mother. If she went, though, Aunt Hager wouldn't have anybody for company but Harriett, and Harriett was the youngest and wildest of the three children. With Pa Williams dead going on ten years, Hager washing every day, Tempy married, and Annjee herself out working, there had been nobody to take much care of the little sister as she grew up. Harriett had had no raising, even though she was smart and in high school. A female child needed care. But she could sing! Lawdy! And dance, too! That was another reason why Aunt Hager didn't like Jimboy. The devil's musicianer, she called him, straight from hell, teaching Harriett buck-and-winging! But when he took his soft-playing guitar and picked out spirituals and old-time Christian hymns on its sweet strings, Hager forgot she was his enemy, and sang and rocked with the rest of them. When Jimboy was home, you couldn't get lonesome or blue.

"Gee, I'll be glad when he comes!" Annjee said to herself. "But if he goes off again, I'll feel like dying in this dead old town. I ain't never been away from here nohow." She spoke aloud to the dim oil-lamp smoking on the table and the sleeping boy on the floor. "I believe I'll go with him next time. I declare I do!" And then, realizing that Jimboy had never once told her when he was leaving or for what destination, she amended her utterance. "I'll follow him, though, as soon as he writes." Because, almost always after he had been away two or three weeks, he would write. "I'll follow him, sure, if he goes off again. I'll leave Sandy here and send money back to mama. Then Harriett could settle down and take care of ma and stop runnin' the streets so much. . . . Yes, that's what I'll do next time!"

This going away was a new thought, and the dark, strong-bodied young woman at the table suddenly began to dream of the cities she had never seen to which Jimboy would lead her. Why, he had been as far north as Canada and as far south as New Orleans, and it wasn't anything for him to go to Chicago or Denver any time! He was a travelling man—and she, Annjee, was too meek and quiet, that's what she was—too stay-at-homish. Never going nowhere, never saying nothing back to those who scolded her or talked about her, not even

sassing white folks when they got beside themselves. And
every colored girl in town said that Mrs. J. J. Rice was no easy
white woman to work for, yet she had been there now five
years, accepting everything without a murmur! Most young
folks, girls and boys, left Stanton as soon as they could for the
outside world, but here she was, Annjelica Williams, going on
twenty-eight, and had never been as far as Kansas City!

"I want to travel," she said to herself. "I want to go places, too."

But that was why Jimboy married her, because she wasn't a
runabout. He'd had enough of those kind of women before he
struck Stanton, he said. St. Louis was full of them, and Chicago running over. She was the first nice girl he'd ever met who
lived at home, so he took her. . . . There were mighty few dark
women had a light, strong, good-looking young husband, really a married husband, like Jimboy, and a little brown kid
like Sandy.

"I'm mighty lucky," Annjee thought, "even if he ain't here."
And two tears of foolish pride fell from the bright eyes in her
round black face. They trickled down on the letter, with its
blue lines and pencil-scrawled message, and some of the words
on the paper began to blur into purple blots because the pencil
had been an indelible one. Quickly she fumbled for a handkerchief to wipe the tears away, when a voice made her start.

"You Annjee!" cried Aunt Hager in the open door. "Go to
bed, chile! Go on! Settin' up here this late, burnin' de light an'
lurin' all sorts o' night-bugs an' creepers into de house!" The
old woman came in out of the dark. "Lawd! I might anigh
stumbled over this boy in de middle o' de flo'! An' you ain't
even took off yo' hat since you got home from work! Is you
crazy? Settin' up here at night with yo' hat on, an' lettin' this
chile catch his death o' cold sleepin' down on de flo' long after
his bedtime!"

Sheepishly Annjee folded her letter and got up. It was true
that she still had on her hat and the sweater she had worn to
Mrs. Rice's. True, too, the whole room was alive with soft-
winged moths fluttering against the hot glass of the light—and

on the kitchen floor a small, brown-skin, infinitely lovable edition of Jimboy lay sprawled contentedly in his grandmother's path, asleep!

"He's my baby!" Annjee said gently, stooping to pick him up. "He's my baby—me and Jimboy's baby!"

IV.

THURSDAY AFTERNOON

Hager had risen at sunrise. On Thursdays she did the Reinharts' washing, on Fridays she ironed it, and on Saturdays she sent it home, clean and beautifully white, and received as pay the sum of seventy-five cents. During the winter Hager usually did half a dozen washings a week, but during the hot season her customers had gone away, and only the Reinharts, on account of an invalid grandmother with whom they could not travel, remained in Stanton.

Wednesday afternoon Sandy, with a boy named Jimmy Lane, called at the back door for their soiled clothes. Each child took a handle and between them carried the large wicker basket seven blocks to Aunt Hager's kitchen. For this service Jimmy Lane received five cents a trip, although Sister Lane had repeatedly said to Hager that he needn't be given anything. She wanted him to learn his Christian duties by being useful to old folks. But Jimmy was not inclined to be Christian. On the contrary, he was a very bad little boy of thirteen, who often led Sandy astray. Sometimes they would run with the basket for no reason at all, then stumble and spill the clothes out on the sidewalk—Mrs. Reinhart's summer dresses, and drawers, and Mr. Reinhart's extra-large B.V.D.'s lying generously exposed to the public. Sometimes, if occasion offered, the youngsters would stop to exchange uncouth epithets with strange little white boys who called them "niggers." Or, again, they might neglect their job for a game of marbles, or a quarter-hour of scrub baseball on a vacant lot; or to tease any little colored girl who might tip timidly by with her hair in tight, well-oiled braids—while the basket of garments would be left forlornly in the street without guardian. But when the clothes were safe in Aunt Hager's kitchen, Jimmy would usually buy candy with his nickel and share it with Sandy before he went home.

After soaking all night, the garments were rubbed through the suds in the morning; and in the afternoon the colored articles were on the line while the white pieces were boiling seriously in a large tin boiler on the kitchen-stove.

"They sho had plenty this week," Hager said to her grandson, who sat on the stoop eating a slice of bread and apple butter. "I's mighty late gettin' 'em hung out to dry, too. Had no business stoppin' this mawnin' to go see sick folks, and me here got all I can do maself! Looks like this warm weather old Mis' Reinhart must change ever' piece from her dress to her shimmy three times a day—sendin' me a washin' like this here!" They heard the screen-door at the front of the house open and slam. "It's a good thing they got me to do it fo' 'em! . . . Sandy, see who's that at de do'."

It was Harriett, home from the country club for the afternoon, cool and slender and pretty in her black uniform with its white collar, her smooth black face and neck powdered pearly, and her crinkly hair shining with pomade. She smelled nice and perfumy as Sandy jumped on her like a dog greeting a favorite friend. Harriett kissed him and let him hang to her arm as they went through the bedroom to the kitchen. She carried a brown cardboard suit-case and a wide straw hat in one hand.

"Hello, mama," she said.

Hager poked the boiling clothes with a vigorous splash of her round stick. The steam rose in clouds of soapy vapor.

"I been waitin' for you, madam!" her mother replied in tones that were not calculated to welcome pleasantly an erring daughter. "I wants to know de truth—was you in town last Monday night or not?"

Harriett dropped her suit-case against the wall. "You seem to have the truth," she said carelessly. "How'd you get it? . . .

Here, Sandy, take this out in the yard and eat it, seed and all."
She gave her nephew a plum she had brought in her pocket. "I
was in town, but I didn't have time to come home. I had to go
to Maudel's because she's making me a dress."

"To Maudel's! . . . Unhuh! An' to de Waiters' Ball, besides
galavantin' up an' down Pearl Street after ten o'clock! I
wouldn't cared so much if you'd told me beforehand, but you
said you didn't come in town 'ceptin' Thursday afternoon, an'
here I was believing yo' lies."

"It's no lies! I haven't been in town before."

"Who brung you here at night anyhow—an' there ain't no
trains runnin'?"

"O, I came in with the cook and some of the boys, mama,
that's who! They hired an auto for the dance. What would be
the use coming home, when you and Annjee go to bed before
dark like chickens?"

"That's all right, madam! Annjee's got sense—savin' her
health an' strength!"

Harriett was not impressed. "For what? To spend her life in
Mrs. Rice's kitchen?" She shrugged her shoulders.

"What you bring yo' suit-case home fo'?"

"I'm quitting the job Saturday," she said. "I've told them
already."

"Quitting!" her mother exclaimed. "What fo'? Lawd, if it
ain't one thing, it's another!"

"What for?" Harriett retorted angrily. "There's plenty what
for! All that work for five dollars a week with what little tips
those pikers give you. And white men insulting you besides,
asking you to sleep with 'em. Look at my finger-nails, all broke
from scrubbing that dining-room floor." She thrust out her
dark slim hands. "Waiting table and cleaning silver, washing
and ironing table-linen, and then scrubbing the floor besides—
that's too much of a good thing! And only three waitresses on
the job. That old steward out there's a regular white folks' nigger. He don't care how hard he works us girls. Well, I'm
through with the swell new Stanton County Country Club this

coming Saturday—I'm telling everybody!" She shrugged her
shoulders again.

"What you gonna do then?"

"Maudel says I can get a job with her."

"Maudel? . . . Where?" The old woman had begun to wring
the clothes dry and pile them in a large dish-pan.

"At the Banks Hotel, chambermaid, for pretty good pay."

Hager stopped again and turned decisively towards her
daughter. "You ain't gonna work in no hotel. You hear me!
They's dives o' sin, that's what they is, an' a child o' mine ain't
goin' in one. If you was a boy, I wouldn't let you go, much less
a girl! They ain't nothin' but strumpets works in hotels."

"Maudel's no strumpet." Harriett's eyes narrowed.

"I don't know if she is or ain't, but I knows I wants you to
stop runnin' with her—I done tole you befo'. . . . Her mammy
ain't none too straight neither, raisin' them chillen in sin. Look
at Sammy in de reform school 'fore he were fifteen for gamb-
lin'. An' de oldest chile, Essie, done gone to Kansas City with
that yaller devil she ain't married. An' Maudel runnin' de
streets night an' day, with you tryin' to keep up with her! . . .
Lawd a mercy! . . . Here, hang up these clothes!"

Her mother pointed to the tin pan on the table filled with
damp, twisted, white underwear. Harriett took the pan in
both hands. It was heavy and she trembled with anger as she
lifted it to her shoulders.

"You can bark at me if you want to, mama, but don't talk
about my friends. I don't care what they are! Maudel'd do anything for me. And her brother's a good kid, whether he's been
in reform school or not. They oughtn't to put him there just
for shooting dice. What's that? I like him, and I like Mrs.
Smothers, too. She's not always scolding people for wanting a
good time and for being lively and trying to be happy."

Hot tears raced down each cheek, leaving moist lines in the
pink powder. Sandy, playing marbles with Buster under the
apple-tree, heard her sniffling as she shook out the clothes and
hung them on the line in the yard.

"You Sandy," Aunt Hager called loudly from the kitchen-door. "Come in here an' get me some water an' cut mo' fire-wood." Her black face was wet with perspiration and drawn from fatigue and worry. "I got to get the rest o' these clothes out yet this evenin'. . . . That chile Harriett's aggravatin' me to death! Help me, Sandy, honey."

They ate supper in silence, for Hager's attempts at conversation with her young daughter were futile. Once the old woman said: "That onery Jimboy's comin' home Saturday," and Harriett's face brightened a moment.

"Gee, I'm glad," she replied, and then her mouth went sullen again. Sandy began uncomfortably to kick the table-leg.

"For Christ's sake!" the girl frowned, and the child stopped, hurt that his favorite aunt should yell at him peevishly for so slight an offense.

"Lawd knows, I wish you'd try an' be mo' like yo' sisters, Annjee an' Tempy," Hager began as she washed the dishes, while Harriett stood near the stove, cloth in hand, waiting to dry them. "Here I is, an old woman, an' you tries ma soul! After all I did to raise you, you don't even hear me when I speak." It was the old theme again, without variation. "Now, there's Annjee, ain't a better chile livin'—if she warn't crazy 'bout Jimboy. An' Tempy married an' doin' well, an' respected ever'where. . . . An' you runnin' wild!"

"Tempy?" Harriett sneered suddenly, pricked by this comparison. "So respectable you can't touch her with a ten-foot pole, that's Tempy! . . . Annjee's all right, working herself to death at Mrs. Rice's, but don't tell me about Tempy. Just because she's married a mail-clerk with a little property, she won't even see her own family any more. When niggers get up in the world, they act just like white folks—don't pay you no mind. And Tempy's that kind of a nigger—she's up in the world now!"

"Close yo' mouth, talking that way 'bout yo' own sister! I ain't asked her to be always comin' home, is I, if she's satisfied in her own house?"

"No, you aren't asking her, mama, but you're always talking about her being so respectable. . . . Well, I don't want to be respectable if I have to be stuck up and dicty like Tempy is. . . . She's colored and I'm colored and I haven't seen her since before Easter. . . . It's not being black that matters with her, though, it's being poor, and that's what we are, you and me and Annjee, working for white folks and washing clothes and going in back doors, and taking tips and insults. I'm tired of it, mama! I want to have a good time once in a while."

"That's 'bout all you does have is a good time," Hager said. "An' it ain't right, an' it ain't Christian, that's what it ain't! An' de Lawd is takin' notes on you!" The old woman picked up the heavy iron skillet and began to wash it inside and out.

"Aw, the church has made a lot of you old Negroes act like Salvation Army people," the girl returned, throwing the dried knives and forks on the table. "Afraid to even laugh on Sundays, afraid for a girl and boy to look at one another, or for people to go to dances. Your old Jesus is white, I guess, that's why! He's white and stiff and don't like niggers!"

Hager gasped while Harriett went on excitedly, disregarding her mother's pain: "Look at Tempy, the highest-class Christian in the family—Episcopal, and so holy she can't even visit her own mother. Seems like all the good-time people are bad, and all the old Uncle Toms and mean, dried-up, long-faced niggers fill the churches. I don't never intend to join a church if I can help it."

"Have mercy on this chile! Help her an' save her from hell-fire! Change her heart, Jesus!" the old woman begged, standing in the middle of the kitchen with uplifted arms. "God have mercy on ma daughter."

Harriett, her brow wrinkled in a steady frown, put the dishes away, wiped the table, and emptied the water with a splash through the kitchen-door. Then she went into the bedroom that she shared with her mother, and began to undress. Sandy saw, beneath her thin white underclothes, the soft black skin of her shapely young body.

"Where you goin'?" Hager asked sharply.

"Out," said the girl.

"Out where?"

"O, to a barbecue at Willow Grove, mama! The boys are coming by in an auto at seven o'clock."

"What boys?"

"Maudel's brother and some fellows."

"You ain't goin' a step!"

A pair of curling-irons swung in the chimney of the lighted lamp on the dresser. Harriett continued to get ready. She was making bangs over her forehead, and the scent of scorching hair-oil drifted by Sandy's nose.

"Up half de night in town Monday, an' de Lawd knows how late ever' night in de country, an' then you comes home to run out agin! . . . You ain't goin'!" continued her mother.

Harriett was pulling on a pair of red silk stockings, bright and shimmering to her hips.

"You quit singin' in de church choir. You say you ain't goin' back to school. You won't keep no job! Now what *is* you gonna do? Yo' pappy said years ago, 'fore he died, you was too purty to 'mount to anything, but I ain't believed him. His last dyin' words was: 'Look out fo' ma baby Harriett.' You was his favourite chile. . . . Now look at you! Runnin' de streets an' wearin' red silk stockings!" Hager trembled." 'Spose yo' pappy was to come back an' see you?"

Harriett powdered her face and neck, pink on ebony, dashed white talcum at each arm-pit, and rubbed her ears with perfume from a thin bottle. Then she slid a light blue dress of many ruffles over her head. The skirt ended midway between the ankle and the knee, and she looked very cute, delicate, and straight, like a black porcelain doll in a Vienna toy shop.

"Some o' Maudel's makin's, that dress—anybody can tell," her mother went on quarrelling. "Short an' shameless as it can be! Regular bad gal's dress, that's what 'tis. . . . What you puttin' it on fo' anyhow, an' I done told you you ain't goin' out? You must think I don't mean ma words. Ain't more'n sixteen last April an' runnin' to barbecues at Willer Grove! De idee!

When I was yo' age, wasn't up after eight o'clock, 'ceptin' Sundays in de church house, that's all. . . . Lawd knows where you young ones is headin'. An' me prayin' an' washin' ma fingers to de bone to keep a roof over yo' head."

The sharp honk of an automobile horn sounded from the street. A big red car, full of laughing brown girls gaily dressed, and coatless, slick-headed black boys in green and yellow silk shirts, drew up at the curb. Somebody squeezed the bulb of the horn a second time and another loud and saucy honk! struck the ears.

"You Sandy," Hager commanded. "Run out there an' tell them niggers to leave here, 'cause Harriett ain't goin' no place."

But Sandy did not move, because his young and slender aunt had gripped him firmly by the collar while she searched feverishly in the dresser-drawer for a scarf. She pulled it out, long and flame-colored, with fiery, silky fringe, before she released the little boy.

"You ain't gwine a step this evenin'!" Hager shouted. "Don't you hear me?"

"O, no?" said Harriett coolly in a tone that cut like knives. "You're the one that says I'm not going—*but I am*!"

Then suddenly something happened in the room—the anger fell like a veil from Hager's face, disclosing aged, helpless eyes full of fear and pain.

"Harriett, honey, I wants you to be good," the old woman stammered. The words came pitiful and low—not a command any longer—as she faced her terribly alive young daughter in the ruffled blue dress and the red silk stockings. "I just wants you to grow up decent, chile. I don't want you runnin' to Willer Grove with them boys. It ain't no place fo' you in the night-time—an' you knows it. You's mammy's baby girl. She wants you to be good, honey, and follow Jesus, that's all."

The baritone giggling of the boys in the auto came across the yard as Hager started to put a timid, restraining hand on her daughter's shoulder—but Harriett backed away.

"You old fool!" she cried. "Lemme go! You old Christian fool!"

She ran through the door and across the sidewalk to the waiting car, where the arms of the young men welcomed her eagerly. The big machine sped swiftly down the street and the rapid sput! sput! sput! of its engine grew fainter and fainter. Finally, the auto was only a red tail-light in the summer dusk. Sandy, standing beside his grandmother in the doorway, watched it until it disappeared.

V.

GUITAR

Throw yo' arms around me, baby,
Like de circle round de sun!
Baby, throw yo' arms around me
Like de circle round de sun,
An' tell yo' pretty papa
How you want yo' lovin' done!

Jimboy was home. All the neighborhood could hear his rich low baritone voice giving birth to the blues. On Saturday night he and Annjee went to bed early. On Sunday night Aunt Hager said: "Put that guitar right up, less'n it's hymns you plans on playin'. An' I don't want too much o' them, 'larmin' de white neighbors."

But this was Monday, and the sun had scarcely fallen below the horizon before the music had begun to float down the alley, over back fences and into kitchen-windows where nice white ladies sedately washed their supper dishes.

Did you ever see peaches
Growin' on a watermelon vine?
Says did you ever see peaches
On a watermelon vine?
Did you ever see a woman
That I couldn't get for mine?

Long, lazy length resting on the kitchen-door-sill, back against the jamb, feet in the yard, fingers picking his sweet guitar, left hand holding against its finger-board the back of an old pocket-knife, sliding the knife upward, downward, getting thus weird croons and sighs from the vibrating strings:

> O, I left ma mother
> An' I cert'ly can leave you.
> Indeed I left ma mother
> An' I cert'ly can leave you,
> For I'd leave any woman
> That mistreats me like you do.

Jimboy, remembering brown-skin mamas in Natchez, Shreveport, Dallas; remembering Creole women in Baton Rouge, Louisiana:

> O, yo' windin' an' yo' grindin'
> Don't have no effect on me,
> Babe, yo' windin' an' yo' grindin'
> Don't have no 'fect on me,
> 'Cause I can wind an' grind
> Like a monkey round a coconut-tree!

Then Harriett, standing under the ripening apple-tree, in the back yard, chiming in:

> Now I see that you don't want me,
> So it's fare thee, fare thee well!
> Lawd, I see that you don't want me,
> So it's fare—thee—well!
> I can still get plenty lovin',
> An' you can go to—Kansas City!

"O, play it, sweet daddy Jimboy!" She began to dance.

Then Hager, from her seat on the edge of the platform covering the well, broke out: "Here, madam! Stop that prancin'! Bad enough to have all this singin' without turnin' de yard into a show-house." But Harriett kept on, her hands picking imaginary cherries out of the stars, her hips speaking an earthly language quite their own.

"You got it, kid," said Jimboy, stopping suddenly, then fingering his instrument for another tune. "You do it like the stage women does. You'll be takin' Ada Walker's place if you keep on."

"Wha! Wha! . . . You chillen sho can sing!" Tom Johnson shouted his compliments from across the yard. And Sarah, beside him on the bench behind their shack, added: "Minds me o' de ole plantation times, honey! It sho do!"

"Unhuh! Bound straight fo' de devil, that's what they is," Hager returned calmly from her place beside the pump. "You an' Harriett both—singin' an' dancin' this stuff befo' these chillens here." She pointed to Sandy and Willie-Mae, who sat on the ground with their backs against the chicken-box. "It's a shame!"

"I likes it," said Willie-Mae.

"Me too," the little boy agreed.

"Naturally you would—none o' you-all's converted yet," countered the old woman to the children as she settled back against the pump to listen to some more.

The music rose hoarse and wild:

I wonder where ma easy rider's gone?
He done left me, put ma new gold watch in pawn.

It was Harriett's voice in plaintive moan to the night sky. Jimboy had taught her that song, but a slight, clay-colored brown boy who had hopped bells at the Clinton Hotel for a couple of months, on his way from Houston to Omaha, discovered its meaning to her. Puppy-love, maybe, but it had hurt when he went away, saying nothing. And the guitar in Jimboy's hands echoed that old pain with an even greater throb than the original ache itself possessed.

Approaching footsteps came from the front yard.

"Lord, I can hear you-all two blocks away!" said Annjee, coming around the house, home from work, with a bundle of

food under her left arm. "Hello! How are you, daddy? Hello,
ma! Gimme a kiss Sandy. . . . Lord, I'm hot and tired and most
played out. This late just getting from work! . . . Here, Jimboy,
come on in and eat some of these nice things the white folks
had for supper." She stepped across her husband's outstretched
legs into the kitchen. "I brought a mighty good piece of cold
ham for you, hon', from Mis' Rice's."

"All right, sure, I'll be there in a minute," the man said, but
he went on playing *Easy Rider*, and Harriett went on singing,
while the food was forgotten on the table until long after Annjee had come outdoors again and sat down in the cool, tired of
waiting for Jimboy to come in to her.

Off and on for nine years, ever since he had married Annjee,
Jimboy and Harriett had been singing together in the evenings.
When they started, Harriett was a little girl with braided hair, and
each time that her roving brother-in-law stopped in Stanton, he
would amuse himself by teaching her the old Southern songs, the
popular rag-time ditties, and the hundreds of varying verses of
the blues that he would pick up in the big dirty cities of the South.
The child, with her strong sweet voice (colored folks called it alto)
and her racial sense of rhythm, soon learned to sing the songs as
well as Jimboy. He taught her the *parse me la*, too, and a few
other movements peculiar to Southern Negro dancing, and sometimes together they went through the buck-and-wing and a few
taps. It was all great fun, and innocent fun except when one
stopped to think, as white folks did, that some of the blues lines
had, not only double, but triple meanings, and some of the dance
steps required very definite movements of the hips. But neither
Harriett nor Jimboy soiled their minds by thinking. It was music,
good exercise—and they loved it.

"Do you know this one, Annjee?" asked Jimboy, calling his
wife's name out of sudden politeness because he had forgotten
to eat her food, had hardly looked at her, in fact, since she
came home. Now he glanced towards her in the darkness
where she sat plump on a kitchen-chair in the yard, apart from
the others, with her back to the growing corn in the garden.

Softly he ran his fingers, light as a breeze, over his guitar strings, imitating the wind rustling through the long leaves of the corn. A rectangle of light from the kitchen-door fell into the yard striking sidewise across the healthy orange-yellow of his skin above the unbuttoned neck of his blue laborer's shirt.

"Come on, sing it with us, Annjee," he said.

"I don't know it," Annjee replied, with a lump in her throat, and her eyes on the silhouette of his long, muscular, animal-hard body. She loved Jimboy too much, that's what was the matter with her! She knew there was nothing between him and her young sister except the love of music, yet he might have dropped the guitar and left Harriett in the yard for a little while to come eat the nice cold slice of ham she had brought him. She hadn't seen him all day long. When she went to work this morning, he was still in bed—and now the blues claimed him.

In the starry blackness the singing notes of the guitar became a plaintive hum, like a breeze in a grove of palmettos; became a low moan, like the wind in a forest of live-oaks strung with long strands of hanging moss. The voice of Annjee's golden, handsome husband on the door-step rang high and far away, lonely-like, crying with only the guitar, not his wife, to understand; crying grotesquely, crying absurdly in the summer night:

> *I got a mule to ride.*
> *I got a mule to ride.*
> *Down in the South somewhere*
> *I got a mule to ride.*

Then asking the question as an anxious, left-lonesome girl-sweetheart would ask it:

> *You say you goin' North.*
> *You say you goin' North.*
> *How 'bout yo' . . . lovin' gal?*
> *You say you goin' North.*

Then sighing in rhythmical despair:

> *O, don't you leave me here.*
> *Babe, don't you leave me here.*
> *Dog-gone yo' comin' back!*
> *Said don't you leave me here.*

On and on the song complained, man-verses and woman-verses, to the evening air in stanzas that Jimboy had heard in the pine-woods of Arkansas from the lumber-camp workers; in other stanzas that were desperate and dirty like the weary roads where they were sung; and in still others that the singer created spontaneously in his own mouth then and there:

> *O, I done made ma bed,*
> *Says I done made ma bed.*
> *Down in some lonesome grave*
> *I done made ma bed.*

It closed with a sad eerie twang.

"That's right decent," said Hager. "Now I wish you-all'd play some o' ma pieces like *When de Saints Come Marchin' In* or *This World Is Not Ma Home*—something Christian from de church."

"Aw, mama, it's not Sunday yet," said Harriett.

"Sing *Casey Jones*," called old man Tom Johnson. "That's ma song."

So the ballad of the immortal engineer with another mama in the Promised Land rang out promptly in the starry darkness, while everybody joined in the choruses.

"Aw, pick it, boy," yelled the old man. "Can't nobody play like you."

And Jimboy remembered when he was a lad in Memphis that W. C. Handy had said: "You ought to make your living out of that, son." But he hadn't followed it up—too many things to see, too many places to go, too many other jobs.

"What song do you like, Annjee?" he asked, remembering her presence again.

"O, I don't care. Any ones you like. All of 'em are pretty." She was pleased and petulant and a little startled that he had asked her.

"All right, then," he said. "Listen to me:"

> *Here I is in de mean ole jail.*
> *Ain't got nobody to go ma bail.*
> *Lonesome an' sad an' chain gang bound—*
> *Ever' friend I had's done turned me down.*

"That's sho it!" shouted Tom Johnson in great sympathy. "Now, when I was in de Turner County Jail . . ."

"Shut up yo' mouth!" squelched Sarah, jabbing her husband in the ribs.

The songs went on, blues, shouts, jingles, old hits: *Bon Bon Buddy, the Chocolate Drop; Wrap Me in Your Big Red Shawl; Under the Old Apple Tree; Turkey in the Straw*—Jimboy and Harriett breaking the silence of the small-town summer night until Aunt Hager interrupted:

"You-all better wind up, chillens, 'cause I wants to go to bed. I ain't used to stayin' 'wake so late, nohow. Play something kinder decent there, son, fo' you stops."

Jimboy, to tease the old woman, began to rock and moan like an elder in the Sanctified Church, patting both feet at the same time as he played a hymn-like, lugubrious tune with a dancing overtone:

> *Tell me, sister,*
> *Tell me, brother,*
> *Have you heard de latest news?*

Then seriously as if he were about to announce the coming of the Judgment:

> *A woman down in Georgia*
> *Got her two sweet-men confused.*

How terrible! How sad! moaned the guitar.

> *One knocked on de front do',*
> *One knocked on de back—*

Sad, sad . . . sad, sad! said the music.

> *Now that woman down in Georgia's*
> *Door-knob is hung with black.*

O, play that funeral march, boy! while the guitar laughed
a dirge.

> *An' de hearse is comin' easy*
> *With two rubber-tired hacks!*

Followed by a long-out, churchlike:

> *Amen . . . !*

Then with rapid glides, groans, and shouts the instrument
screamed of a sudden in profane frenzy, and Harriett began to
ball-the-jack, her arms flopping like the wings of a headless pi-
geon, the guitar strings whining in ecstasy, the player rocking
gaily to the urgent music, his happy mouth crying: "Tack 'em
on down, gal! Tack 'em on down, Harrie!"

But Annjee had risen.

"I wish you'd come in and eat the ham I brought you," she said
as she picked up her chair and started towards the house. "And
you, Sandy! Get up from under that tree and go to bed." She spoke
roughly to the little fellow, whom the songs had set a-dreaming.
Then to her husband: "Jimboy, I wish you'd come in."

The man stopped playing, with a deep vibration of the strings
that seemed to echo through the whole world. Then he leaned
his guitar against the side of the house and lifted straight up in
his hairy arms Annjee's plump, brown-black little body while

he kissed her as she wriggled like a stubborn child, her soft breasts rubbing his hard body through the coarse blue shirt.

"You don't like my old songs, do you, baby? You don't want to hear me sing 'em," he said, laughing. "Well, that's all right. I like you, anyhow, and I like your ham, and I like your kisses, and I like everything you bring me. Let's go in and chow down." And he carried her into the kitchen, where he sat with her on his knees as he ate the food she so faithfully had brought him from Mrs. J. J. Rice's dinner-table.

Outside, Willie-Mae went running home through the dark. And Harriett pumped a cool drink of water for her mother, then helped her to rise from her low seat, Sandy aiding from behind, with both hands pushing firmly in Aunt Hager's fleshy back. Then the three of them came into the house and glanced, as they passed through the kitchen, at Annjee sitting on Jimboy's lap with both dark arms tight around his neck.

"Looks like you're clinging to the Rock of Ages," said Harriett to her sister. "Be sure you don't slip, old evil gal!"

But at midnight, when the owl that nested in a tree near the corner began to hoot, they were all asleep—Annjee and Jimboy in one room, Harriett and Hager in another, with Sandy on the floor at the foot of his grandmother's bed. Far away on the railroad line a whistle blew, lonesome and long.

VI.

WORK

The sunflowers in Willie-Mae's back yard were taller than Tom Johnson's head, and the hollyhocks in the fence corners were almost as high. The nasturtiums, blood-orange and gold, tumbled over themselves all around Madam de Carter's house. Aunt Hager's sweet-william, her pinks, and her tiger-lilies were abloom and the apples on her single tree would soon be ripe. The adjoining yards of the three neighbors were gay with flowers. "Watch out for them dogs!" his grandmother told Sandy hourly, for the days had come when the bright heat made gentle animals go mad. Bees were heavy with honey, great green flies hummed through the air, yellow-black butterflies suckled at the rambling roses . . . and watermelons were on the market.

The Royal African Knights and Ladies of King Solomon's Scepter were preparing a drill for the September Emancipation celebration, a "Drill of All Nations," in which Annjee was to represent Sweden. It was not to be given for a month or more, but the first rehearsal would take place tonight.

"Sandy," his mother said, shaking him early in the morning as he lay on his pallet at the foot of Aunt Hager's bed, "listen here! I want you to come out to Mis' Rice's this evening and help me get through the dishes so's I can start home early, in time to wash and dress myself to go to the lodge hall. You hears me?"

"Yes'm," said Sandy, keeping his eyes closed to the bright stream of morning sunlight entering the window. But half an hour later, when Jimboy kicked him and said: "Hey, bo! You wanta go fishin'?" he got up at once, slid into his pants; and

together they went out in the garden to dig worms. It was seldom that his father took him anywhere, and, of course, he
wanted to go. Sandy adored Jimboy, but Jimboy, amiable and
indulgent though he was, did not often care to be bothered
with his ten-year-old son on his fishing expeditions.

Harriett had gone to her job, and Hager had long been at
the tubs under the apple-tree when the two males emerged
from the kitchen-door. "Huh! You ain't workin' this mawnin',
is you?" the old woman grunted, bending steadily down, then
up, over the wash-board.

"Nope," her tall son-in-law answered. "Donahoe laid me
off yesterday on account o' the white bricklayers said they
couldn't lay bricks with a nigger."

"Always something to keep you from workin'," panted Hager.

"Sure is," agreed Jimboy pleasantly. "But don't worry, me
and Sandy's gonna catch you a mess o' fish for supper today.
How's that, ma?"

"Don't need no fish," the old woman answered. "An' don't
come ma-in' me! Layin' round here fishin' when you ought to
be out makin' money to take care o' this house an' that chile o'
your'n." The suds rose foamy white about her black arms as
the clothes plushed up and down on the zinc wash-board.
"Lawd deliver me from a lazy darky!"

But Jimboy and Sandy were already behind the tall corn,
digging for bait near the back fence.

"Don't never let no one woman worry you," said the boy's
father softly, picking the moist wriggling worms from the up-
turned loam. "Treat 'em like chickens, son. Throw 'em a little
corn and they'll run after you, but don't give 'em too much. If
you do, they'll stop layin' and expect you to wait on 'em."

"Will they?" asked Sandy.

The warm afternoon sun made the river a languid sheet of
muddy gold, glittering away towards the bridge and the flour-
mills a mile and a half off. Here in the quiet, on the end of a
rotting jetty among the reeds, Jimboy and his son sat silently.
A long string of small silver fish hung down into the water,

keeping fresh, and the fishing-lines were flung far out in the stream, waiting for more bites. Not a breeze on the flat brown-gold river, not a ripple, not a sound. But once the train came by behind them, pouring out a great cloud of smoke and cinders and shaking the jetty.

"That's Number Five," said Jimboy. "Sure is flyin'," as the train disappeared between rows of empty box-cars far down the track, sending back a hollow clatter as it shot past the flour-mills, whose stacks could be dimly seen through the heat haze. Once the engine's whistle moaned shrilly.

"She's gone now," said Jimboy as the last click of the wheels died away. And, except for the drone of a green fly about the can of bait, there was again no sound to disturb the two fishermen.

Jimboy gazed at his lines. Across the river Sandy could make out, in the brilliant sunlight, the gold of wheat-fields and the green of trees on the hills. He wondered if it would be nice to live over there in the country.

"Man alive!" his father cried suddenly, hauling vigorously at one of the lines. "Sure got a real bite now. . . . Look at this catfish." From the water he pulled a large flopping lead-colored creature, with a fierce white mouth bleeding and gaping over the hook.

"He's on my line!" yelled Sandy. "I caught him!"

"Pshaw!" laughed Jimboy. "You was setting there dreaming."

"No, I wasn't!"

But just then, at the mills, the five-o'clock whistles blew. "Oh, gee, dad!" cried the boy, frightened. "I was s'posed to go to Mis' Rice's to help mama, and I come near forgetting it. She wants to get through early this evenin' to go to the lodge meeting. I gotta hurry and go help her."

"Well, you better beat it then, and I'll look out for your line like I been doing and bring the fishes home."

So the little fellow balanced himself across the jetty, scrambled up the bank, and ran down the railroad track towards town. He was quite out of breath when he reached the foot of Penrose Street, with Mrs. Rice's house still ten blocks away, so he walked awhile, then ran again, down the long residential street, with its large houses sitting in green shady lawns far back from the sidewalk. Sometimes a sprinkler attached to a long rubber hose, sprayed fountain-like jets of cold water on the thirsty grass. In one yard three golden-haired little girls were playing under an elm-tree, and in another a man and some children were having a leisurely game of croquet.

Finally Sandy turned into a big yard. The delicious scent of frying beefsteak greeted the sweating youngster as he reached the screen of the white lady's kitchen-door. Inside, Annjee was standing over the hot stove seasoning something in a saucepan, beads of perspiration on her dark face, and large damp spots under the arms of her dress.

"You better get here!" she said. "And me waiting for you for the last hour. Here, take this pick and break some ice for the tea." Sandy climbed up on a stool and raised the ice-box lid while his mother opened the oven and pulled out a pan of golden-brown biscuits. "Made these for your father," she remarked. "The white folks ain't asked for 'em, but they like 'em, too, so they can serve for both. . . . Jimboy's crazy about biscuits. . . . Did he work today?"

"No'm," said Sandy, jabbing at the ice. "We went fishing."

At that moment Mrs. Rice came into the kitchen, tall and blond, in a thin flowered gown. She was a middle-aged white woman with a sharp nasal voice.

"Annjee, I'd like the potatoes served just as they are in the casserole. And make several slices of very thin toast for my father. Now, be sure they *are* thin!"

"Yes, m'am," said Annjee stirring a spoonful of flour into the frying-pan, making a thick brown gravy.

"Old thin toast," muttered Annjee when Mrs. Rice had gone back to the front. "Always bothering round the kitchen! Here 'tis lodge-meeting night—dinner late anyhow—and she coming telling me to stop and make toast for the old man! He ain't too indigestible to eat biscuits like the rest of 'em. . . . White folks sure is a case!" She laid three slices of bread on top of the stove. "So spoiled with colored folks waiting on 'em all their days! Don't know what they'll do in heaven, 'cause I'm gonna sit down up there myself."

Annjee took the biscuits, light and brown, and placed some on a pink plate she had warmed. She carried them, with the butter and jelly, into the dining-room. Then she took the steak from the warmer, dished up the vegetables into gold-rimmed serving-dishes, and poured the gravy, which smelled deliciously onion-flavored.

"Gee, I'm hungry," said the child, with his eyes on the big steak ready to go in to the white people.

"Well, just wait," replied his mother. "You come to work, not to eat. . . . Whee! but it's hot today!" She wiped her wet face and put on a large white bungalow apron that had been hanging behind the door. Then she went with the iced tea and a pitcher of water into the dining-room, struck a Chinese gong, and came back to the kitchen to get the dishes of steaming food, which she carried in to the table.

It was some time before she returned from waiting on the table; so Sandy, to help her, began to scrape out the empty pans and put them to soak in the sink. He ate the stewed corn that had stuck in the bottom of one, and rubbed a piece of bread in the frying-pan where the gravy had been. His mother came out with the water-pitcher, broke some ice for it, and returned to the dining-room where Sandy could hear laughter, and the clinking of spoons in tea-glasses, and women talking. When Annjee came back into the kitchen, she took four custards from the ice-box and placed them on gold-rimmed plates.

"They're about through," she said to her son. "Sit down and I'll fix you up."

Sandy was very hungry and he hoped Mrs. Rice's family hadn't eaten all the steak, which had looked so good with its brown gravy and onions.

Shortly, his mother returned carrying the dishes that had been filled with hot food. She placed them on the kitchen-table in front of Sandy, but they were no longer full and no longer hot. The corn had thickened to a paste, and the potatoes were about gone; but there was still a ragged piece of steak left on the platter.

"Don't eat it all," said Annjee warningly. "I want to take some home to your father."

The bell rang in the dining-room. Annjee went through the swinging door and returned bearing a custard that had been but little touched.

"Here, sonny—the old man says it's too sweet for his stomach, so you can have this." She set the yellow cornstarch before Sandy. "He's seen these ripe peaches out here today and he wants some, that's all. More trouble than he's worth, po' old soul, and me in a hurry!" She began to peel the fruit. "Just like a chile, 'deed he is!" she added, carrying the sliced peaches into the dining-room and leaving Sandy with a plate of food before him, eating slowly. "When you rushing to get out, seems like white folks tries theirselves."

In a moment she returned, ill-tempered, and began to scold Sandy for taking so long with his meal.

"I asked you to help me so's I can get to the lodge on time, and you just set and chew and eat! . . . Here, wipe these dishes, boy!" Annjee began hurriedly to lay plates in a steaming row on the shelf of the sink; so Sandy got up and, between mouthfuls of pudding, wiped them with a large dish-towel.

Soon Mrs. Rice came into the kitchen again, briskly, through the swinging door and glanced about her. Sandy felt ashamed for the white woman to see him eating a left-over pudding from her table, so he put the spoon down.

"Annjee," the mistress said sharply. "I wish you wouldn't put quite so much onion in your sauce for the steak. I've mentioned it to you several times before, and you know very well we don't like it."

"Yes, m'am," said Annjee.

"And do *please* be careful that our drinking water is cold before meals are served. . . . You were certainly careless tonight. You must think more about what you are doing, Annjee."

Mrs. Rice went out again through the swinging door, but

Sandy stood near the sink with a burning face and eyes that
had suddenly filled with angry tears. He couldn't help it—
hearing his sweating mother reprimanded by this tall white
woman in the flowered dress. Black, hard-working Annjee answered: "Yes, m'am," and that was all—but Sandy cried.

"Dry up," his mother said crossly when she saw him, thinking he was crying because she had asked him to work. "What's
come over you, anyway?—can't even wipe a few plates for me
and act nice about it!"

He didn't answer. When the dining-room had been cleared
and the kitchen put in order, Annjee told him to empty the
garbage while she wrapped in newspapers several little bun-
dles of food to carry to Jimboy. Then they went out the back
door, around the big house to the street, and trudged the fourteen blocks to Aunt Hager's, taking short cuts through alleys,
passing under arc-lights that sputtered whitely in the deepen-
ing twilight, and greeting with an occasional "Howdy" other
poor colored folks also coming home from work.

"How are you, Sister Jones?"

"Right smart, I thank yuh!" as they passed.

Once Annjee spoke to her son. "Evening's the only time we
niggers have to ourselves!" she said. "Thank God for night . . .
'cause all day you gives to white folks."

VII.

WHITE FOLKS

When they got home, Aunt Hager was sitting in the cool of the evening on her new porch, which had been rebuilt for thirty-five dollars added to the mortgage. The old woman was in her rocking-chair, with Jimboy, one foot on the ground and his back against a pillar, lounging at her feet. The two were quarrelling amicably over nothing as Annjee and Sandy approached.

"Good-evenin', you-all," said Annjee. "I brought you a nice piece o' steak, Jimboy-sugar, and some biscuits to go with it. Come on in and eat while I get dressed to go to the drill practice. I got to hurry."

"We don't want no steak now," Jimboy answered without moving. "Aunt Hager and me had fresh fish for supper and egg-corn-bread and we're full. We don't need nothin' more."

"Oh! . . ." said Annjee disappointedly. "Well, come on in anyhow, honey, and talk while I get dressed." So he rose lazily and followed his wife into the house.

Shortly, Sister Johnson, pursued by the ever-present Willie-Mae, came through the blue-grey darkness from next door. "Good-evenin', Sister Williams; how you been today?"

"Tolable," answered Hager, " 'ceptin' I's tired out from washin' an' rinsin'. Have a seat. . . . You Sandy, go in de house an' get Sister Johnson a settin'-chair. . . . Where's Tom?"

"Lawd, chile, he done gone to bed long ago. That there sewer-diggin' job ain't so good fer a man old as Tom. He 'bout played out. . . . I done washed fer Mis' Cohn maself today. . . . Umh! dis cheer feels good! . . . Looked like to me she had near 'bout fifty babies' diddies in de wash. You know she done got twins, 'sides dat young-'un born last year."

The conversation of the two old women rambled on as their grandchildren ran across the front yard laughing, shrieking, wrestling; catching fire-flies and watching them glow in closed fists, then releasing them to twinkle in the sultry night-air.

Harriett came singing out of the house and sat down on the edge of the porch. "Lord, it's hot! . . . How are you, Mis' Johnson? I didn't see you in the dark."

"Jest tolable, chile," said the old woman, "but I can't kick. Honey, when you gits old as I is, you'll be doin' well if you's livin' a-tall, de way you chillens runs round now days! How come you ain't out to some party dis evenin'?"

"O, there's no party tonight," said Harriett laughing. "Besides, this new job of mine's a heart-breaker, Mis' Johnson. I got to stay home and rest now. I'm kitchen-girl at that New Albert Restaurant, and time you get through wrestling with pots and arguing with white waitresses and colored cooks, you don't feel much like running out at night. But the shifts aren't bad, though, food's good, and—well, you can't expect everything." She shrugged her shoulders against the two-by-four pillar on which her back rested.

"Long's it keeps you off de streets, I's glad," said Hager, rocking contentedly. "Maybe I can git you goin' to church agin now."

"Aw, I don't like church," the girl replied.

"An', chile, I can't blame you much," said Sister Johnson, fumbling in the pocket of her apron. "De way dese churches done got now days. . . . Sandy, run in de house an' ask yo' pappy fo' a match to light ma pipe. . . . It ain't 'Come to Jesus' no mo' a-tall. Ministers dese days an' times don't care nothin' 'bout po' Jesus. 'Stead o' dat it's rally dis an' collection dat, an' de aisle wants a new carpet, an' de pastor needs a 'lectric fan fer his red-hot self." The old sister spat into the yard. "Money! That's all 'tis! An' white folkses' religion—Lawd help! 'Taint no use in mentionin' them."

"True," agreed Hager.

"Cause if de gates o' heaven shuts in white folkses' faces like de do's o' dey church in us niggers' faces, it'll be too bad! Yes, sir! One thing sho, de Lawd ain't prejudiced!"

"No," said Hager; "but He don't love ugly, neither in niggers nor in white folks."

"Now, talking about white folks' religion," said Annjee, emerging from the house with a fresh white dress on, "why, Mis' Rice where I work don't think no more about playing bridge on Sunday than she does about praying—and I ain't never seen her pray yet."

"You're nuts," said Jimboy behind her. "People's due to have a little fun on Sundays. That's what's the matter with colored folks now—work all week and then set up in church all day Sunday, and don't even know what's goin' on in the rest of the world."

"Huh!" grunted Hager.

"Well, we won't argue, daddy," Annjee smiled. "Come on and walk a piece with me, sweetness. Here 'tis nearly nine and I should a been at the hall at eight, but colored folks are always behind the clock. Come on, Jimboy."

"Good-bye, mama," yelled Sandy from the lawn as his parents strolled up the street together.

"Jimboy's right," said Harriett. "Darkies do like the church too much, but white folks don't care nothing about it at all. They're too busy getting theirs out of this world, not from God. And I don't blame 'em, except that they're so mean to niggers. They're right, though, looking out for themselves . . . and yet I hate 'em for it. They don't have to mistreat us besides, do they?"

"Honey, don't talk that way," broke in Hager. "It ain't Christian, chile. If you don't like 'em, pray for 'em, but don't feel evil against 'em. I was in slavery, Harrie, an' I been knowin' white folks all ma life, an' they's good as far as they can see—but when it comes to po' niggers, they just can't see far, that's all."

Harriett opened her mouth to reply, but Jimboy, who left

Annjee at the corner and had returned to the porch, beat her to
it. "We too dark for 'em, ma," he laughed. "How they gonna see
in the dark? You colored folks oughta get lighter, that's what!"
   "Shut up yo' mouth, you yaller rooster!" said Sister Johnson.
"White folks is white folks, an' dey's mean! I can't help what
Hager say," the old woman disagreed emphatically with her
crony. "Ain't I been knowin' crackers sixty-five years, an' ain't
dey de cause o' me bein' here in Stanton 'stead o' in ma home
right today? De dirty buzzards! Ain't I nussed t'ree of 'em up
from babies like ma own chillens, and ain't dem same t'ree boys
done turned round an' helped run me an' Tom out o' town?"
   The old sister took a long draw on her corn-cob pipe, and a
fiery red spot glowed in its bowl, while Willie-Mae and Sandy
stopped playing and sat down on the porch as she began a tale
they had all heard at least a dozen times.
   "I's tole you 'bout it befo', ain't I?" asked Sister Johnson.
   "Not me," lied Jimboy, who was anxious to keep her going.
   "No, you haven't," Harriett assured her.
   "Well, it were like dis," and the story unwound itself, the pre-
liminary details telling how, as a young freed-girl after the Civil
War, Sister Johnson had gone into service for a white planter's
family in a Mississippi town near Vicksburg. While attached to
this family, she married Tom Johnson, then a field-hand, and
raised five children of her own during the years that followed,
besides caring for three boys belonging to her white mistress,
nursing them at her black breasts and sometimes leaving her
own young ones in the cabin to come and stay with her white
charges when they were ill. These called her mammy, too, and
when they were men and married, she still went to see them and
occasionally worked for their families.
   "Now, we niggers all lived at de edge o' town in what de
whites called Crowville, an' most of us owned little houses an'
farms, an' we did right well raisin' cotton an' sweet 'taters an'
all. Now, dat's where de trouble started! We was doin' too
well, an' de white folks said so! But we ain't paid 'em no 'ten-
tion, jest thought dey was talkin' fer de pastime of it. . . . Well,
we all started fixin' up our houses an' paintin' our fences, an'

Crowville looked kinder decent-like when de white folks 'gin
to 'mark, so's we servants could hear 'em, 'bout niggers livin'
in painted houses an' dressin' fine like we was somebody! . . .
Well, dat went on fer some time wid de whites talkin' an' de
coloreds doin' better'n better year by year, sellin' mo' cotton
ever' day an' gittin' nice furniture an' buyin' pianers, till by an'
by a prosp'rous nigger named John Lowdins up an' bought
one o' dese here new autimobiles—an' dat settled it! . . . A
white man in town one Sat'day night tole John to git out o'dat
damn car 'cause a nigger ain't got no business wid a autimo-
bile nohow! An' John say: 'I ain't gonna git out!' Den de white
man, what's been drinkin', jump up on de runnin'-bo'ad an'
bust John in de mouth fer talkin' back to him—he a white
man, an' Lowdins nothin' but a nigger. 'De very idee!' he say,
and hit John in de face six or seven times. Den John drawed
his gun! One! two! t'ree! he fiah, hit dis old red-neck cracker
in de shoulder, but he ain't dead! Aint nothin' meant to kill a
cracker what's drunk. But John think he done kilt this white
man, an' so he left him kickin' in de street while he runs that
car o' his'n lickety-split out o' town, goes to Vicksburg, an'
catches de river boat. . . . Well, sir! Dat night Crowville's
plumb full o' white folks wid dogs an' guns an' lanterns, shoutin'
an' yellin' an' scarin' de wits out o' us coloreds an' wakin' us
up way late in de night-time lookin' fer John, an' dey don't
find him. . . . Den dey say dey gwine teach dem Crowville niggers a lesson, all of 'em, paintin' dey houses an' buyin' cars an'
livin' like white folks, so dey comes to our do's an' tells us to
leave our houses—git de hell out in de fields, 'cause dey don't
want to kill nobody there dis evenin'! . . . Well, sir! Niggers in
night-gowns an' underwear an' shimmies, half-naked an'
barefooted, was runnin' ever' which way in de dark, scratchin'
up dey legs in de briah patches, fallin' on dey faces, scared to
death! Po' ole Pheeny, what ain't moved from her bed wid de
paralytics fo' six years, dey made her daughters carry her out,
screamin' an' walleyed, an' set her in de middle o' de cotton-
patch. An' Brian, what was sleepin' naked, jumps up an' grabs
his wife's apron and runs like a rabbit with not another blessed

thing on! Chillens squallin' ever'where, an' mens a-pleadin' an' a-cussin', an' womens cryin' 'Lawd 'a' Mercy' wid de whites of dey eyes showin'! . . . Den looked like to me 'bout five hundred white mens took torches an' started burnin' wid fiah ever' last house, an' hen-house, an' shack, an' barn, an' privy, an' shed, an' cow-slant in de place! An' all de niggers, when de fiah blaze up, was moanin' in de fields, callin' on de Lawd fer help! An' de fiah light up de whole country clean back to de woods! You could smell fiah, an' you could see it red, an' taste de smoke, an' feel it stingin' yo' eyes. An' you could hear de bo'ads a-fallin' an' de glass a-poppin', an' po' animals roastin' an' fryin' an' a-tearin' at dey halters. An' one cow run out, fiah all ovah, wid her milk streamin' down. An' de smoke roll up, de cotton-fields were red . . . an' dey ain't been no mo' Crowville after dat night. No, sir! De white folks ain't left nothin' fer de niggers, not nary bo'ad standin' one 'bove another, not even a dog-house. . . . When it were done— nothin' but ashes! . . . De white mens was ever'where wid guns, scarin' de po' blacks an' keepin' 'em off, an' one of 'em say: 'I got good mind to try yo'-all's hide, see is it bullet proof— gittin' so prosp'rous, paintin' yo' houses an' runnin ovah white folks wid yo' damn gasoline buggies! Well, after dis you'll damn sight have to bend yo' backs an' work a little!' . . . Dat's what de white man say. . . . But we didn't—not yit! 'Cause ever' last nigger moved from there dat Sunday mawnin'. It were right funny to see ole folks what ain't never been out o' de backwoods pickin' up dey feet an' goin'. Ma Bailey say: 'De Lawd done let me live eighty years in one place, but ma next eighty'll be spent in St. Louis.' An' she started out walkin' wid neither bag nor baggage. . . . An' me an' Tom took Willie-Mae an' went to Cairo, an' Tom started railroad-workin' wid a gang; then we come on up here, been five summers ago dis August. We ain't had not even a rag o' clothes when we left Crowville—so don't tell me 'bout white folks bein' good, Hager, 'cause I knows 'em. . . . Yes, indeedy, I really knows 'em. . . . Dey done made us leave our home."

The old woman knocked her pipe against the edge of the

porch, emptying its dead ashes into the yard, and for a moment no one spoke. Sandy, trembling, watched a falling star drop behind the trees. Then Jimboy's deep voice, like a bitter rumble in the dark, broke the silence. "I know white folks, too," he said. "I lived in the South." "And I ain't never been South," added Harriett hoarsely, "but I know 'em right here . . . and I hate 'em!" "De Lawd hears you," said Hager. "I don't care if He does hear me, mama! You and Annjee are too easy. You just take whatever white folks give you—*coon* to your face, and *nigger* behind your backs—and don't say nothing. You run to some white person's back door for every job you get, and then they pay you one dollar for five dollars' worth of work, and fire you whenever they get ready." "They do that all right," said Jimboy. "They don't mind firin' you. Wasn't I layin' brick on the *Daily Leader* building and the white union men started sayin' they couldn't work with me because I wasn't in the union? So the boss come up and paid me off. 'Good man, too,' he says to me, 'but I can't buck the union.' So I said I'd join, but I knew they wouldn't let me before I went to the office. Anyhow, I tried. I told the guys there I was a bricklayer and asked 'em how I was gonna work if I couldn't be in the union. And the fellow who had the cards, secretary I guess he was, says kinder sharp, like he didn't want to be bothered: 'That's your look-out, big boy, not mine.' So you see how much the union cares if a black man works or not." "Ain't Tom had de same trouble?" affirmed Sister Johnson. "Got put off de job mo'n once on 'count o' de white unions." "O, they've got us cornered, all right," said Jimboy. "The white folks are like farmers that own all the cows and let the niggers take care of 'em. Then they make you pay a sweet price for skimmed milk and keep the cream for themselves—but I reckon cream's too rich for rusty-kneed niggers anyhow!" They laughed. "That's a good one!" said Harriett. "You know old man Wright, what owns the flour-mill and the new hotel—how he made his start off colored women working in his canning factory? Well, when he built that orphan home for colored and gave it to the city last year, he had the whole place made just about the size of the dining-room at his own house. They got the little niggers in that asylum cooped up like chickens. And the reason he built it was to get the colored babies out of the city home, with its nice playgrounds, because he thinks the two races oughtn't to mix! But he don't care how hard he works his colored help in that canning factory of his, does he? Wasn't I there thirteen hours a day in tomato season? Nine cents an hour and five cents overtime after ten hours—and you better work overtime if you want to keep the job! . . . As for the races mixing—ask some of those high yellow women who work there. They know a mighty lot about the races mixing!"

"Most of 'em lives in de Bottoms, where de sportin' houses are," said Hager. "It's a shame de way de white mens keeps them sinful places goin'."

"It ain't Christian, is it?" mocked Harriett. . . . "White folks!" . . . And she shrugged her shoulders scornfully. Many disagreeable things had happened to her through white folks. Her first surprising and unpleasantly lasting impression of the pale world had come when, at the age of five, she had gone alone one day to play in a friendly white family's yard. Some mischievous small boys there, for the fun of it, had taken hold of her short kinky braids and pulled them, dancing round and round her and yelling: "Blackie! Blackie! Blackie!" while she screamed and tried to run away. But they held her and pulled her hair terribly, and her friends laughed because she *was* black and she *did* look funny. So from that time on, Harriett had been uncomfortable in the presence of whiteness, and that early hurt had grown with each new incident into a rancor that she could not hide and a dislike that had become pain.

Now, because she could sing and dance and was always amusing, many of the white girls in high school were her friends. But when the three-thirty bell rang and it was time to go home, Harriett knew their polite "Good-bye" was really a kind way of saying: "We can't be seen on the streets with a

colored girl." To loiter with these same young ladies had been
all right during their grade-school years, when they were all
younger, but now they had begun to feel the eyes of young
white boys staring from the windows of pool halls, or from
the tennis-courts near the park—so it was not proper to be
seen with Harriett.

But a very unexpected stab at the girl's pride had come only
a few weeks ago when she had gone with her class-mates, on
tickets issued by the school, to see an educational film of the
under-sea world at the Palace Theatre, on Main Street. It was
a special performance given for the students, and each class
had had seats allotted to them beforehand; so Harriett sat
with her class and had begun to enjoy immensely the strange
wonders of the ocean depths when an usher touched her on
the shoulder.

"The last three rows on the left are for colored," the girl in
the uniform said.

"I—But—But I'm with my class," Harriett stammered.
"We're all supposed to sit here."

"I can't help it," insisted the usher, pointing towards the rear
of the theatre, while her voice carried everywhere. "Them's the
house rules. No argument now—you'll have to move."

So Harriett rose and stumbled up the dark aisle and out into
the sunlight, her slender body hot with embarrassment and
rage. The teacher saw her leave the theatre without a word of
protest, and none of her white classmates defended her for
being black. They didn't care.

"All white people are alike, in school and out," Harriett
concluded bitterly, as she told of her experiences to the folks
sitting with her on the porch in the dark.

Once, when she had worked for a Mrs. Leonard Baker on
Martin Avenue, she accidentally broke a precious cut-glass
pitcher used to serve some out-of-town guests. And when she
tried to apologize for the accident, Mrs. Baker screamed in
a rage: "Shut up, you impudent little black wench! Talking
back to me after breaking up my dishes. All you darkies are

alike—careless sluts—and I wouldn't have a one of you in my house if I could get anybody else to work for me without paying a fortune. You're all impossible."

"So that's the way white people feel," Harriett said to Aunt Hager and Sister Johnson and Jimboy, while the two children listened. "They wouldn't have a single one of us around if they could help it. It don't matter to them if we're shut out of a job. It don't matter to them if niggers have only the back row at the movies. It don't matter to them when they hurt our feelings without caring and treat us like slaves down South and like beggars up North. No, it don't matter to them. . . . White folks run the world, and the only thing colored folks are expected to do is work and grin and take off their hats as though it don't matter. . . . O, I hate 'em!" Harriett cried, so fiercely that Sandy was afraid. "I hate white folks!" she said to everybody on the porch in the darkness. "You can pray for 'em if you want to, mama, but I hate 'em! . . . I hate white folks! . . I hate 'em all!"

VIII.

DANCE

Mrs. J. J. Rice and family usually spent ten days during the August heat at Lake Dale, and thither they had gone now, giving Annjee a forced vacation with no pay. Jimboy was not working, and so his wife found ten days of rest without income not especially agreeable. Nevertheless, she decided that she might as well enjoy the time; so she and Jimboy went to the country for a week with Cousin Jessie, who had married one of the colored farmers of the district. Besides, Annjee thought that Jimboy might help on the farm and so make a little money. Anyway, they would get plenty to eat, because Jessie kept a good table. And since Jessie had eight children of her own, they did not take Sandy with them—eight were enough for a woman to be worried with at one time!

Aunt Hager had been ironing all day on the Reinharts' clothes—it was Friday. At seven o'clock Harriett came home, but she had already eaten her supper at the restaurant where she worked.

"Hello, mama! Hy, Sandy!" she said, but that was all, because she and her mother were not on the best of terms. Aunt Hager was attempting to punish her youngest daughter by not allowing her to leave the house after dark, since Harriett, on Tuesday night, had been out until one o'clock in the morning with no better excuse than a party at Maudel's. Aunt Hager had threatened to whip her then and there that night.

"You ain't had a switch on yo' hide fo' three years, but don't think you's gettin' too big fo' me not to fan yo' behind, madam. 'Spare de rod an' spoil de chile,' that's what de Bible say, an'

Lawd knows you sho is spoiled! De idee of a young gal yo' age stayin' out till one o'clock in de mawnin', an' me not knowed where you's at. . . . Don't you talk back to me! . . . You rests in this house ever' night this week an' don't put yo' foot out o' this yard after you comes from work, that's what you do. Lawd knows I don't know what I's gonna do with you. I works fo' you an' I prays fo' you, an' if you don't mind, I's sho gonna whip you, even if you is goin' on seventeen years old!"

Tonight as soon as she came from work Harriett went into her mother's room and lay across the bed. It was very warm in the little four-room house, and all the windows and doors were open.

"We's got some watermelon here, daughter," Hager called from the kitchen. "Don't you want a nice cool slice?"

"No," the girl replied. She was fanning herself with a palm-leaf fan, her legs in their cheap silk stockings hanging over the side of the bed, and her heels kicking the floor. Benbow's Band played tonight for the dance at Chaver's Hall, and everybody was going—but her. Gee, it was hard to have a Christian mother! Harriett kicked her slippers off with a bang and rolled over on her stomach, burying her powdery face in the pillows. . . . Somebody knocked at the back door.

A boy's voice was speaking excitedly to Hager: "Hemorrhages . . . and papa can't stop 'em . . . she's coughin' something terrible . . . says can't you please come over and help him"—frightened and out of breath.

"Do, Jesus!" cried Hager. "I'll be with you right away, chile. Don't worry." She rushed into the bedroom to change her apron. "You Harriett, listen; Sister Lane's taken awful sick an' Jimmy says she's bleedin' from de mouth. If I ain't back by nine o'clock, see that that chile Sandy's in de bed. An' you know you ain't to leave this yard under no circumstances. . . . Po' Mis' Lane! She sho do have it hard." In a whisper: "I 'spects she's got de T. B., that what I 'spects!" And the old woman hustled out to join the waiting youngster. Jimmy was leaning against the door, looking at Sandy, and neither of the boys knew what to say. Jimmy Lane wore his mother's cast-off shoes to school, and Sandy used to tease him, but tonight he didn't tease his friend about his shoes.

"You go to bed 'fore it gets late," said his grandmother, starting down the alley with Jimmy.

"Yes'm," Sandy called after her. "So long, Jim!" He stood under the apple-tree and watched them disappear.

Aunt Hager had scarcely gotten out of sight when there was a loud knock at the front door, and Sandy ran around the house to see Harriett's boy friend, Mingo, standing in the dusk outside the screen-door, waiting to be let in.

Mingo was a patent-leather black boy with wide, alive nostrils and a mouth that split into a lighthouse smile on the least provocation. His body was heavy and muscular, resting on bowed legs that curved backward as though the better to brace his chunky torso; and his hands were hard from mixing concrete and digging ditches for the city's new water-mains.

"I know it's tonight, but I can't go," Sandy heard his aunt say at the door. They were speaking of Benbow's dance. "And his band don't come here often, neither. I'm heart-sick having to stay home, dog-gone it all, especially this evening!"

"Aw, come on and go anyway," pleaded Mingo.

"After I been savin' up my dough for two weeks to take you, and got my suit cleaned and pressed and all. Heck! If you couldn't go and knew it yesterday, why didn't you tell me? That's a swell way to treat a fellow!"

"Because I wanted to go," said Harriett; "and still want to go. . . . Don't make so much difference about mama, because she's mad anyhow . . . but what could we do with this kid? We can't leave him by himself." She looked at Sandy, who was standing behind Mingo listening to everything.

"You can take me," the child offered anxiously, his eyes dancing at the delightful prospect. "I'll behave, Harrie, if you take me, and I won't tell on you either. . . . Please lemme go, Mingo. I ain't never seen a big dance in my life. I wanta go."

"Should we?" asked Harriett doubtfully, looking at her boy friend standing firmly on his curved legs.

"Sure, if we got to have him . . . damn 'im!" Mingo replied.

"Better the kid than no dance. Go git dressed." So Harriett made a dash for the clothes-closet, while Sandy ran to get a clean waist from one of his mother's dresser-drawers, and Mingo helped him put it on, cussing softly to himself all the while. "But it ain't your fault, pal, is it?" he said to the little boy.

"Sure not," Sandy replied. "I didn't tell Aunt Hager to make Harrie stay home. I tried to 'suade grandma to let her go," the child lied, because he liked Mingo. "I guess she won't care about her goin' to just one dance." He wanted to make everything all right so the young man wouldn't be worried. Besides, Sandy very much wanted to go himself.

"Let's beat it," Harriett shrilled excitedly before her dress was fastened, anxious to be gone lest her mother come home. She was powdering her face and neck in the next room, nervous, happy, and afraid all at once. The perfume, the voice, and the pat, pat, pat of the powder-puff came out to the waiting gentleman.

"Yo' car's here, madam," mocked Mingo. "Step right this way and let's be going!"

> *Wonder where ma easy rider's gone—*
> *He done left me, put ma new gold watch in pawn!*

Like a blare from hell the second encore of *Easy Rider* filled every cubic inch of the little hall with hip-rocking notes. Benbow himself was leading and the crowd moved like jelly-fish dancing on individual sea-shells, with Mingo and Harriett somewhere among the shakers. But they were not of them, since each couple shook in a world of its own, as, with a weary wail, the music abruptly ceased.

Then, after scarcely a breath of intermission, the band struck up again with a lazy one-step. A tall brown boy in a light tan suit walked his partner straight down the whole length of the floor and, when he reached the corner, turned leisurely in one spot, body riding his hips, eyes on the ceiling, and his girl shaking her full breasts against his pink silk shirt.

Then they recrossed the width of the room, turned slowly, repeating themselves, and began again to walk rhythmically down the hall, while the music was like a lazy river flowing between mountains, carving a canyon coolly, calmly, and without insistence. The *Lazy River One-Step* they might have called what the band was playing as the large crowd moved with the greatest ease about the hall. To drum-beats barely audible, the tall boy in the tan suit walked his partner round and round time after time, revolving at each corner with eyes uplifted, while the piano was the water flowing, and the high, thin chords of the banjo were the mountains floating in the clouds. But in sultry tones, alone and always, the brass cornet spoke harshly about the earth.

Sandy sat against the wall in a hard wooden folding chair. There were other children scattered lonesomely about on chairs, too, watching the dancers, but he didn't seem to know any of them. When the music stopped, all the chairs quickly filled with loud-talking women and girls in brightly colored dresses who fanned themselves with handkerchiefs and wiped their sweating brows. Sandy thought maybe he should give his seat to one of the women when he saw Maudel approaching.

"Here, honey," she said. "Take this dime and buy yourself a bottle of something cold to drink. I know Harriett ain't got you on her mind out there dancin'. This music is certainly righteous, chile!" She laughed as she handed Sandy a coin and closed her pocketbook. He liked Maudel, although he knew his grandmother didn't. She was a large good-natured brown-skinned girl who walked hippishly and used too much rouge on her lips. But she always gave Sandy a dime, and she was always laughing.

He went through the crowd towards the soft-drink stand at the end of the hall. "Gimme a bottle o' cream soda," he said to the fat orange-colored man there, who had his sleeves rolled up and a white butcher's-apron covering his barrel-like belly. The man put his hairy arms down into a zinc tub full of ice and water and began pulling out bottles, looking at their caps, and then dropping them back into the cold liquid.

"Don't seem like we got no cream, sonny. How'd a lemon do you?" he asked above the bedlam of talking voices.

"Naw," said Sandy. "It's too sour."

On the improvised counter of boards the wares displayed consisted of cracker-jacks, salted peanuts, a box of gum, and Sen Sens, while behind the counter was a lighted oil-stove holding a tin pan full of spare-ribs, sausage, and fish; and near it an ice-cream freezer covered with a brown sack. Some cases of soda were on the floor beside the zinc tub filled with bottles, in which the man was still searching.

"Nope, no cream," said the fat man.

"Well, gimme a fish sandwich then," Sandy replied, feeling very proud because some kids were standing near, looking at him as he made his purchase like a grown man.

"Buy me one, too," suggested a biscuit-colored little girl in a frilly dirty-white dress.

"I only got a dime," Sandy said. "But you can have half of mine." And he gallantly broke in two parts the double square of thick bread, with its hunk of greasy fish between, and gravely handed a portion to the grinning little girl.

"Thanks," she said, running away with the bread and fish in her hands.

"Shame on you!" teased a small boy, rubbing his forefingers at Sandy. "You got a girl! You got a girl!"

"Go chase yourself!" Sandy replied casually, as he picked out the bones and smacked his lips on the sweet fried fish. The orchestra was playing another one-step, with the dancers going like shuttles across the floor. Sandy saw his Aunt Harriett and a slender yellow boy named Billy Sanderlee doing a series of lazy, intricate steps as they wound through the crowd from one end of the hall to the other. Certain less accomplished couples were watching them with admiration.

Sandy, when he had finished eating, decided to look for the wash-room, where he could rinse his hands, because they were greasy and smelled fishy. It was at the far corner of the hall. As he pushed open the door marked GENTS, a thick grey cloud of cigarette-smoke drifted out. The stench of urine and gin and a crowd of men talking, swearing, and drinking licker surrounded the little boy as he elbowed his way towards the wash-bowls. All the fellows were shouting loudly to one another and making fleshy remarks about the women they had danced with.

"Boy, you ought to try Velma," a mahogany-brown boy yelled. "She sure can go."

"Hell," answered a whisky voice somewhere in the smoke. "That nappy-headed black woman? Gimme a high yaller for mine all de time. I can't use no coal!"

"Well, de blacker de berry, de sweeter de juice," protested a slick-haired ebony youth in the center of the place. . . . "Ain't that right, sport?" he demanded of Sandy, grabbing him jokingly by the neck and picking him up.

"I guess it is," said the child, scared, and the men laughed.

"Here, kid, buy yourself a drink," the slick-headed boy said, slipping Sandy a nickel as he set him down gently at the door. "And be sure it's pop—not gin."

Outside, the youngster dried his wet hands on a handkerchief, blinked his smoky eyes, and immediately bought the soda, a red strawberry liquid in a long, thick bottle.

Suddenly and without warning the cornet blared at the other end of the hall in an ear-splitting wail: "Whaw! . . . Whaw! . . . Whaw! . . . Whaw!" and the snare-drum rolled in answer. A pause . . . then the loud brassy notes were repeated and the banjo came in, "Plinka, plink, plink," like timid drops of rain after a terrific crash of thunder. Then quite casually, as though nothing had happened, the piano lazied into a slow drag, with all the other instruments following. And with the utmost nonchalance the drummer struck into time.

"Ever'body shake!" cried Benbow, as a ribbon of laughter swirled round the hall.

Couples began to sway languidly, melting together like candy in the sun as hips rotated effortlessly to the music. Girls snuggled pomaded heads on men's chests, or rested powdered chins on men's shoulders, while wild young boys put both arms tightly around their partners' waists and let their hands hang down carelessly over female haunches. Bodies moved ever so easily together—ever so easily, as Benbow turned towards his musicians and cried through cupped hands: "Aw, screech it, boys!"

A long, tall, gangling gal stepped back from her partner, adjusted her hips, and did a few easy, gliding steps all her own before her man grabbed her again.

"Eu-o-oo-ooo-oooo!" moaned the cornet titillating with pain, as the banjo cried in stop-time, and the piano sobbed aloud with a rhythmical, secret passion. But the drums kept up their hard steady laughter—like somebody who don't care.

"I see you plowin', Uncle Walt," called a little autumn-leaf brown with switching skirts to a dark-purple man grinding down the center of the floor with a yellow woman. Two short prancing blacks stopped in their tracks to quiver violently. A bushy-headed girl threw out her arms, snapped her fingers, and began to holler: "Hey! . . . Hey!" while her perspiring partner held doggedly to each hip in an effort to keep up with her. All over the hall, people danced their own individual movements to the scream and moan of the music.

"Get low . . . low down . . . down!" cried the drummer, bouncing like a rubber ball in his chair. The banjo scolded in diabolic glee, and the cornet panted as though it were out of breath, and Benbow himself left the band and came out on the floor to dance slowly and ecstatically with a large Indian-brown woman covered with diamonds.

"Aw, do it, Mister Benbow!" one of his admirers shouted frenziedly as the hall itself seemed to tremble.

"High yallers, draw nigh! Brown-skins, come near!" somebody squalled. "But black gals, stay where you are!"

"Whaw! Whaw! Whaw!" mocked the cornet—but the steady tomtom of the drums was no longer laughter now, no longer even pleasant: the drum-beats had become sharp with surly sound, like heavy waves that beat angrily on a granite rock. And under the dissolute spell of its own rhythm the music had got quite beyond itself. The four black men in Benbow's wandering band were exploring depths to which mere sound had no business to go. Cruel, desolate, unadorned was their music now, like the body of a ravished woman on the sun-baked earth; violent and hard, like a giant standing over his bleeding mate in the blazing sun. The odors of bodies, the stings of flesh, and the utter emptiness of soul when all is done—these things the piano and the drums, the cornet and the twanging banjo insisted on hoarsely to a beat that made the dancers move, in that little hall, like pawns on a frenetic checker-board.

"Aw, play it, Mister Benbow!" somebody cried. The earth rolls relentlessly, and the sun blazes for ever on the earth, breeding, breeding. But why do you insist like the earth, music? Rolling and breeding, earth and sun for ever relentlessly. But why do you insist like the sun? Like the lips of women? Like the bodies of men, relentlessly?

"Aw, play it, Mister Benbow!"

But why do you insist, music?

Who understands the earth? Do you, Mingo? Who understands the sun? Do you, Harriett? Does anybody know—among you high yallers, you jelly-beans, you pinks and pretty daddies, among you sealskin browns, smooth blacks, and chocolates-to-the-bone—does anybody know the answer?

"Aw, play it, Benbow!"

"It's midnight. De clock is strikin' twelve, an' . . ."

"Aw, play it, Mister Benbow!"

During intermission, when the members of the band stopped making music to drink gin and talk to women, Harriett and Mingo bought Sandy a box of cracker-jacks and another bottle of soda and left him standing in the middle of the floor holding both. His young aunt had forgotten time, so Sandy decided to go upstairs to the narrow unused balcony that ran the length of one side of the place. It was dusty up there, but a few broken chairs stood near the railing and he sat on one of them. He leaned his arms on the banister, rested his chin in his hands, and when the music started, he looked down on the mass of moving couples crowding the floor. He had a clear view of the

energetic little black drummer eagle-rocking with staccato reg-
ularity in his chair as his long, thin sticks descended upon the
tightly drawn skin of his small drum, while his foot patted the
pedal of his big bass-drum, on which was painted in large red
letters: "BENBOW'S FAMOUS KANSAS CITY BAND."

As the slow shuffle gained in intensity (and his cracker-jacks
gave out), Sandy looked down drowsily on the men and
women, the boys and girls, circling and turning beneath him.
Dresses and suits of all shades and colors, and a vast confusion
of bushy heads on swaying bodies. Faces gleaming like circus
balloons—lemon-yellow, coal-black, powder-grey, ebony-black,
blue-black faces; chocolate, brown, orange, tan, creamy-gold
faces—the room full of floating balloon faces—Sandy's eyes
were beginning to blur with sleep—colored balloons with
strings, and the music pulling the strings. No! Girls pulling the
strings—each boy a balloon by a string. Each face a balloon.

Sandy put his head down on the dusty railing of the gallery.
An odor of hair-oil and fish, of women and sweat came up to
him as he sat there alone, tired and a little sick. It was very
warm and close, and the room was full of chatter during the
intervals. Sandy struggled against sleep, but his eyes were just
about to close when, with a burst of hopeless sadness, the *St.
Louis Blues* spread itself like a bitter syrup over the hall. For a
moment the boy opened his eyes to the drowsy flow of sound,
long enough to pull two chairs together; then he lay down on
them and closed his eyes again. Somebody was singing:

St. Louis woman with her diamond rings . . .

as the band said very weary things in a loud and brassy
manner and the dancers moved in a dream that seemed to
have forgotten itself:

Got ma man tied to her apron-strings . . .

Wah! Wah! Wah! . . . The cornet laughed with terrible rude-
ness. Then the drums began to giggle and the banjo whined an

insulting leer. The piano said, over and over again: "St. Louis! That big old dirty town where the Mississippi's deep and wide, deep and wide . . ." and the hips of the dancers rolled.

Man's got a heart like a rock cast in de sea . . .

while the cynical banjo covered unplumbable depths with a plinking surface of staccato gaiety, like the sparkling bubbles that rise on deep water over a man who has just drowned himself:

Or else he never would a gone so far from me . . .

then the band stopped with a long-drawn-out wail from the cornet and a flippant little laugh from the drums.

A great burst of applause swept over the room, and the musicians immediately began to play again. This time just blues, not the *St. Louis*, nor the *Memphis*, nor the *Yellow Dog*—but just the plain old familiar blues, heart-breaking and extravagant, ma-baby's-gone-from-me blues.

Nobody thought about anyone else then. Bodies sweatily close, arms locked, cheek to cheek, breast to breast, couples rocked to the pulse-like beat of the rhythm, yet quite oblivious each person of the other. It was true that men and women were dancing together, but their feet had gone down through the floor into the earth, each dancer's alone—down into the center of things—and their minds had gone off to the heart of loneliness, where they didn't even hear the words, the sometimes lying, sometimes laughing words that Benbow, leaning on the piano, was singing against this background of utterly despondent music:

> *When de blues is got you,*
> *Ain't no use to run away.*
> *When de blue-blues got you,*
> *Ain't no use to run away,*
> *'Cause de blues is like a woman*
> *That can turn yo' good hair grey.*

Umn-ump! . . . Umn! . . . Umn-ump!

> *Well, I tole ma baby,*
> *Says baby, baby, babe, be mine,*
> *But ma baby was deceitful.*
> *She must a thought that I was blind.*

De-da! De-da! . . . De da! De da! Dee!

> *O, Lawdy, Lawdy, Lawdy,*
> *Lawdy, Lawdy, Lawd . . . Lawd . . . Lawd!*
> *She quit me fo' a Texas gambler,*
> *So I had to git another broad.*

Whaw-whaw! . . . Whaw-whaw-whaw! As though the laughter of a cornet could reach the heart of loneliness.

These mean old weary blues coming from a little orchestra of four men who needed no written music because they couldn't have read it. Four men and a leader—Rattle Benbow from Galveston; Benbow's buddy, the drummer, from Houston; his banjoist from Birmingham; his cornetist from Atlanta; and the pianist, long-fingered, sissyfied, a coal-black lad from New Orleans who had brought with him an exaggerated rag-time which he called jazz.

"I'm jazzin' it, creepers!" he sometimes yelled as he rolled his eyes towards the dancers and let his fingers beat the keys to a frenzy. . . . But now the piano was cryin' the blues!

Four homeless, plug-ugly niggers, that's all they were, playing mean old loveless blues in a hot, crowded little dance-hall in a Kansas town on Friday night. Playing the heart out of loneliness with a wide-mouthed leader, who sang everybody's troubles until they became his own. The improvising piano, the whanging banjo, the throbbing bass-drum, the hard-hearted little snare-drum, the brassy cornet that laughed, "Whaw-whaw-whaw. . . . Whaw!" were the waves in this lonesome sea of harmony from which Benbow's melancholy voice rose:

You gonna wake up some mawnin'
An' turn yo' smilin' face.
Wake up some early mawnin',
Says turn yo' smilin' face,
Look at yo' sweetie's pillow—
An' find an empty place!

Then the music whipped itself into a slow fury, an awk-ward, elemental, foot-stamping fury, with the banjo running terrifiedly away in a windy moan and then coming back again, with the cornet wailing like a woman who don't know what it's all about:

Then you gonna call yo' baby,
Call yo' lovin' baby dear—
But you can keep on callin',
'Cause I won't be here!

And for a moment nothing was heard save the shuf-shuf-shuffle of feet and the immense booming of the bass-drum like a living vein pulsing at the heart of loneliness. "Sandy! . . . Sandy! . . . My stars! Where is that child? . . . Has anybody seen my little nephew?" All over the hall. . . . "Sandy! . . . Oh-o-o, Lord!" Finally, with a sigh of relief: "You little brat, darn you, hiding up here in the balcony where no-body could find you! . . . Sandy, wake up! It's past four o'clock and I'll get killed."

Harriett vigorously shook the sleeping child, who lay stretched on the dusty chairs; then she began to drag him down the narrow steps before he was scarcely awake. The hall was almost empty and the chubby little black drummer was waddling across the floor carrying his drums in canvas cases. Someone was switching off the lights one by one. A mustard-colored man stood near the door quarrelling with a black woman. She began to cry and he slapped her full in the mouth, then turned his back and left with another girl of maple-sugar brown. Harriett jerked Sandy past this linked couple and pulled the boy down the long flight of stairs into the street, where Mingo stood waiting, with a lighted cigarette making a white line against his black skin.

"You better git a move on," he said. "Daylight ain't holdin' itself back for you!" And he told the truth, for the night had already begun to pale.

Sandy felt sick at the stomach. To be awakened precipitately made him cross and ill-humored, but the fresh, cool air soon caused him to feel less sleepy and not quite so ill. He took a deep breath as he trotted rapidly along on the sidewalk beside his striding aunt and her boy friend. He watched the blue-grey dawn blot out the night in the sky; and then pearl-grey blot out the blue, while the stars faded to points of dying fire. And he listened to the birds chirping and trilling in the trees as though they were calling the sun. Then, as he became fully awake, the child began to feel very proud of himself, for this was the first time he had ever been away from home all night.

Harriett was fussing with Mingo. "You shouldn't've kept me out like that," she said. "Why didn't you tell me what time it was? . . . I didn't know."

And Mingo came back: "Hey, didn't I try to drag you away at midnight and you wouldn't come? And ain't I called you at one o'clock and you said: 'Wait a minute'—dancin' with some yaller P. I. from St. Joe, with your arms round his neck like a life-preserver? . . . Don't tell me I didn't want to leave, and me got to go to work at eight o'clock this mornin' with a pick and shovel when the whistle blows! What de hell?"

But Harriett did not care to quarrel now when there would be no time to finish it properly. She was out of breath from hurrying and almost in tears. She was afraid to go home.

"Mingo, I'm scared."

"Well, you know what you can do if your ma puts you out," her escort said quickly, forgetting his anger. "I can take care of you. We could get married."

"Could we, Mingo?"

"Sure!"

She slipped her hand in his. "Aw, daddy!" and the pace became much less hurried.

When they reached the corner near which Harriett lived, she lifted her dark little purple-powdered face for a not very lingering kiss and sent Mingo on his way. Then she frowned anxiously and ran on. The sky was a pale pearly color, waiting for the warm gold of the rising sun.

"I'm scared to death!" said Harriett. "Lord, Sandy, I hope ma ain't up! I hope she didn't come home last night from Mis' Lane's. We shouldn't've gone, Sandy . . . I guess we shouldn't've gone." She was breathing hard and Sandy had to run fast to keep up with her. "Gee, I'm scared!"

The grass was diamond-like with dew, and the red bricks of the sidewalk were damp, as the small boy and his young aunt hurried under the leafy elms along the walk. They passed Madam de Carter's house and cut through the wet grass into their own yard as the first rays of the morning sun sifted through the trees. Quietly they tiptoed towards the porch; quickly and quietly they crossed it; and softly, ever so softly, they opened the parlor door.

In the early dusk the oil-lamp still burned on the front-room table, and in an old arm-chair, with the open Bible on her lap, sat Aunt Hager Williams, a bundle of switches on the floor at her feet.

IX.

CARNIVAL

Between the tent of Christ and the tents of sin there stretched scarcely a half-mile. Rivalry reigned: the revival and the carnival held sway in Stanton at the same time. Both were at the south edge of town, and both were loud and musical in their activities. In a dirty white tent in the Hickory Woods the Reverend Duke Braswell conducted the services of the Lord for the annual summer tent-meeting of the First Ethiopian Baptist Church. And in Jed Galoway's meadow lots Swank's Combined Shows, the World's Greatest Midway Carnival, had spread canvas for seven days of bunko games and cheap attractions. The old Negroes went to the revival, and the young Negroes went to the carnival, and after sundown these August evenings the mourning songs of the Christians could be heard rising from the Hickory Woods while the profound syncopation of the minstrel band blared from Galoway's Lots, strangely intermingling their notes of praise and joy.

Aunt Hager with Annjee and Sandy went to the revival every night (Sandy unwillingly), while Jimboy, Harriett, and Maudel went to the carnival. Aunt Hager prayed for her youngest daughter at the meetings, but Harriett had not spoken to her mother, if she could avoid it, since the morning after the dance, when she had been whipped. Since their return from the country Annjee and Jimboy were not so loving towards each other, either, as they had been before. Jimboy tired of Jessie's farm, so he came back to town three days before his wife returned. And now the revival and the carnival widened the breach between the Christians and the sinners in Aunt

Hager's little household. And Sandy would rather have been with the sinners—Jimboy and Harriett—but he wasn't old enough; so he had to go to meetings until, on Thursday morning, when he and Buster were climbing over the coal-shed in the back yard, Sandy accidentally jumped down on a rusty nail, which penetrated the heel of his bare foot. He set up a wail, cried until noon over the pain, and refused to eat any dinner; so finally Jimboy said that if he would only hush hollering he'd take him to the carnival that evening.

"Yes, take de rascal," said Aunt Hager. "He ain't doin' no good at de services, wiggling and squirming so's we can't hardly hear de sermon. He ain't got religion in his heart, that chile!"

"I hope he ain't," said his father, yawning.

"All you wants him to be is a good-fo'-nothin' rounder like you is," retorted Hager. And she and Jimboy began their daily quarrel, which lasted for hours, each of them enjoying it immensely. But Sandy kept pulling at his father and saying: "Hurry up and let's go," although he knew well that nothing really started at the carnival until sundown. Nevertheless, about four o'clock, Jimboy said: "All right, come on," and they started out in the hot sun towards Galoway's Lots, the man walking tall and easy while the boy hobbled along on his sore foot, a rag tied about his heel.

At the old cross-bar gate on the edge of town, through which Jed Galoway drove his cows to pasture, there had been erected a portable arch strung with electric lights spelling out "SWANK'S SHOWS" in red and yellow letters, but it was not very impressive in the day-time, with the sun blazing on it, and no people about. And from this gate, extending the whole length of the meadow on either side, like a roadway, were the tents and booths of the carnival: the Galatea illusion, the seal and sea-lion circus, the Broadway musical-comedy show, the freaks, the games of chance, the pop-corn- and lemonade-stands, the colored minstrels, the merry-go-round, the fun house, the hoochie-coochie, the Ferris wheel, and, at the far end, a canvas tank under a tiny platform high in the air from

which the World's Most Dangerous and Spectacular High
Dive took place nightly at ten-thirty.

"We gonna stay to see that, ain't we, papa?" Sandy asked.

"Sure," said Jimboy. "But didn't I tell you there wouldn't be
nothin' runnin' this early in the afternoon? See! Not even the
band playin', and ain't a thing open but the freak-show and I'll
bet all the freaks asleep." But he bought Sandy a bag of peanuts and planked down twenty cents for two tickets into the
sultry tent where a perspiring fat woman and a tame-looking
wild-man were the only attractions to be found on the plat-
forms. The sword-swallower was not yet at work, nor the electric marvel, nor the human glass-eater. The terrific sun beat
fiercely through the canvas on this exhibit of two lone human
abnormalities, and the few spectators in the tent kept wiping
their faces with their handkerchiefs.

Jimboy struck up a conversation with the Fat Woman, a
pink and white creature who said she lived in Columbus,
Ohio; and when Jimboy said he'd been there, she was interested. She said she had always lived right next door to colored
people at home, and she gave Sandy a postcard picture of herself for nothing, although it had "10¢" marked on the back.
She kept saying she didn't see how anybody could stay in Kansas and it a dry state where a soul couldn't even get beer except
from a bootlegger.

When Sandy and his father came out, they left the row of
tents and went across the meadow to a clump of big shade-
trees beneath which several colored men who worked with the
show were sitting. A blanket had been spread on the grass,
and a crap game was going on to the accompaniment of much
arguing and good-natured cussing. But most of the men were
just sitting around not playing, and one or two were stretched
flat on their faces, asleep. Jimboy seemed to know several of
the fellows, so he joined in their talk while Sandy watched the
dice roll for a while, but since the boy didn't understand the
game, he decided to go back to the tents.

"All right, go ahead," said his father. "I'll pick you up later when the lights are lit and things get started; then we can go in the shows."

Sandy limped off, walking on the toe of his injured foot. In front of the sea-lion circus he found Earl James, a little white boy in his grade at school; the two of them went around together for a while, looking at the large painted canvas pictures in front of the shows or else lying on their stomachs on the ground to peep under the tents. When they reached the minstrel-show tent near the end of the midway, they heard a piano tinkling within and the sound of hands clapping as though someone was dancing.

"Jeezus! Let's see this," Earl cried, so the two boys got down on their bellies, wriggled under the flap of the tent on one side, and looked in.

A battered upright piano stood on the ground in front of the stage, and a fat, bald-headed Negro was beating out a rag. A big white man in a checkered vest was leaning against the piano, derby on head, and a long cigar stuck in his mouth. He was watching a slim black girl, with skirts held high and head thrown back, prancing in a mad circle of crazy steps. Two big colored boys in red uniforms were patting time, while another girl sat on a box, her back towards the peeping youngsters staring up from under the edge of the tent. As the girl who was dancing whirled about, Sandy saw that it was Harriett.

"Pretty good, ain't she, boss?" yelled the wrinkle-necked Negro at the piano as he pounded away.

The white man nodded and kept his eyes on Harriett's legs. The two black boys patting time were grinning from ear to ear.

"Do it, Miss Mama!" one of them shouted as Harriett began to sashay gracefully.

Finally she stopped, panting and perspiring, with her lips smiling and her eyes sparkling gaily. Then she went with the white man and the colored piano-player behind the canvas curtains to the stage. One of the show-boys put his arms around the girl sitting on the box and began tentatively to feel her breasts.

"Don't be so fresh, hot papa," she said. And Sandy recognized Maudel's voice, and saw her brown face as she leaned back to look at the show-man. The boy in the red suit bent over and kissed her several times, while the other fellow kept imitating the steps he had just seen Harriett performing.

"Let's go," Earl said to Sandy, rolling over on the ground. The two small boys went on to the next tent, where one of the carnival men caught them, kicked their behinds soundly, and sent them away.

The sun was setting in a pink haze, and the showgrounds began to take on an air of activity. The steam calliope gave a few trial hoots, and the merry-go-round circled slowly without passengers. The paddle-wheels and the get-'em-hot men, the lemonade-sellers and the souvenir-vendors were opening their booths to the evening trade. A barker began to ballyhoo in front of the freak-show. By and by there would be a crowd. The lights came on along the Midway, the Ferris wheel swept languidly up into the air, and when Sandy found his father, the colored band had begun to play in front of the minstrel show.

"I want to ride on the merry-go-round," Sandy insisted. "And go in the Crazy House." So they did both; then they bought hamburger sandwiches with thick slices of white onion and drank strawberry soda and ate pop-corn with butter on it. They went to the sea-lion circus, tried to win a Kewpie doll at the paddle-wheel booth, and watched men losing money on the hidden pea, then trying to win it back at four-card monte behind the Galatea attraction. And all the while Sandy said nothing to his father about having seen Harriett dancing in the minstrel tent that afternoon.

Sandy had lived too long with three women not to have learned to hold his tongue about the private doings of each of them. When Annjee paid two dollars a week on a blue silk shirt for his father at Cohn's cut-rate credit store, and Sandy saw her make the payments, he knew without being told that the matter was never to be mentioned to Aunt Hager. And if his grandmother sometimes threw Harriett's rouge out in the alley, Sandy saw it with his eyes, but not with his mouth.

Because he loved all three of them—Harriett and Annjee and Hager—he didn't carry tales on any one of them to the others. Nobody would know he had watched his Aunt Harrie dancing on the carnival lot today in front of a big fat white man in a checkered vest while a Negro in a red suit played the piano.

"We got a half-dollar left for the minstrel show," said Jimboy. "Come on, let's go." And he pulled his son through the crowd that jammed the long Midway between the booths. All the bright lights of the carnival were on now, and everything was running full blast. The merry-go-round whirled to the ear-splitting hoots of the calliope; bands blared; the canvas paintings of snakes and dancing-girls, human skeletons, fire-eaters, billowed in the evening breeze; pennants flapped, barkers shouted, acrobats twirled in front of a tent; a huge paddle-wheel clicked out numbers. Folks pushed and shoved and women called to their children not to get lost. In the air one smelled the scent of trampled grass, peanuts, and hot dogs, animals and human bodies.

The large white man in the checkered vest was making the ballyhoo in front of the minstrel show, his expansive belly turned towards the crowd that had been attracted by the band. One hand pointed towards a tawdry group of hard-looking Negro performers standing on the platform.

"Here we have, ladies and gents, Madam Caledonia Watson, the Dixie song-bird; Dancing Jenkins, the dark strutter from Jacksonville; little Lizzie Roach, champeen coon-shouter of Georgia; and last, but not least, Sambo and Rastus, the world's funniest comedians. Last performance this evening! . . . Strike her up, perfesser! . . . Come along, now, folks!"

The band burst into sound, Madam Watson and Lizzie Roach opened their brass-lined throats, the men dropped into a momentary clog-dance, and then the whole crowd of performers disappeared into the tent. The ticket-purchasing townspeople followed through the public opening beneath a gaudily painted sign picturing a Mississippi steamboat in the moonlight, and two black bucks shooting gigantic dice on a street-corner.

Jimboy and Sandy followed the band inside and took seats, and soon the frayed curtain rose, showing a plantation scene in the South, where three men, blackened up, and two women in bandannas sang longingly about Dixie. Then Sambo and Rastus came out with long wooden razors and began to argue and shoot dice, but presently the lights went out and a ghost appeared and frightened the two men away, causing them to leave all the money on the stage. (The audience thought it screamingly funny—and just like niggers.) After that one of the women sang a ragtime song and did the eagle-rock. Then a man with a banjo in his hands began to play, but until then the show had been lifeless.

"Listen to him," Jimboy said, punching Sandy. "He's good!"

The piece he was picking was full of intricate runs and trills long drawn out, then suddenly slipping into tantalizing rhythms. It ended with a vibrant whang!—and the audience yelled for more. As an encore he played a blues and sang innumerable verses, always ending:

> *An' Ah can't be satisfied,*
> *'Cause all Ah love has*
> *Done laid down an' died.*

And to Sandy it seemed like the saddest music in the world—but the white people around him laughed.

Then the stage lights went on, the band blared, and all the black actors came trooping back, clapping their hands before the cotton-field curtain as each one in turn danced like fury, vigorously distorting agile limbs into the most amazing positions, while the scene ended with the fattest mammy and the oldest uncle shaking jazzily together.

The booths were all putting out their lights as the people poured through the gate towards town. Sandy hobbled down the road beside his father, his sore heel, which had been forgotten all evening, paining him terribly until Jimboy picked him up and carried him on his shoulder. Automobiles and buggies whirled past them in clouds of gritty dust, and young boys calling vulgar words hurried after tittering girls. When Sandy and his father reached home, Aunt Hager and Annjee had not yet returned from the revival. Jimboy said he thought maybe they had stopped at Mrs. Lane's to sit up all night with the sick woman, so Sandy spread his pallet on the floor at the foot of his grandmother's bed and went to sleep. He did not hear his Aunt Harriett when she came home, but late in the night he woke up with his heel throbbing painfully, his throat dry, and his skin burning, and when he tried to bend his leg, it hurt him so that he began to cry.

Harriett, awakened by his moans, called drowsily: "What's the matter, honey?"

"My foot," said Sandy tearfully.

So his young aunt got out of bed, lit the lamp, and helped him to the kitchen, where she heated a kettle of water, bathed his heel, and covered the nail-wound with vaseline. Then she bound it with a fresh white rag.

"Now that ought to feel better," she said as she led him back to his pallet, and soon they were both asleep again.

The next morning when Hager came from the sickbed of her friend, she sent to the butcher-shop for a bacon rind, cut from it a piece of fat meat, and bound it to Sandy's heel as a cure.

"Don't want you havin' de blood-pisen here," she said. "An' don't you run round an' play on that heel. Set out on de porch an' study yo' reader, 'cause school'll be startin' next month." Then she began Mrs. Reinhart's ironing.

The next day, Saturday, the last day of the carnival, Jimboy carried the Reinharts' clothes home for Hager, since Sandy was crippled and Jimmy Lane's mother was down in bed. But after delivering the clothes Jimboy did not come home for supper. When Annjee and Hager wanted to leave for the revival in the early evening, they asked Harriett if she would stay home with the little boy, for Sandy's heel had swollen purple where the rusty nail had penetrated and he could hardly walk at all.

"You been gone ever' night this week," Hager said to the girl. "An' you ain't been anear de holy tents where de Lawd's word is preached; so you ought to be willin' to stay home one night with a po' little sick boy."

"Yes'm," Harriett muttered in a noncommittal tone. But shortly after her mother and Annjee had gone, she said to her nephew: "You aren't afraid to stay home by yourself, are you?"

And Sandy answered: "Course not, Aunt Harrie."

She gave him a hot bath and put a new piece of fat meat on his festering heel. Then she told him to climb into Annjee's bed and go to sleep, but instead he lay for a long time looking out the window that was beside the bed. He thought about the carnival—the Ferris wheel sweeping up into the air, and the minstrel show. Then he remembered Benbow's dance a few weeks ago and how his Aunt Harriett had stood sullenly the next morning while Hager whipped her—and hadn't cried at all, until the welts came under her silk stockings. . . . Then he wondered what Jimmy Lane would do if his sick mother died from the T. B. and he were left with nobody to take care of him, because Jimmy's step-father was no good. . . . Eu-uuu! His heel hurt! . . . When school began again, he would be in the fifth grade, but he wished he'd hurry up and get to high school, like Harriett was. . . . When he got to be a man, he was going to be a railroad engineer. . . . Gee, he wasn't sleepy—and his heel throbbed painfully.

In the next room Harriett had lighted the oil-lamp and was moving swiftly about taking clothes from the dresser-drawers and spreading them on the bed. She thought Sandy was asleep, he knew—but he couldn't go to sleep the way his foot hurt him. He could see her through the doorway folding her dresses in little piles and he wondered why she was doing that. Then she took an old suit-case from the closet and began to pack it, and when it was full, she pulled a new bag from under the bed, and into it she dumped her toilet-articles, powder, vaseline, nail-polish, straightening comb, and several pairs of old stockings rolled in balls. Then she sat down on the bed between the two closed suit-cases for a long time with her hands in her lap and her eyes staring ahead of her.

Finally she rose and closed the bureau-drawers, tidied up

the confusion she had created, and gathered together the discarded things she had thrown on the floor. Then Sandy heard her go out into the back yard towards the trash-pile. When she returned, she put on a tight little hat and went into the kitchen to wash her hands, throwing the water through the back door. Then she tip-toed into the room where Sandy was lying and kissed him gently on the head. Sandy knew that she thought he was asleep, but in spite of himself he suddenly threw his arms tightly around her neck. He couldn't help it.

"Where you going, Aunt Harriett?" he said, sitting up in bed, clutching the girl.

"Honey, you won't tell on me, will you?" Harriett asked.

"No," he answered, and she knew he wouldn't. "But where are you going, Aunt Harrie?"

"You won't be afraid to stay here until grandma comes?"

"No," burying his face on her breast. "I won't be afraid."

"And you won't forget Aunt Harrie?"

"Course not."

"I'm leaving with the carnival," she told him.

For a moment they sat close together on the bed. Then she kissed him, went into the other room and picked up her suitcases—and the door closed.

X.

PUNISHMENT

Old white Dr. McDillors, beloved of all the Negroes in Stanton, came on Sunday morning, swabbed Sandy's festering foot with iodine, bound it up, and gave him a bottle of green medicine to take, and by the middle of the week the boy was able to hobble about again without pain; but Hager continued to apply fat meat instead of following the doctor's directions.

When Harriett didn't come back, Sandy no longer slept on a pallet on the floor. He slept in the big bed with his grandma Hager, and the evenings that followed weren't so jolly, with his young aunt off with the carnival, and Jimboy spending most of his time at the pool hall or else loafing on the station platform watching the trains come through—and nobody playing music in the back yard.

They went to bed early these days, and after that eventful week of carnival and revival, a sore heel, and a missing Aunt Harriett, the muscles of Sandy's little body often twitched and jerked in his sleep and he would awaken suddenly from dreaming that he heard sad raggy music playing while a woman shouted for Jesus in the Gospel tent, and a girl in red silk stockings cried because the switches were cutting her legs. Sometimes he would lie staring into the darkness a long time, while Aunt Hager lay snoring at his side. And sometimes in the next room, where Annjee and Jimboy were, he could hear the slow rhythmical creaking of the bedsprings and the low moans of his mother, which he already knew accompanied the grown-up embraces of bodily love. And sometimes through the window he could see the moonlight glinting on the tall, tassel-crowned stalks of corn in the garden. Perhaps he would toss and turn until he had awakened Aunt Hager and she would say drowsily: "What's de matter with you, chile? I'll put you back on de flo' if you can't be still!" Then he would go to sleep again, and before he knew it, the sun would be flooding the room with warm light, and the coffee would be boiling on the stove in the kitchen, and Annjee would have gone to work.

Summer days were long and drowsy for grown-ups, but for Sandy they were full of interest. In the mornings he helped Aunt Hager by feeding the chickens, bringing in the water for her wash-tubs and filling the buckets from which they drank. He chopped wood, too, and piled it behind the kitchen-stove; then he would take the broom and sweep dust-clean the space around the pump and under the apple-tree where he played. Perhaps by that time Willie-Mae would come over or Buster would be there to shoot marbles. Or maybe his grandmother would send him to the store to get a pound of sugar or ten cents' worth of meal for dinner, and on the way there was certain to be an adventure. Yesterday he had seen two bad little boys from the Bottoms, collecting scrap-iron and junk in the alleys, get angry at each other and pretend to start a fight.

The big one said to the smaller one: "I'm a fast-black and you know I sho won't run! Jest you pick up that piece o' iron that belongs to me. Go ahead, jest you try!"

And the short boy replied: "I'm your match, long skinny! Strike me an' see if you don't get burnt up!" And then they started to play the dozens, and Sandy, standing by, learned several new and very vulgar words to use when talking about other people's mothers.

The tall kid said finally: "Aw, go on, you little clay-colored nigger, you looks too much like mustard to me anyhow!" Picking up the disputed piece of scrap-iron, he proceeded on his quest for junk, looking into all the trash-piles and garbage-cans along the alley, but the smaller of the two boys took his gunny-sack and went in the opposite direction alone.

"Be careful, sissy, and don't break your dishes," his late companion called after his retreating buddy, and Sandy carefully memorized the expression to try on Jimmy Lane some time—that is, if Jimmy's mother got well, for Mrs. Lane now was in the last stages of consumption. But if she got better, Sandy was going to tell her son to be careful and not break his dishes—always wearing his mother's shoes, like a girl.

By that time he had forgotten what Hager sent him to the store to buy, and instead of getting meal he bought washing-powder. When he came home, after nearly an hour's absence, his grandmother threatened to cut an elm switch, but she satisfied herself instead by scolding him for staying so long, and then sending him back to exchange the washing-powder for meal—and she waiting all that time to make corn dumplings to put in the greens!

In the afternoon Sandy played in his back yard or next door at the Johnsons', but Hager never allowed him outside their block. The white children across the street were frequently inclined to say "Nigger," so he was forbidden to play there. Usually Buster, who looked like a white kid, and Willie-Mae, who couldn't have been blacker, were his companions. The three children would run at hide-and-seek, in the tall corn; or they would tag one another in the big yard, or play house under the apple-tree.

Once when they were rummaging in the trash-pile to see what they could find, Sandy came across a pawn ticket which he took into the kitchen to Hager. It was for a watch his Aunt Harriett had pawned the Saturday she ran away.

Sometimes in the late afternoon the children would go next door to Madam de Carter's and she would give them ginger cookies and read to them from the *Bible Story Reader*. Madam de Carter looked very pompous and important in her silk waist as she would put on her *pince-nez* and say: "Now, children, seat yourselves and preserve silence while I read you-all this moralizing history of Samson's treacherous hair. Now, Buster, who were Samson? Willie-Mae, has you ever heard of Delilah?"

Sometimes, if Jimboy was home, he would take down his

old guitar and start the children to dancing in the sunlight—but then Hager would always call Sandy to pump water or go to the store as soon as she heard the music.

"Out there dancin' like you ain't got no raisin'!" she would say. "I tells Jimboy 'bout playin' that ole ragtime here! That's what ruint Harriett!"

And on Sundays Sandy went to Sabbath school at the Shiloh Baptist Church, where he was given a colored picture card with a printed text on it. The long, dull lessons were taught by Sister Flora Garden, who had been to Wilberforce College, in Ohio. There were ten little boys in Sandy's class, ranging from nine to fourteen, and they behaved very badly, for Miss Flora Garden, who wore thick-lensed glasses on her roach-colored face, didn't understand little boys.

"Where was Moses when the lights went out?" Gritty Smith asked her every Sunday, and she didn't even know the answer.

Sandy didn't think much of Sunday-school, and frequently instead of putting his nickel in the collection basket he spent it for candy, which he divided with Buster—until one very hot Sunday Hager found it out. He had put a piece of the sticky candy in his shirt-pocket and it melted, stuck, and stained the whole front of his clean clothes. When he came home, with Buster behind him, the first thing Hager said was: "What's all this here stuck up in yo' pocket?" and Buster commenced to giggle and said Sandy had bought candy.

"Where'd you get the money, sir?" demanded Aunt Hager searchingly of her grandson.

"I—we—er—Madam Carter gimme a nickel," Sandy replied haltingly, choosing the first name he could think of, which would have been all right had not Madam de Carter herself stopped by the house, almost immediately afterwards, on her way home from church.

"Is you give Sandy a nickel to buy candy this mawnin'?" Hager asked her as soon as she entered the parlor.

"Why, no, Sister Williams, I isn't. I had no coins about me a-tall at services this morning."

"Umn-huh! I thought so!" said Hager. "You Sandy!"

The little boy, guilt written all over his face, came in from the front porch, where he had been sitting with his father after Buster went home.

"Where'd you tell me you got that nickel this mawnin'?" And before he could answer, she spat out: "I'm gonna whip you!"

"Jehovah help us! Children sure is bad these days," said Madam de Carter, shaking her head as she left to go next door to her own house. "They sure *are* bad," she added, self-consciously correcting her English.

"I'm gonna whip you," Hager continued, sitting down amazed in her plush chair. "De idee o' with-holdin' yo' Sunday-school money from de Lawd an' buyin' candy."

"I only spent a penny," Sandy lied, wriggling.

"How you gwine get so much candy fo' a penny that you has some left to gum up in yo' pocket? Tell me that, how you gonna do it?"

Sandy, at a loss for an answer, was standing with lowered eyelids, when the screen door opened and Jimboy came in. Sandy looked up at him for aid, but his father's usually amiable face was stern this time.

"Come here!" he said. The man towered very tall above the little fellow who looked up at him helplessly.

"I's gwine whip him!" interposed Hager.

"Is that right, you spent your Sunday-school nickel for candy?" Jimboy demanded gravely.

Sandy nodded his head. He couldn't lie to his father, and had he spoken now, the sobs would have come.

"Then you told a lie to your grandma—and I'm ashamed of you," his father said.

Sandy wanted to turn his head away and escape the slow gaze of Jimboy's eyes, but he couldn't. If Aunt Hager would only whip him, it would be better; then maybe his father wouldn't say any more. But it was awful to stand still and listen to Jimboy talk to him this way—yet there he stood, stiffly holding back the sobs.

"To take money and use it for what it ain't s'posed to be

used is the same as stealing," Jimboy went on gravely to his son. "That's what you done today, and then come home and lie about it. Nobody's ugly as a liar, you know that! . . . I'm not much, maybe. Don't mean to say I am. I won't work a lot, but what I do I do honest. White folks gets rich lyin' and stealin'— and some niggers gets rich that way, too—but I don't need money if I got to get it dishonest, with a lot o' lies trailing behind me, and can't look folks in the face. It makes you feel dirty! It's no good! . . . Don't I give you nickels for candy whenever you want 'em?"

The boy nodded silently, with the tears trickling down his chin.

"And don't I go with you to the store and buy you ice-cream and soda-pop any time you ask me?"

The child nodded again.

"And then you go and take the Sunday-school nickel that your grandma's worked hard for all the week, spend it on candy, and come back home and lie about it. So that's what you do! And then lie!"

Jimboy turned his back and went out on the porch, slamming the screen door behind him. Aunt Hager did not whip her grandson, but returned to the kitchen and left him standing disgraced in the parlor. Then Sandy began to cry, with one hand in his mouth so no one could hear him, and when Annjee came home from work in the late afternoon, she found him lying across her bed, head under the pillows, still sobbing because Jimboy had called him a liar.

XI

SCHOOL

Some weeks later the neighbors were treated to an early morning concert:

> *I got a high yaller*
> *An' a little short black,*
> *But a brown-skin gal*
> *Can bring me right on back!*
> *I'm singin' brown-skin!*
> *Lawdy! . . . Lawd!*
> *Brown-skin! . . . O, ma Lawd!*

"It must be Jimboy," said Hager from the kitchen. "A lazy coon, settin' out there in the cool singin', an' me in here sweatin' and washin' maself to dust!"

> *Kansas City Southern!*
> *I mean de W. & A.!*
> *I'm gonna ride de first train*
> *I catch goin' out ma way.*
> *I'm got de railroad blues—*

"I wish to God you'd go on, then!" mumbled Hager over the wash-boilers.

> *But I ain't got no railroad fare!*
> *I'm gwine to pack ma grip an'*
> *Beat ma way away from here!*

"Learn me how to pick a cord, papa," Sandy begged as he sat beside his father under the apple-tree, loaded with ripe fruit.

"All right, look a-here! . . . You put your thumb like this. . . ." Jimboy began to explain. "But, doggone, your fingers ain't long enough yet!"

Still they managed to spend a half-day twanging at the old instrument, with Sandy trying to learn a simple tune.

The sunny August mornings had become September mornings, and most of Aunt Hager's "white folks" had returned from their vacations; her kitchen was once more a daily laundry. Great boilers of clothes steamed on the stove and, beside the clothes, pans of apple juice boiled to jelly, and the peelings of peaches simmered to jam.

There was no news from the runaway Harriett. . . . Mrs. Lane died one sultry night, with Hager at the bedside, and was buried by the lodge with three hacks and a fifty-dollar coffin. . . . The following week the Drill of All Nations, after much practising by the women, was given with great success and Annjee, dressed in white and wrapped in a Scandinavian flag, marched proudly as Sweden. . . . Madam de Carter's house was now locked and barred, as she had departed for Oklahoma to organize branches of the lodge there. . . . Tempy had stopped to see Hager one afternoon, but she didn't stay long. She told her mother she was out collecting rents and that she and her husband were buying another house. . . . Willie-Mae had a new calico dress. . . . Buster had learned to swear better than Sandy. . . . And next Monday was to be the opening of the new school term.

Sandy hated even to think about going back to school. He was having much fun playing, and Jimboy had been teaching him to box. Then the time to go to classes came.

"Wash yo' face good, sir, put on yo' clean waist, an' polish yo' shoes," Aunt Hager said bright and early, " 'cause I don't want none o' them white teachers sayin' I sends you to school dirty as a 'cuse to put you back in de fourth grade. You hear me, sir!"

"Yes'm," Sandy replied.

This morning he was to enter the "white" fifth grade, having passed last June from the "colored" fourth, for in Stanton the Negro children were kept in separate rooms under colored teachers until they had passed the fourth grade. Then, from the fifth grade on, they went with the other children, and the teachers were white.

When Sandy arrived on the school grounds with his face shining, he found the yard already full of shouting kids. On the girls' side he saw Willie-Mae jumping rope. Sandy found Earl and Buster and some boys whom he knew playing mumble-peg on the boys' side, and he joined them. When the bell rang, they all crowded into the building, as the marching-lines had not yet been formed. Miss Abigail Minter, the principal, stood at the entrance, and there were big signs on all the room doors marking the classes. Sandy found the fifth-grade room upstairs and went in shyly. It was full of whispering youngsters huddled in little groups. He saw two colored children among them, both girls whom he didn't know, but there were no colored boys. Soon the teacher rapped briskly on her desk, and silence ensued.

"Take seats, all of you, please," she rasped out. "Anywhere now until we get order." She rapped again impatiently with the ruler. "Take seats at once." So the children each selected a desk and sat down, most of the girls at the front of the room and most of the boys together at the back, where they could play and look out the windows.

Then the teacher, middle-aged and wearing glasses, passed out tiny slips of paper to each child in the front row, with the command that they be handed backwards, so that every student received one slip.

"Now, write your names on the paper, turning it longways," she said. "Nothing but your names, that's all I want today. You will receive forms to fill out later, but I want to get your seats assigned this morning, however."

Amid much confusion and borrowing of pencils, the slips were finally signed in big awkward letters, and collected by the teacher, who passed up and down the aisles. Then she went to

her desk, and there was a delightful period of whispering and
wriggling as she sorted the slips and placed them in alphabeti-
cal order. Finally she finished.

"Now," she said, "each child rise as I call out your names,
so I can see who you are."

The teacher stood up with the papers in her hand.

"Mary Atkins . . . Carl Dietrich . . . Josephine Evans," she
called slowly glancing up after each name. "Franklin Rhodes . . .
James Rogers." Sandy stood up quickly. "Ethel Shortlidge . . .
Roland Thomas." The roll-call continued, each child standing
until he had been identified, then sitting down again.

"Now," the teacher said, "everybody rise and make a line
around the walls. Quietly! No talking! As I call your names
this time, take seats in order, starting with number one in the
first row near the window. . . . Mary Atkins . . . Carl
Dietrich. . . ." The roll was repeated, each child taking a seat
as she had commanded. When all but four of the children were
seated, the two colored girls and Sandy still were standing.

"Albert Zwick," she said, and the last white child sat down
in his place. "Now," said the teacher, "you three colored children take the seats behind Albert. You girls take the first two,
and you," pointing to Sandy, "take the last one. . . . Now I'm
going to put on the board the list of books to buy and I want
all of you to copy them correctly." And she went on with her
details of schoolroom routine.

One of the colored girls turned round to Sandy and whispered: "She just put us in the back cause we're niggers." And
Sandy nodded gravely. "My name's Sadie Butler and she's put
me behind the Z cause I'm a nigger."

"An old heifer!" said the first little colored girl, whispering
loudly. "I'm gonna tell my mama." But Sandy felt like crying.
And he was beginning to be ashamed of crying because he was
no longer a small boy. But the teacher's putting the colored
children in the back of the room made him feel like crying.

At lunch-time he came home with his list of books, and
Aunt Hager pulled her wet arms out of the tub, wiped her
hands, and held them up in horror.

"Lawdy! Just look! Something else to spend money for. Ever' year more an' more books, an' chillens learn less an' less! Used to didn't have nothin' but a blue-backed speller, and now look ahere—a list as long as ma arm! Go out there in de yard an' see is yo' pappy got any money to give you for 'em, 'cause I ain't."

Sandy found Jimboy sitting dejectedly on the well-stoop in the sunshine, with his head in his hands. "You got any money, papa?" he asked.

Jimboy looked at the list of books written in Sandy's childish scrawl and slowly handed him a dollar and a half.

"You see what I got left, don't you?" said his father as he turned his pants-pockets inside out, showing the little boy a jack-knife, a half-empty sack of Bull Durham, a key, and a dime. But he smiled, and took Sandy awkwardly in his arms and kissed him. "It's all right, kid."

That afternoon at school they had a long drill on the multiplication table, and then they had a spelling-match, because the teacher said that would be a good way to find out what the children knew. For the spelling-bee they were divided into two sides—the boys and the girls, each side lining up against an opposite wall. Then the teacher gave out words that they should have learned in the lower grades. On the boys' side everyone was spelled down except Sandy, but on the girls' side there were three proud little white girls left standing and Sandy came near spelling them down, too, until he put the *e* before *i* in "chief," and the girls' side won, to the disgust of the boys, and the two colored girls, who wanted Sandy to win.

After school Sandy went uptown with Buster to buy books, but there was so large a crowd of children in the bookstore that it was five o'clock before he was waited on and his list filled. When he reached home, Aunt Hager was at the kitchen-stove frying an eggplant for supper.

"You stayin' out mighty long," she said without taking her attention from the stove.

"Where's papa?" Sandy asked eagerly. He wanted to show Jimboy his new books—a big geography, with pictures of

animals in it, and a *Nature Story Reader* that he knew his father would like to see.

"Look in yonder," said Hager, pointing towards Annjee's
bedroom.

Sandy rushed in, then stopped, because there was no one
there. Suddenly a queer feeling came over him and he put his
books down on the bed. Jimboy's clothes were no longer hanging against the wall where his working-shirts and overalls
were kept. Then Sandy looked under the bed. His father's old
suit-case was not there either, nor his work-shoes, nor his Sunday patent-leathers. And the guitar was missing.

"Where's papa?" he asked again, running back to the kitchen.

"Can't you see he ain't here?" replied his grandmother, busily turning slices of eggplant with great care in the skillet.
"Gone—that's where he is—a lazy nigger. Told me to tell Annjee he say goodbye, 'cause his travellin' blues done come
on . . . ! Huh! Jimboy's yo' pappy, chile, but he sho ain't worth
his salt! . . . an' I's right glad he's took his clothes an' left here,
maself."

XII.

HARD WINTER

September passed and the corn-stalks in the garden were cut. There were no more apples left on the trees, and chilly rains came to beat down the falling leaves from the maples and the elms. Cold and drearily wet October passed, too, with no hint of Indian summer or golden forests. And as yet there was no word from the departed Jimboy. Annjee worried herself sick as usual, hoping every day that a letter would come from this wandering husband whom she loved. And each night she hurried home from Mrs. Rice's, looked on the parlor table for the mail, and found none. Harriett had not written, either, since she went away with the carnival, and Hager never mentioned her youngest daughter's name. Nor did Hager mention Jimboy except when Annjee asked her, after she could hold it no longer: "Are you sure the mail-man ain't left me a letter today?" And then Aunt Hager would reply impatiently: "You think I'd a et it if he did? You know that good-for-nothin', upsettin' scoundrel ain't wrote!"

But in spite of daily disappointments from the postal service Annjee continued to rush from Mrs. Rice's hot kitchen as soon after dinner as she could and to trudge through the chill October rains, anxious to feel in the mail-box outside her door, then hope against hope for a letter inside on the little front-room table—which would always be empty. She caught a terrible cold tramping through the damp streets, forgetting to button her cloak, then sitting down with her wet shoes on when she got home, a look of dumb disappointment in her eyes, too tired and unhappy to remove her clothes.

"You's a fool," said her mother, whose tongue was often much sharper than the meaning behind it. "Mooning after a worthless nigger like Jimboy. I tole you years ago he were no good, when he first come, lookin' like he ought to be wearin' short pants, an' out here courtin' you. Ain't none o' them bell-hoppin', racehoss-followin' kind o' darkies worth havin', an' that's all Jimboy was when you married him an' he ain't much mo'n that now. An' you older'n he is, too!"

"But you know why I married, don't you?"

"You Sandy, go outdoors an' get me some wood fo' this stove. . . . Yes, I knows why, because he were de father o' that chile you was 'bout to bring here, but I don't see why it couldn't just well been some o' these steady, hard-workin' Stanton young men's what was courtin' you at de same time. . . . But, chile or no chile, I couldn't hear nothin' but Jimboy, Jimboy, Jimboy! I told you you better stay in de high school an' get your edication, but no, you had to marry this Jimboy. Now you see what you got, don't you?"

"Well, he ain't been so bad, ma! And I don't care, I love him!"

"Umn-huh! Try an' live on love, daughter! Just try an' live on love. . . . You's made a mistake, that's all, honey. . . . But I guess there ain't no use talkin' 'bout it now. Take off yo' wet shoes 'fore you catch yo' death o' cold!"

On Thanksgiving at Mrs. Rice's, so Annjee reported, they had turkey with chestnut dressing; but at Aunt Hager's she and Sandy had a nice juicy possum, a present from old man Logan, parboiled and baked sweet and brown with yams in the pan. Aunt Hager opened a jar of peach preserves. And she told Sandy to ask Jimmy Lane in to dinner because, since his mother died, he wasn't faring so well and the people he was staying with didn't care much about him. But since Jimmy had quit school, Sandy didn't see him often; and the day before Thanksgiving he couldn't find him at all, so they had no company to help them eat the possum.

The week after Thanksgiving Annjee fell ill and had to go to bed. She had the grippe, Aunt Hager said, and she began to dose her with quinine and to put hot mustard-plasters on her

back and gave her onion syrup to drink, but it didn't seem to
do much good, and finally she had to send Sandy for Dr.
McDillors.

"System's all run down," said the doctor. "Heavy cold on
the chest—better be careful. And stay in the bed!" But the
warning was unnecessary. Annjee felt too tired and weak ever
to rise, and only the mail-man's whistle blowing at somebody
else's house would cause her to try to lift her head. Then she
would demand weakly: "Did he stop here?"

Hager's home now was like a steam laundry. The kitchen
was always hung with lines of clothes to dry, and in the late
afternoon and evenings the ironing-board was spread from the
table to a chair-back in the middle of the floor. All of the old
customers were sending their clothes to Hager again during
the winter. And since Annjee was sick, bringing no money into
the house on Saturdays, the old woman had even taken an
extra washing to do. Being the only wage-earner, Hager kept
the suds flying—but with the wet weather she had to dry the
clothes in the kitchen most of the time, and when Sandy came
home from school for lunch, he would eat under dripping lines
of white folks' garments while he listened to his mother coughing in the next room.

In the other rooms of the house there were no stoves, so the
doors were kept open in order that the heat might pass through
from the kitchen. They couldn't afford to keep more than one
fire going; therefore the kitchen was living-room, dining-room,
and work-room combined. In the mornings Sandy would jump
out of bed and run with his clothes in his hands to the kitchen-
stove, where his grandmother would have the fire blazing, the
coffee-pot on, and a great tub of water heating for the washings. And in the evenings after supper he would open his geography and read about the strange countries far away, the book
spread out on the oilcloth-covered kitchen-table. And Aunt
Hager, if her ironing was done, would sit beside the stove and
doze, while Annjee tossed and groaned in her chilly bedroom.
Only in the kitchen was it really bright and warm.

In the afternoons when Sandy came home from school he

would usually find Sister Johnson helping Hager with her ironing, and keeping up a steady conversation.

"Dis gonna be a hard winter. De papers say folks is out o'
work ever' where, an', wid all dis sleet an' rain, it's a terror fo'
de po' peoples, I tells you! Now, ma Tom, he got a good job
tendin' de furnace at de Fair Buildin', so I ain't doin' much
washin' long as he's workin'—but so many colored men's out
o' work here, wid Christmas comin', it sho is too bad! An' you,
Sis Williams, wid yo' daughter sick in bed! Any time yo'
clothes git kinder heavy fo' you, I ain't mind helpin' you out.
Jest send dis chile atter me or holler 'cross de yard if you kin
make me hear! . . . How you press dis dress, wid de collar turn
up or down? Which way do Mis' Dunset like it?"

"I always presses it down," returned Hager, who was ironing handkerchiefs and towels on the table. "Better let me iron
that, an' you take these here towels."

"All right," agreed Sister Johnson, "'cause you knows how
yo' white folks likes dey things, an' I don't. Folks have so many
different ways!"

"Sho do," said Hager. "I washed for a woman once what
even had her sheets starched."

"But you's sure got a fine repertation as a washer, Sis Williams. One o' de white ladies what I washes fo' say you washes
beautiful."

"I reckon white folks does think right smart of me," said
Hager proudly. "They always likes you when you tries to do
right."

"When you tries to do yo' work right, you means. Dey ain't
carin' nothin' 'bout you 'yond workin' fo' 'em. Ain't dey got all
de little niggers settin' off in one row at dat school whar Sandy
an' Willie-Mae go at? I's like Harriett—ain't got no time fo'
white folks maself, 'ceptin' what little money dey pays me. You
ain't been run out o' yo' home like I is, Hager. . . . Sandy, make
haste go fetch my pipe from over to de house, an' don't stay all
day playin' wid Willie-Mae! Tote it here quick! . . . An' you
oughter hear de way white folks talks 'bout niggers. Says dey's
lazy, an' says dey stinks, an' all. Huh! Dey ought to smell

dey-selves! You's smelled white peoples when dey gets to sweatin' ain't you? Smells jest like sour cream, only worser, kinder sickenin' like. And some o' dese foriners what's been eating garlic—phew! Lawdy!"

When Sandy returned with the pipe, the conversation had shifted to the deaths in the colored community. "Hager, folks dyin' right an' left already dis winter. We's had such a bad fall, dat's de reason why. You know dat no-'count Jack Smears passed away last Sunday. Dey had his funeral yesterday an' I went. Good thing he belonged to de lodge, too, else he'd been buried in de po'-field, 'cause he ain't left even de copper cents to put on his eyes. Lodge beared his funeral bill, but I heard more'n one member talkin' 'bout how dey was puttin' a ten-dollar nigger in a hundred-dollar coffin! . . . An' his wife were at de funeral. Yes, sir! A hussy! After she done left him last year wid de little chillens to take care of, an' she runnin' round de streets showin' off. Dere she sot, big as life, in front wid de moaners, long black veil on her face and done dyed her coat black, an' all de time Reverend Butler been preachin' 'bout how holy Jack were, she turn an' twist an' she coughed an' she whiffled an' blowed an' she wiped—tryin' her best to cry an' couldn't, deceitful as she is! Then she jest broke out to screamin', but warn't a tear in her eye; makin' folks look at her, dat's all, 'cause she ain't cared nothin' 'bout Jack. She been livin' in de Bottoms since last Feb'ary wid a young bell-hop ain't much older'n her own son, Bert!"

"Do Jesus!" said Hager. "Some womens is awful."

"Worse'n dat," said Sister Johnson. . . . "Lawdy! Listen at dat sleet beatin' on dese winders! Sho gwine be a real winter! An' how time do pass. Ain't but t'ree mo' weeks till Christmas!"

"Truth!" said Sandy's grandmother. "An' we ain't gwine have no money a-tall. Ain't no mo'n got through payin' ma taxes good, an' de interest on ma mortgage, when Annjee get sick here! Lawd, I tells you, po' colored womens have it hard!"

"Sho do!" said Sister Johnson, sucking at her pipe as she ironed. "How long you been had this house, Sis Williams?"

"Fo' nigh on forty years, ever sence Cudge an' me come here

from Montgomery. An' I been washin' fo' white folks ever' week de Lawd sent sence I been here, too. Bought this house washin', and made as many payments myself as Cudge come near; an' raised ma chillens washin'; an' when Cudge taken sick an' laid on his back for mo'n a year, I taken care o' him washin'; an' when he died, paid de funeral bill washin', cause he ain't belonged to no lodge. Sent Tempy through de high school and edicated Annjee till she marry that onery pup of a Jimboy, an' Harriett till she left home. Yes, sir. Washin', an' here I is with me arms still in de tub! . . . But they's one mo' got to go through school yet, an' that's ma little Sandy. If de Lawd lets me live, I's gwine make a edicated man out o' him. He's gwine be another Booker T. Washington." Hager turned a voluminous white petticoat on the ironing-board as she carefully pressed its embroidered hem. "I ain't never raised no boy o' ma own yet, so I wants this one o' Annjee's to 'mount to something. I wants him to know all they is to know, so's he can help this black race o' our'n to come up and see de light and take they places in de world. I wants him to be a Fred Douglass leadin' de people, that's what, an' not followin' in de tracks o' his good-for-nothin' pappy, worthless an' wanderin' like Jimboy is."

"O, don't say that, ma," Annjee cried weakly from her bed in the other room. "Jimboy's all right, but he's just too smart to do this heavy ditch-digging labor, and that's all white folks gives the colored a chance at here in Stanton; so he had to leave."

"There you go excitin' yo'self agin, an' you sick. I thought you was asleep. I ain't meant nothin', honey. Course he's all right," Hager said to quiet her daughter, but she couldn't resist mumbling: "But I ain't seen him doin' you no good."

"Well, he ain't beat her, has he?" asked Sister Johnson, who, for the sake of conversation, often took a contrary view-point. "I's knowed many a man to beat his wife. Tom used to tap me a few times 'fo' I found out a way to stop him, but dat ain't nedder here nor dere!" She folded a towel decisively and gave it a vigorous rub with the hot iron. "Did I ever tell you 'bout de man lived next do' to us in Cairo what cut his wife in de stomach wid a razor an' den stood ovah her when de doctor was sewin' her up moanin': 'I don't see why I cut her in de stomach! O, Lawd! She always told me she ain't want to be cut in de stomach!' . . . An' it warn't two months atter dat dat he done sliced her in de stomach agin when she was tryin' to git away from him! He were a mean nigger, that man were!"

"Annjee, is you taken yo' medicine yet? It's past fo' o'clock," Hager called. "Sandy, here, take this fifteen cents, chile, and run to de store an' get me a soup bone. I gwine try an' make a little broth for yo' mother. An' don't be gone all day neither, 'cause I got to send these clothes back to Mis' Dunset." Hager was pressing out the stockings as she turned her attention to the conversation again. "They tells me, Sister Johnson, that Seth Jones done beat up his wife something terrible."

"He did, an' he oughter! She was always stayin' way from home an' settin' up in de church, not even cookin' his meals, an' de chillens runnin' ragged in de street."

"She's a religious frantic, ain't she?" asked Hager. . . . "You Sandy, hurry up, sir! an' go get that soup bone!"

"No, chile, 'tain't that," said Sister Johnson. "She ain't carin' so much 'bout religion. It's Reverend Butler she's runnin' atter. Ever' time de church do' opens, there she sets in de preacher's mouth, tryin' to 'tract de shepherd from his sheep. She de one what taken her husband's money an' bought Reverend Butler dat gold-headed walkin'-cane he's got. I ain't blame Seth fer hittin' her bap on de head, an' she takin' his money an' buyin' canes fer ministers!"

"Sadie Butler's in my school," said Sandy, putting on his stocking cap. "Reverend Butler's her stepfather."

"Shut up! You hears too much," said Hager. "Ain't I told you to go on an' get that soup bone?"

"Yes'm. I'm going."

"An' I reckon I'll be movin' too," said Sister Johnson, placing the iron on the stove. "It's near 'bout time to be startin' Tom's supper. I done told Willie-Mae to peel de taters 'fo' I come ovah here, but I spects she ain't done it. Dat's de worse black gal to get to work! Soon as she eat, she run outdo's to de privy to keep from washin' de dishes!"

Sandy started to the store, and Sister Johnson, with on old coat over her head, scooted across the back yard to her door. It was a chill December afternoon and the steady sleet stung Sandy in the face as he ran along, but the air smelled good after the muggy kitchen and the stale scent of Annjee's sickroom. Near the corner Sandy met the mail-man, his face red with cold.

"Got anything for us?" asked the little boy.

"No," said the man as he went on without stopping.

Sandy wished his mother would get well soon. She looked so sad lying there in bed. And Aunt Hager was always busy washing and ironing. His grandmother didn't even have time to mend his stockings any more and there were great holes in the heels when he went to school. His shoes were worn out under the bottoms, too. Yesterday his mother had said: "Honey, you better take them high brown shoes of mine from underneath the bed and put 'em on to keep your feet dry this wet weather. I can't afford to buy you none now, and you ain't got no rubbers."

"You want me to wear old women's shoes like Jimmy Lane?" Sandy objected. "I won't catch cold with my feet wet."

But Hager from the kitchen overruled his objections. "Put on them shoes, sir, an' don't argue with yo' mother, an' she sick in de bed! Put 'em on an' hush yo' mouth, till you get something better."

So this morning at recess Sandy had to fight a boy for calling him "sissy" on account of his mother's shoes he was wearing.

But only a week and a half more and the Christmas vacation would come! Uptown the windows were already full of toys, dolls, skates, and sleds. Sandy wanted a Golden Flyer sled for Christmas. That's all he wanted—a Golden Flyer with flexible rudders, so you could guide it easy. Boy! Wouldn't he come shooting down that hill by the Hickory Woods where the fellows coasted every year! They cost only four dollars and ninety-five cents and surely his grandma could afford that for him, even if his mother was sick and she had just paid her taxes. Four ninety-five—but he wouldn't want anything else if Aunt Hager would buy that sled for Santa Claus to bring him! Every day, after school, he passed by the store, where many sleds were displayed, and stood for a long time looking at this Golden Flyer of narrow hard-wood timbers varnished a shiny yellow. It had bright red runners and a beautiful bar with which to steer.

When he told Aunt Hager about it, all she said was: "Boy, is you crazy?" But Annjee smiled from her bed and answered: "Wait and see." Maybe they would get it for him—but Santa Claus was mean to poor kids sometimes, Sandy knew, when their parents had no money.

"Fifteen cents' worth of hamburger," he said absent-mindedly to the butcher when he reached the market. . . . And when Sandy came home, his grandmother whipped him for bringing ground meat instead of the soup bone for which she had sent him.

So the cold days passed, heavy and cloudy, with Annjee still in bed, and the kitchen full of garments hanging on lines to dry because, out of doors, the frozen rain kept falling. Always in Hager's room a great pile of rough-dried clothes eternally waited to be ironed. Sandy helped his grandmother as much as he could, running errands, bringing in coal and wood, pumping water in the mornings before school, and sitting by his mother in the evenings, reading to her from his *Nature Story Reader* when it wasn't too cold in her bedroom.

Annjee was able to sit up now and she said she felt better, but she looked ashen and tired. She wanted to get back to work, so she would have a little money for Christmas and be able to help Hager with the doctor's bill, but she guessed she couldn't. And she was still worrying about Jimboy. Three months had passed since he went away—a longer time than usual that he hadn't written. Maybe something *had* happened to him. Maybe he was out of work and hungry, because this was a hard winter. *Maybe he was dead!*

"O, my God, no!" Annjee cried as the thought struck her.

But one Sunday morning, ten days before Christmas, the door-bell rang violently and a special-delivery boy stood on the front porch. Annjee's heart jumped as she sat up in bed. She had seen the youngster approaching from the window. Word from Jimboy surely—or word about him!

"Ma! Sandy! Go quick and see what it is!"

"Letter for Mrs. Annjelica Rogers," said the boy, stamping the snow from his feet. "Sign here."

While Sandy held the door open, letting the cold wind blow through the house, Hager haltingly scrawled something on the boy's pink pad. Then, with the child behind her, the old woman hurried to her daughter's bed with the white envelope.

"It's from him!" Annjee cried; "I know it's from Jimboy," as she tore open the letter with trembling fingers.

A scrap of dirty tablet-paper fell on the quilt, and Annjee quickly picked it up. It was written in pencil in a feminine hand.

DEAR SISTER,

I am stranded in Memphis, Tenn. and the show has gone on to New Orleans. I can't buy anything to eat because I am broke and don't know anybody in this town. Annjee, please send me my fare to come home and mail it to the Beale Street Colored Hotel. I'm sending my love to you and mama.

Your baby sister,
HARRIETT

XIII.

CHRISTMAS

"Po' little thing," said Hager. "Po' little thing. An' here we ain't
got no money." The night before, on Saturday, Hager had bought
a sack of flour, a chunk of salt pork, and some groceries. Old Dr.
McDillors had called in the afternoon, and she had paid him, too.

"I reckon it would take mo'n thirty dollars to send fo' Harriett, an' Lawd knows we ain't got three dollars in de house."

Annjee lay limply back on her pillows staring out of the
window at the falling snow. She had been crying.

"But never mind," her mother went on, "I's gwine see Mr.
John Frank tomorrow an' see can't I borry a little mo' money
on this mortgage we's got with him."

So on Monday morning the old lady left her washing and
went uptown to the office of the money-lender, but the clerk
there said Mr. Frank had gone to Chicago and would not be
back for two weeks. There was nothing the clerk could do
about it, since he himself could not lend money.

That afternoon Annjee sat up in bed and wrote a long letter
to Harriett, telling her of their troubles, and before she sealed
it, Sandy saw his mother slip into the envelope the three one-
dollar bills that she had been guarding under her pillow.

"There goes your Santa Claus," she said to her son, "but
maybe Harriett's hungry. And you don't want Aunt Harrie to
be hungry, do you?"

"No'm," Sandy said.

The grey days passed and Annjee was able to get up and sit beside the kitchen-stove while her mother ironed. Every afternoon

Sandy went downtown to look at the shop windows, gay with Christmas things. And he would stand and stare at the Golden Flyer sleds in Edmondson's hardware-shop. He could feel himself coasting down a long hill on one of those light, swift, red and yellow coasters, the envy of all the other boys, white and colored, who looked on.

When he went home, he described the sled minutely to Annjee and Aunt Hager and wondered aloud if that might be what he would get for Christmas. But Hager would say: "Santa Claus are just like other folks. He don't work for nothin'!" And his mother would add weakly from her chair: "This is gonna be a slim Christmas, honey, but mama'll see what she can do." She knew his heart was set on a sled, and he could tell that she knew; so maybe he would get it.

One day Annjee gathered her strength together, put a woollen dress over her kimono, wrapped a heavy cloak about herself, and went out into the back yard. Sandy, from the window, watched her picking her way slowly across the frozen ground towards the outhouse. At the trash-pile near the alley fence she stopped and, stooping down, began to pull short pieces of boards and wood from the little pile of lumber that had been left there since last summer by the carpenters who had built the porch. Several times in her labor she rose and leaned weakly against the back fence for support, and once Sandy ran out to see if he could help her, but she told him irritably to get back in the house out of the weather or she would put him to bed without any supper. Then, after placing the boards that she had succeeded in unearthing in a pile by the path, she came wearily back to the kitchen, trembling with cold.

"I'm mighty weak yet," she said to Hager, "but I'm sure much better than I was. I don't want to have the grippe no more. . . . Sandy, look in the mail-box and see has the mailman come by yet."

As the little boy returned empty-handed, he heard his mother talking about old man Logan, who used to be a carpenter.

"Maybe he can make it," she was saying, but stopped when she heard Sandy behind her. "I guess I'll lay back down now."

Aunt Hager wrung out the last piece of clothes that she had been rinsing. "Yes, chile," she said, "you go on and lay down. I's gwine make you some tea after while." And the old woman went outdoors to take from the line the frozen garments blowing in the sharp north wind.

After supper that night Aunt Hager said casually: "Well, I reckon I'll run down an' see Brother Logan a minute whilst I got nothin' else to do. Sandy, don't you let de fire go out, and take care o' yo' mama."

"Yes'm," said the little boy, drawing pictures on the oilcloth-covered table with a pin. His grandmother went out the back door and he looked through the frosty window to see which way she was going. The old woman picked up the boards that his mother had piled near the alley fence, and with them in her arms she disappeared down the alley in the dark.

After a little, Aunt Hager returned puffing and blowing.

"Can he do it?" Annjee demanded anxiously from the bedroom when she heard her mother enter.

"Yes, chile," Hager answered. "Lawd, it sho is cold out yonder! Whee! Lemme git here to this stove!"

That night it began to snow again. The great heavy flakes fell with languid gentility over the town and silently the whiteness covered everything. The next morning the snow froze to a hard sparkling crust on roofs and ground, and in the late afternoon when Sandy went to return the Reinharts' clothes, you could walk on top of the snow without sinking.

At the back door of the Reinharts' house a warm smell of plum-pudding and mince pies drifted out as he waited for the cook to bring the money. When she returned with seventy-five cents, she had a nickel for Sandy, too. As he slid along the street, he saw in many windows gay holly wreaths with red berries and big bows of ribbon tied to them. Sandy wished he could buy a holly wreath for their house. It might make his mother's room look cheerful. At home it didn't seem like Christmas with the kitchen full of drying clothes, and no Christmas-tree.

Sandy wondered if, after all, Santa Claus might, by some good fortune, bring him that Golden Flyer sled on Christmas morning. How fine this hard snow would be to coast on, down the long hill past the Hickory Woods! How light and swift he would fly with his new sled! Certainly he had been a good boy, carrying Aunt Hager's clothes for her, waiting on his mother when she was in bed, emptying the slops and cutting wood every day. And at night when he said his prayers:

> *Now I lay me down to sleep.*
> *Pray the Lord my soul to keep.*
> *If I should die before I wake,*
> *Pray the Lord my soul to take. . . .*

he had added with great earnestness: "And let Santa bring me a Golden Flyer sled, please, Lord. Amen."

But Sandy knew very well that there wasn't really any Santa Claus! He knew in his heart that Hager and his mother were Santa Claus—and that they didn't any money. They were poor people. He was wearing his mama's shoes, as Jimmy Lane had once done. And his father and Harriett, who used to make the house gay, laughing and singing, were far away somewhere. . . . There wasn't any Santa Claus.

"I don't care," he said, tramping over the snow in the twilight on his way from the Reinharts'.

Christmas Eve. Candles and poinsettia flowers. Wreaths of evergreen. Baby trees hung with long strands of tinsel and fragile ornaments of colored glass. Sandy passed the windows of many white folks' houses where the curtains were up and warm floods of electric light made bright the cozy rooms. In Negro shacks, too, there was the dim warmth of oil-lamps and Christmas candles glowing. But at home there wasn't even a holly wreath. And the snow was whiter and harder than ever on the ground.

Tonight, though, there were no clothes drying in the kitchen when he went in. The ironing-board had been put away behind the door, and the whole place was made tidy and clean. The fire blazed and crackled in the little range; but nothing else said Christmas—no laughter, no tinsel, no tree.

Annjee had been about all day, still weak, but this afternoon she had made a trip to the store for a quarter's worth of mixed candies and nuts and a single orange, which she had hidden away until morning. Hager had baked a little cake, but there was no frosting on it such as there had been in other years, and there were no strange tissue-wrapped packages stuck away in the corners of trunks and drawers days ahead of time.

Although the little kitchen was warm enough, the two bedrooms were chilly, and the front room was freezing-cold because they kept the door there closed all the time. It was hard to afford a fire in one stove, let alone two, Aunt Hager kept saying, with nobody working but herself.

"I's thinking about Harriett," she remarked after their Christmas Eve supper as she rocked before the fire, "and how I's always tried to raise her right."

"And I'm thinking about—well, there ain't no use mentionin' him," Annjee said.

A sleigh slid by with jingling bells and shouts of laughter from the occupants, and a band of young people passed on their way to church, singing carols. After a while another sleigh came along with a jolly sound.

"Santa Claus!" said Annjee, smiling at her serious little son. "You better hurry and go to bed, because he'll be coming soon. And be sure to hang up your stocking."

But Sandy was afraid that she was fooling, and, as he pulled off his clothes, he left his stockings on the floor, stuck into the women's shoes he had been wearing. Then, leaving the bedroom door half open so that the heat and a little light from the kitchen would come in, he climbed into his mother's bed. But he wasn't going to close his eyes yet. Sandy had discovered long ago that you could hear and see many things by not going to sleep when the family expected you to; therefore he remained awake tonight.

His mother was talking to Aunt Hager now: "I don't think

he'll charge us anything, do you, ma?" And the old woman answered: "No, chile, Brother Logan's been tryin' to be ma beau for twenty years, an' he ain't gonna charge us nothin'."

Annjee came into the half-dark bedroom and looked at Sandy, lying still on the side of the bed towards the window. Then she took down her heavy coat from the wall and, sitting on the edge of a chair, began to pull on her rubbers. In a few moments he heard the front door close softly. His mother had gone out.

Where could she be going, he wondered, this time of night? He heard her footsteps crunching the hard snow and, rolling over close to the window, he pulled aside the shade a little and looked out. In the moonlight he saw Annjee moving slowly down the street past Sister Johnson's house, walking carefully over the snow like a very weak woman.

"Mama's still sick," the child thought, with his nose pressed against the cold window-pane. "I wish I could a bought her a present today."

Soon an occasional snore from the kitchen told Sandy that Hager dozed peacefully in her rocker beside the stove. He sat up in bed, wrapped a quilt about his shoulders, and remained looking out the window, with the shade hanging behind his back.

The white snow sparkled in the moonlight, and the trees made striking black shadows across the yard. Next door at the Johnsons' all was dark and quiet, but across the street, where white folks lived, the lights were burning brightly and a big Christmas-tree with all its candles aglow stood in the large bay window while a woman loaded it with toys. Sandy knew that four children lived there, three boys and a girl, whom he had often watched playing on the lawn. Sometimes he wished he had a brother or sister to play with him, too, because it was very quiet in a house with only grown-ups about. And right now it was dismal and lonely to be by himself looking out the window of a cold bedroom on Christmas Eve.

Then a woman's cloaked figure came slowly back past Sister Johnson's house in the moonlight, and Sandy saw that it was his mother returning, her head down and her shadow moving blackly on the snow. You could hear the dry grate of her heels on the frozen whiteness as she walked, leaning forward, dragging something heavy behind her. Sandy prepared to lie down quickly in bed again, but he kept his eyes against the windowpane to see what Annjee was pulling, and, as she came closer to the house, he could distinguish quite clearly behind her a solid, home-made sled bumping rudely over the snow.

Before Annjee's feet touched the porch, he was lying still as though he had been asleep a long time.

The morning sunlight was tumbling brightly into the windows when Sandy opened his eyes and blinked at the white world outside.

"Aren't you ever going to get up?" asked Annjee, smiling timidly above him. "It's Christmas morning, honey. Come see what Santa Claus brought you. Get up quick."

But he didn't want to get up. He knew what Santa Claus had brought him and he wanted to stay in bed with his face to the wall. It wasn't a Golden Flyer sled—and now he couldn't even hope for one any longer. He wanted to pull the covers over his head and cry, but, "Boy! You ain't up yet?" called Aunt Hager cheerily from the kitchen. "De little Lawd Jesus is in His manger fillin' all de world with light. An' old Santa done been here an' gone! Get out from there, chile, an' see!"

"I'm coming, grandma," said Sandy slowly, wiping his tear-filled eyes and rolling out of bed as he forced his mouth to smile wide and steady at the few little presents he saw on the floor—for the child knew he was expected to smile.

"O! A sled!" he cried in a voice of mock surprise that wasn't his own at all; for there it stood, heavy and awkward, against the wall and beside it on the floor lay two picture-books from the ten-cent store and a pair of white cotton gloves. Above the sled his stocking, tacked to the wall, was partly filled with candy, and the single orange peeped out from the top.

But the sled! Home-made by some rough carpenter, with strips of rusty tin nailed along the wooden runners, and a piece of clothes-line to pull it with!

"It's fine," Sandy lied, as he tried to lift it and place it on the floor as you would in coasting; but it was very heavy, and too wide for a boy to run with in his hands. You could never get a swift start. And a board was warped in the middle.

"It's a nice sled, grandma," he lied. "I like it, mama."

"Mr. Logan made it for you," his mother answered proudly, happy that he was pleased. "I knew you wanted a sled all the time."

"It's a nice sled," Sandy repeated, grinning steadily as he held the heavy object in his hands. "It's an awful nice sled."

"Well, make haste and look at de gloves, and de candy, and them pretty books, too," called Hager from the kitchen, where she was frying strips of salt pork. "My, you sho is a slow chile on Christmas mawnin'! Come 'ere and lemme kiss you." She came to the bedroom and picked him up in her arms. "Christmas gift to Hager's baby chile! Come on, Annjee, bring his clothes out here behind de stove an' bring his books, too. . . . This here's Little Red Riding Hood and the Wolf, and this here's Hansee and Gretsle on de cover—but I reckon you can read 'em better'n I can. . . . Daughter, set de table. Breakfast's 'bout ready now. Look in de oven an' see 'bout that cornbread. . . . Lawd, this here Sandy's just like a baby lettin' ole Hager hold him and dress him. . . . Put yo' foot in that stocking, boy!" And Sandy began to feel happier, sitting on his grandmother's lap behind the stove.

Before noon Buster had come and gone, showing off his new shoes and telling his friend about the train he had gotten that ran on a real track when you wound it up. After dinner Willie-Mae appeared bringing a naked rag doll and a set of china dishes in a blue box. And Sister Johnson sent them a mince pie as a Christmas gift.

Almost all Aunt Hager's callers knocked at the back door, but in the late afternoon the front bell rang and Annjee sent Sandy through the cold parlor to answer it. There on the porch stood his Aunt Tempy, with several gaily wrapped packages in her arms. She was almost a stranger to Sandy, yet she kissed him peremptorily on the forehead as he stood in the doorway.

Then she came through the house into the kitchen, with much the air of a mistress of the manor descending to the servants' quarters.

"Land sakes alive!" said Hager, rising to kiss her.

Tempy hugged Annjee, too, before she sat down, stiffly, as though the house she was in had never been her home. To little black Willie-Mae she said nothing.

"I'm sorry I couldn't invite you for Christmas dinner today, but you know how Mr. Siles is," Tempy began to explain to her mother and sister. "My husband is home so infrequently, and he doesn't like a house full of company, but of course Dr. and Mrs. Glenn Mitchell will be in later in the evening. They drop around any time. . . . But I had to run down and bring you a few presents. . . . You haven't seen my new piano yet, have you, mother? I must come and take you home with me some nice afternoon." She smiled appropriately, but her voice was hard.

"How is you an' yo' new church makin' it?" asked Hager, slightly embarrassed in the presence of her finely dressed society daughter.

"Wonderful!" Tempy replied. "Wonderful! Father Hill is so dignified, and the services are absolutely refined! There's never anything niggerish about them—so you know, mother, they suit me."

"I's glad you likes it," said Hager.

There was an awkward silence; then Tempy distributed her gifts, kissed them all as though it were her Christian duty, and went her way, saying that she had calls to make at Lawyer and Mrs. Moore's, and Professor Booth's, and Madam Temple's before she returned home. When she had gone, everybody felt relieved—as though a white person had left the house. Willie-Mae began to play again, and Hager pushed her feet out of her shoes once more, while Annjee went into the bedroom and lay down.

Sandy sat on the floor and untied his present, wrapped in several thicknesses of pink tissue paper, and found, in a bright Christmas box, a big illustrated volume of *Andersen's Fairy*

Tales decorated in letters of gold. With its heavy pages and fine pictures, it made the ten-cent-store books that Hager had bought him appear cheap and thin. It made his mother's sled look cheap, too, and shamed all the other gifts the ones he loved had given him.

"I don't want it," he said suddenly, as loud as he could. "I don't want Tempy's old book!" And from where he was sitting, he threw it with all his might underneath the stove.

Hager gasped in astonishment. "Pick that up, sir," she cried amazed. "Yo' Aunt Tempy done bought you a fine purty book an' here you throwin' it un'neath de stove in de ashes! Lawd have mercy! Pick it up, I say, this minute!"

"I won't!" cried Sandy stubbornly. "I won't! I like my sled what you-all gave me, but I don't want no old book from Tempy! I won't pick it up!"

Then the astonished Hager grabbed him by the scruff of the neck and jerked him to his feet.

"Do I have to whip you yet this holy day? . . . Pick up that book, sir!"

"No!" he yelled.

She gave him a startled rap on the head with the back of her hand. "Talkin' sassy to yo' old grandma an' tellin' her no!"

"What is it?" Annjee called from the bedroom, as Sandy began to wail.

"Nothin'," Hager replied, " 'ceptin' this chile's done got beside hisself an' I has to hit him—that's all!"

But Sandy was not hurt by his grandmother's easy rap. He was used to being struck on the back of the head for misdemeanors, and this time he welcomed the blow because it gave him, at last, what he had been looking for all day—a sufficient excuse to cry. Now his pent-up tears flowed without ceasing while Willie-Mae sat in a corner clutching her rag doll to her breast, and Tempy's expensive gift lay in the ashes beneath the stove.

XIV.

RETURN

After Christmas there followed a period of cold weather, made bright by the winter sun shining on the hard crusty snow, where children slid and rolled, and over which hay-wagons made into sleighs on great heavy runners drove jingling into town from the country. There was skating on the frozen river and fine sledding on the hills beyond the woods, but Sandy never went out where the crowds were with his sled, because he was ashamed of it.

After New Year's Annjee went back to work at Mrs. Rice's, still coughing a little and still weak. But with bills to pay and Sandy in need of shoes and stockings and clothes to wear to school, she couldn't remain idle any longer. Even with her mother washing and ironing every day except the Sabbath, expenses were difficult to meet, and Aunt Hager was getting pretty old to work so hard. Annjee thought that Tempy ought to help them a little, but she was too proud to ask her. Besides, Tempy had never been very affectionate towards her sisters even when they were all girls together—but she ought to help look out for their mother. Hager, however, when Annjee brought up the subject of Tempy's help, said that she was still able to wash, thank God, and wasn't depending on any of her children for anything—not so long as white folks wore clothes.

At school Sandy passed all of his mid-year tests and, along with Sadie Butler, was advanced to the fifth A, but the other colored child in the class, a little fat girl named Mary Jones, failed and had to stay behind. Mary's mother, a large sulphur-yellow woman who cooked at the Drummer's Hotel, came to

the school and told the teacher, before all the children, just
what she thought of her for letting Mary fail—and her thoughts
were not very complimentary to the stiff, middle-aged white
lady who taught the class. The question of color came up, too,
during the discussion.

"Look at ma chile settin' back there behind all de white
ones," screamed the sulphur-yellow woman. "An' me payin' as
much taxes as anybody! You treats us colored folks like we
ain't citizerzens—that's what you does!" The argument had to
be settled in the principal's office, where the teacher went with
the enraged mother, while the white children giggled that a
fat, yellow colored lady should come to school to quarrel about
her daughter's not being promoted. But the colored children in
the class couldn't laugh.

St. Valentine's day came and Sadie Butler sent Sandy a big red
heart. But for Annjee, "the mail-man passed and didn't leave no
news," because Jimboy hadn't written yet, nor had Harriett
thanked her for the three dollars she had mailed to Memphis
before Christmas. There were no letters from anybody.

The work at Mrs. Rice's was very heavy, because Mrs.
Rice's sister, with two children, had come from Indiana to
spend the winter, and Annjee had to cook for them and clean
their rooms, too. But she was managing to save a little money
every week. She bought Sandy a new blue serge suit with a
Norfolk coat and knickerbocker pants. And then he sat up
very stiffly in Sterner's studio and had his picture taken.

The freckled-faced white boy, Paul Biggers, who sat across
from Sandy in school, delivered the *Daily Leader* to several
streets in Sandy's neighborhood, and Sandy sometimes went
with him, helping to fold and throw the papers in the various doorways. One night it was almost seven o'clock when he
got home.

"I had a great mind not to wait for you," said Aunt Hager,
who had long had the table set for supper. "Wash yo' face an'
hands, sir! An' brush that snow off yo' coat 'fo' you hang it up."

His grandmother took a pan of hot spoon-bread from the
oven and put it on the table, where the little oil-lamp glowed

warmly and the plain white dishes looked clean and inviting. On the stove there was a skillet full of fried apples and bacon, and Hager was making a pot of tea.

"Umn-nn! Smells good!" said Sandy, speaking of everything at once as he slid into his chair. "Gimme a lot o' apples, grandma."

"Is that de way you ask fo' 'em, sir? Can't you say please no mo'?"

"Please, ma'am," said the boy, grinning, for Hager's sharpness wasn't serious, and her old eyes were twinkling.

While they were eating, Annjee came in from work with a small bucket of oyster soup in her hands. They heated this and added it to their supper, and Sandy's mother sat down in front of the stove, with her feet propped up on the grate to dry quickly. It was very comfortable in the little kitchen.

"Seems like the snow's melting," said Annjee. "It's kinder sloppy and nasty underfoot. . . . Ain't been no mail today, has they?"

"No, honey," said Hager. "Leastwise, I been washin' so hard ain't had no time to look in de box. Sandy, run there to de front do' an' see. But I knows there ain't nothin', nohow."

"Might be," said Annjee as Sandy took a match and went through the dark bedroom and parlor to the front porch. There was no mail. But Sandy saw, coming across the slushy dirty-white snow towards the house, a slender figure approaching in the gloom. He waited, shivering in the doorway a moment to see who it was; then all at once he yelled at the top of his lungs: "Aunt Harrie's here!"

Pulling her by the hand, after having kissed and hugged and almost choked her, he ran back to the kitchen. "Look, here's Aunt Harrie!" he cried. "Aunt Harrie's home!" And Hager turned from the table, upsetting her tea, and opened wide her arms to take her to her bosom.

"Ma chile!" she shouted. "Done come home again! Ma baby chile come home!"

Annjee hugged and kissed Harriett, too, as her sister sat on Hager's knees—and the kitchen was filled with sound, warm and free and loving, for the prodigal returned.

"Ma chile's come back!" her mother repeated over and over. "Thank de Lawd! Ma chile's back!"

"You want some fried apples, Harrie?" asked Sandy, offering her his plate. "You want some tea?"

"No, thank you, honey," she replied when the excitement had subsided and Aunt Hager had released her, with her little black hat askew and the powder kissed off one side of her face. She got up, shook herself, and removed her hat to brush down her hair, but she kept her faded coat on as she laid her little purse of metal mesh on the table. Then she sat down on the chair that Annjee offered her near the fire. She was thinner and her hair had been bobbed, giving her a boyish appearance, like the black pages in old Venetian paintings. But her lips were red and there were two little spots of rouge burning on each cheek, although her eyes were dark with heavy shadows as though she had been ill.

Hager was worried. "Has you been sick, chile?" she asked.

"No, mama," Harriett said. "I've been all right—just had a hard time, that's all. I got mad, and quit the show in Memphis, and they wouldn't pay me—so that was that! The minstrels left the carnival for the winter and started playing the theatres, and the new manager was a cheap skate. I couldn't get along with him."

"Did you get my letter and the money?" Annjee asked. "We didn't have no more to send you, and afterwards, when you didn't write, I didn't know if you got it."

"I got it and meant to thank you, sis, but I don't know—just didn't get round to it. But, anyway, I'm out of the South now. It's a hell—I mean it's an awful place if you don't know anybody! And more hungry niggers down there! I wonder who made up that song about *Dear Old Southland*. There's nothing dear about it that I can see. Good God! It's awful! . . . But I'm back." She smiled. "Where's Jim-boy? . . . O, that's right, Annjee—you told me in the letter. But I sort-a miss him around here. Lord, I hope he didn't go to Memphis!"

"Did you find a job down there?" Annjee asked, looking at her sister's delicate hands.

"Sure, I found a *job* all right," Harriett replied in a tone that made Annjee ask no more questions. "Jobs are like hen's teeth—try and find 'em." And she shrugged her shoulders as Sandy had so often seen her do, but she no longer seemed to him like a little girl. She was grown-up and hard and strange now, but he still loved her.

"Aunt Harrie, I passed to the fifth A," he announced proudly.

"That's wonderful," she answered. "My, but you're smart! You'll be a great man some day, sure, Sandy."

"Where's yo' suit-case, honey?" Hager interrupted, too happy to touch her food on the table or to take her eyes away from the face of her returned child. "Didn't you bring it back with you? Where is it?"

"Sure, I got it. . . . But I'm gonna live at Maudel's this time, mama. . . . I left it at the station. I didn't think you-all'd want me here." She tried to make the words careless-like, but they were pitifully forced.

"Aw, honey!" Annjee cried, the tears coming.

The shadow of inner pain passed over Hager's black face, but the only reply she made was: "You's growed up now, chile. I reckon you knows what you's doin'. You's been ten thousand miles away from yo' mammy, an' I reckon you knows. . . . Come on, Sandy, let's we eat." Slowly the old woman returned to the cold food on her plate. "Won't you eat something with us, daughter?"

Harriett's eyes lowered and her shoulders drooped. "No, mama, thank you. I'm—not hungry."

Then a long, embarrassing silence followed while Hager gulped at her tea, Sandy tried to swallow a mouthful of bread that seemed to choke him, and Annjee stared stupidly at the stove.

Finally Harriett said: "I got to go now." She stood up to button her coat and put on her hat. Then she took her metal purse from the table.

"Maudel'll be waiting for me, but I'll be seeing you-all again soon, I guess. Good-bye, Sandy honey! I got to go. . . . Annjee, I got to go now. . . . Good-bye, mama!" She was trembling. As she bent down to kiss Hager, her purse slipped out of her

hands and fell in a little metal heap on the floor. She stooped
to pick it up.

"I got to go now."

A tiny perfume-bottle in the bag had broken from the fall,
and as she went through the cold front room towards the door,
the odor of cheap and poignant drugstore violets dripped
across the house.

XV

ONE BY ONE

You could smell the spring.

"'Tain't gwine be warm fo' weeks yet!" Hager said.

Nevertheless, you could smell the spring. Little boys were already running in the streets without their overcoats, and the ground-hog had seen its shadow. Snow remained in the fence corners, but it had melted on the roofs. The yards were wet and muddy, but no longer white.

It was a sunny afternoon in late March that a letter came. On his last delivery the mail-man stopped, dropped it in the box—and Sandy saw him. It was addressed to his mother and he knew it must be from Jimboy.

"Go on an' take it to her," his grandma said, as soon as she saw the boy coming with it in his hand. "I knows that's what you want to do. Go on an' take it." And she bent over her ironing again.

Sandy ran almost all the way to Mrs. Rice's, dropping the letter more than once on the muddy sidewalk, so excited he did not think to put it in his pocket. Into the big yard and around to the white lady's back door he sped—and it was locked! He knocked loudly for a long time, and finally an upper window opened and Annjee, a dust-rag around her head, looked down, squinting in the sunlight.

"Who's there?" she called stridently, thinking of some peddler or belated tradesman for whom she did not wish to stop her cleaning.

Sandy pantingly held up the letter and was about to say something when the window closed with a bang. He could hear his mother almost falling down the back stairs, she was coming so fast. Then the key turned swiftly in the lock, the door opened, and, without closing it, Annjee took the letter from him and tore it open where she stood.

"It's from Jimboy!"

Sandy stood on the steps looking at his mother, her bosom heaving, her sleeves rolled up, and the white cloth tied about her head, doubly white against her dark-brown face.

"He's in Detroit, it says. . . . Umn! I ain't never seen him write such a long letter. 'I had a hard time this winter till I landed here,' it says, 'but things look pretty good now, and there is lots of building going on and plenty of work opening up in the automobile plants . . . a mighty lot of colored folks here . . . hope you and Sandy been well. Sorry couldn't send you nothing Xmas, but I was in St. Paul broke. . . . Kiss my son for me. . . . Tell ma hello even if she don't want to hear it. Your loving husband, Jimboy Rogers.' "

Annjee did her best to hold the letter with one hand and pick up Sandy with the other, but he had grown considerably during the winter and she was still a little weak from her illness; so she bent down to his level and kissed him several times before she re-read the letter.

"From your daddy!" she said. "Umn-mn. . . . Come on in here and warm yourself. Lemme see what he says again!" . . . She lighted the gas oven in the white kitchen and sat down in front of it with her letter, forgetting the clock and the approaching time for Mrs. Rice's dinner, forgetting everything. "A letter from my daddy! From my far-off sugar-daddy!"

"From *my* daddy," corrected Sandy. . . . "Say, gimme a nickel to buy some marbles, mama. I wanta go play."

Without taking her eyes from the precious note Annjee fumbled in her apron and found a coin. "Take it and go on!" she said.

It was a dime. Sandy skipped around the house and down the street in the chilly sunshine. He decided to stop at Buster's for a while before going home, since he had to pass there anyway, and he found his friend in the house trying to carve boats from clothes-pins with a rusty jack-knife.

Buster's mother was a seamstress, and, after opening the front door and greeting Sandy with a cheery "Hello," she returned to her machine and a friend who was calling on her. She was a tall young light-mulatto woman, with skin like old ivory. Maybe that was why Buster was so white. But her husband was a black man who worked on the city's garbage-trucks and was active politically when election time came, getting colored men to vote Republican. Everybody said he made lots of money, but that he wasn't really Buster's father.

The golden-haired child gave Sandy a butcher-knife and together they whacked at the clothes-pins. You could hear the two women talking plainly in the little sewing-room, where the machine ran between snatches of conversation.

"Yes," Buster's mother was saying, "I have the hardest time keeping that boy colored! He goes on just like he was white. Do you know what he did last week? Cut all the blossoms off my geranium plants here in the house, took them to school, and gave them to Dorothy Marlow, in his grade. And you know who Dorothy is, don't you? Senator Marlow's daughter! . . . I said: 'Buster, if you ever cut my flowers to carry to any little girl again, I'll punish you severely, but if you cut them to carry to little white girls, I don't know what I'll do with you. . . . Don't you know they hang colored boys for things like that?' I wanted to scare him—because you know there might be trouble even among kids in school over such things. . . . But I had to laugh."

Her friend laughed too. "He's a hot one, taking flowers to the women already, and a white girl at that! You've got a fast-working son, Elvira, I must say. . . . But, do you know, when you first moved here and I saw you and the boy going in and out, I thought sure you were both white folks. I didn't know you was colored till my husband said: 'That's Eddie's wife!' You-all sure looked white to me."

The machine started to whir, making the conversation inaudible for a few minutes, and when Sandy caught their words again, they were talking about the Elks' club-house that the colored people were planning to build.

"Can you go out?" Sandy demanded of Buster, since they were making no headway with the tough clothes-pins and dull knives.

"Maybe," said Buster. "I'll go see." And he went into the other room and asked his mother.

"Put on your overcoat," she commanded. "It's not summer yet. And be back in here before dark."

"All right, Vira," the child said.

The two children went to Mrs. Rumford's shop on the corner and bought three cents' worth of candy and seven cents' worth of peewees with which to play marbles when it got warm. Then Sandy walked back past Buster's house with him and they played for a while in the street before Sandy turned to run home.

Aunt Hager was making mush for supper. She sent him to the store for a pint bottle of milk as soon as he arrived, but he forgot to take the bottle and had to come back for it.

"You'd forget yo' head if it wasn't tied to you!" the old woman reminded him.

They were just finishing supper when Annjee got home with two chocolate éclairs in her coat-pocket, mashed together against Jimboy's letter.

"Huh! I'm crazy!" she said, running her hand down into the sticky mess. "But listen, ma! He's got a job and is doing well in Detroit, Jimboy says. . . . And I'm going to him!"

"You what?" Hager gasped, dropping her spoon in her mush-bowl. "What you sayin'?"

"I said I'm going to him, ma! I got to!" Annjee stood with her coat and hat still on, holding the sticky letter. "I'm going where my heart is, ma! . . . Oh, not today." She put her arms around her mother's neck. "I don't mean today, mama, nor next week. I got to save some money first. I only got a little now. But I mean I'm going to him soon's I can. I can't help it, ma—I love him!"

"Lawd, is you foolish!" cried Hager. "What's you gwine do with this chile, trapesin' round after Jimboy? What you gwine do if he leaves you in Detroiter or wherever he are? What you gwine do then? You loves him! Huh!"

"But he ain't gonna leave me in Detroit, 'cause I'm going with him everywhere he goes," she said, her eyes shining. "He ain't gonna leave me no more!"

"An' Sandy?"

"Couldn't he stay with you, mama? And then maybe we'd come back here and live, Jimboy and me, some time, when we get a little money ahead, and could pay off the mortgage on the house. . . . But there ain't no use arguing, mama, I got to go!"

Hager had never seen Annjee so positive before; she sat speechless, looking at the bowl of mush.

"I got to go where it ain't lonesome and where I ain't unhappy— and that's where Jimboy is! I got to go soon as I can."

Hager rose to put some water on the stove to heat for the dishes.

"One by one you leaves me—Tempy, then Harriett, then you," she said. "But Sandy's gonna stick by me, ain't you, son? He ain't gwine leave his grandma."

The youngster looked at Hager, moving slowly about the kitchen putting away the supper things.

"And I's gwine to make a fine man out o' you, Sandy. I's gwine raise one chile right yet, if de Lawd lets me live—just one chile right!" she murmured.

That night the March wind began to blow and the window-panes rattled. Sandy woke up in the dark, lying close and warm beside his mother. When he went back to sleep again, he dreamed that his Aunt Tempy's Christmas book had been turned into a chariot, and that he was riding through the sky with Tempy standing very dignifiedly beside him as he drove. And he couldn't see anybody down on earth, not even Hager.

When his mother rolled out at six o'clock to go to work, he woke up again, and while she dressed, he lay watching his breath curl mistily upwards in the cold room. Outside the

window it was bleak and grey and the March wind, humming
through the leafless branches of the trees, blew terrifically. He
heard Aunt Hager in the kitchen poking at the stove, making
up a blaze to start the coffee boiling. Then the front door closed
when his mother went out and, as the door slammed, the wind
howled fiercely. It was nice and warm in bed, so he lay under
the heavy quilts half dreaming, half thinking, until his grandmother shook him to get up. And many were the queer, dream-
drowsy thoughts that floated through his mind—not only that
morning, but almost every morning while he lay beneath the
warm quilts until Hager had called him three or four times to
get ready for school.

He wondered sometimes whether if he washed and washed
his face and hands, he would ever be white. Someone had
told him once that blackness was only skin-deep. . . . And
would he ever have a big house with electric lights in it, like
his Aunt Tempy—but it was mostly white people who had
such fine things, and they were mean to colored. . . . Some
white folks were nice, though. Earl was nice at school, but
not the little boys across the street, who called him "nigger"
every day . . . and not Mrs. Rice, who scolded his mother. . . .
Aunt Harrie didn't like any white folks at all. . . . But Jesus
was white and wore a long, white robe, like a woman's, on
the Sunday-school cards. . . . Once Jimmy Lane said: "God
damn Jesus" when the teacher scolded him for not knowing
his Bible lesson. He said it out loud in church, too, and the
church didn't fall down on him, as Sandy thought it might. . . .
Grandma said it was a sin to cuss and swear, but all the fellows at school swore—and Jimboy did, too. But every time
Sandy said "God damn," he felt bad, because Aunt Hager
said God was mighty good and it was wrong to take His
name in vain. But he would like to learn to say "God damn"
without feeling anything like most boys said it—just "God
damn! . . . God damn! . . . God damn!" without being
ashamed of himself. . . . The Lord never seemed to notice,
anyhow. . . . And when he got big, he wanted to travel like

Jimboy. He wanted to be a railroad engineer, but Harriett
had said there weren't any colored engineers on trains. . . .
What would he be, then? Maybe a doctor; but it was more
fun being an engineer and travelling far away.

Sandy wished Annjee would take him with her when she
went to join Jimboy—but then Aunt Hager would be all by
herself, and grandma was so nice to him he would hate to
leave her alone. Who would cut wood for her then? . . . But
when he got big, he would go to Detroit. And maybe New
York, too, where his geography said they had the tallest buildings in the world, and trains that ran under the river. . . . He
wondered if there were any colored people in New York. . . .
How ugly African colored folks looked in the geography—
with bushy heads and wild eyes! Aunt Hager said her mother
was an African, but she wasn't ugly and wild; neither was
Aunt Hager; neither was little dark Willie-Mae, and they were
all black like Africans. . . . And Reverend Braswell was as
black as ink, but he knew God. . . . God didn't care if people
were black, did He? . . . What was God? Was He a man or a
lamb or what? Buster's mother said God was a light, but Aunt
Hager said He was a King and had a throne and wore a
crown—she intended to sit down by His side by and by. . . .
Was Buster's father white? Buster was white and colored both.
But he didn't look like he was colored. What made Buster not
colored? . . . And what made girls different from boys? . . .
Once when they were playing house, Willie-Mae told him
how girls were different from boys, but they didn't know why.
Now Willie-Mae was in the seventh grade and had hard little breasts that stuck out sharp-like, and Jimmy Lane said
dirty things about Willie-Mae. . . . Once he asked his mother
what his navel was for and she said, "Layovers to catch med-
dlers." What did that mean? . . . And how come ladies got
sick and stayed in bed when they had babies? Where did babies come from, anyhow? Not from storks—a fairy-story like
Santa Claus. . . . Did God love people who told fairy-stories
and lied to kids about storks and Santa Claus? . . . Santa Claus
was no good, anyhow! God damn Santa Claus for not bring-

ing him the sled he wanted Christmas! It was all a lie about
Santa Claus!

The sound of Hager pouring coal on the fire and dragging
her wash-tubs across the kitchen-floor to get ready for work
broke in on Sandy's drowsy half-dreams, and as he rolled over
in bed, his grandmother, hearing the springs creak, called
loudly: "You Sandy! Get up from there! It's seven and past!
You want to be late gettin' to yo' school?"

"Yes'm, I'm coming, grandma!" he said under the quilts.
"But it's cold in here."

"You knows you don't dress in yonder! Bring them clothes
on out behind this stove, sir."

"Yes'm." So with a kick of the feet his covers went flying
back and Sandy ran to the warmth of the little kitchen, where
he dressed, washed, and ate. Then he yelled for Willie-Mae—
when he felt like it—or else went on to school without her,
joining some of the boys on the way.

So spring was coming and Annjee worked diligently at Mrs.
Rice's day after day. Often she did something extra for Mrs.
Rice's sister and her children—pressed a shirtwaist or ironed
some stockings—and so added a few quarters or maybe even a
dollar to her weekly wages, all of which she saved to help carry
her to Jimboy in Detroit.

For ten years she had been cooking, washing, ironing,
scrubbing—and for what? For only the few weeks in a year, or
a half-year, when Jimboy would come home from some strange
place and take her in his strong arms and kiss her and murmur: "Annjee, baby!" That's what she had been working for—
then the dreary months were as nothing, and the hard years
faded away. But now he had been gone all winter, and, from
his letter, he might not come back soon, because he said Detroit was a fine place for colored folks. . . . But Stanton—well,
Annjee thought there must surely be better towns, where a
woman wouldn't have to work so hard to live. . . . And where
Jimboy was.

So before the first buds opened on the apple-tree in the back yard, Annjee had gone to Detroit, leaving Sandy behind with his grandmother. And when the apple blossoms came in full bloom, there was no one living in the little house but a grey-headed old woman and her grandchild.

"One by one they leaves you," Hager said slowly. "One by one yo' chillen goes."

XVI.

NOTHING BUT LOVE

"A year ago tonight was de storm what blowed ma porch away! You 'members, honey? . . . Done seem like this year took more'n ma porch, too. My baby chile's left home an' gone to stay down yonder in de Bottoms with them triflin' Smothers family, where de piano's goin' night an' day. An' yo' mammy's done gone a-trapesin' after Jimboy. . . . Well, I thanks de Lawd you ain't gone too. You's mighty little an' knee-high to a duck, but you's ma stand-by. You's all I got, an' you ain't gwine leave yo' old grandma, is you?"

Hager had turned to Sandy in these lonely days for comfort and companionship. Through the long summer evenings they sat together on the front porch and she told her grandchild stories. Sometimes Sister Johnson came over and sat with them for a while smoking. Sometimes Madam de Carter, full of chatter and big words about the lodge and the race, would be there. But more often the two were alone—the black washwoman with the grey hair and the little brown boy. Slavery-time stories, myths, folk-tales like the Rabbit and the Tar Baby; the war, Abe Lincoln, freedom; visions of the Lord; years of faith and labor, love and struggle filled Aunt Hager's talk of a summer night, while the lightning-bugs glowed and glimmered and the katydids chirruped, and the stars sparkled in the far-off heavens.

Sandy was getting to be too big a boy to sit in his grandmother's lap and be rocked to sleep as in summers gone by;

now he sat on a little stool beside her, leaning his head on her legs when he was tired. Or else he lay flat on the floor of the porch listening, and looking up at the stars. Tonight Hager talked about love.

"These young ones what's comin' up now, they calls us ole fogies, an' handkerchief heads, an' white folks' niggers 'cause we don't get mad an' rar' up in arms like they does 'cause things is kinder hard, but, honey, when you gets old, you knows they ain't no sense in gettin' mad an' sourin' yo' soul with hatin' peoples. White folks is white folks, an' colored folks is colored, an' neither one of 'em is bad as t'other make out. For mighty nigh seventy years I been knowin' both of 'em, an' I ain't never had no room in ma heart to hate neither white nor colored. When you starts hatin' people, you gets uglier than they is—an' I ain't never had no time for ugliness, 'cause that's where de devil comes in—in ugliness!

"They talks 'bout slavery time an' they makes out now like it were de most awfullest time what ever was, but don't you believe it, chile, 'cause it weren't all that bad. Some o' de white folks was just as nice to their niggers as they could be, nicer than many of 'em is now, what makes 'em work for less than they needs to eat. An' in those days they had to feed 'em. An' they ain't every white man beat his slaves neither! Course I ain't sayin' 'twas no paradise, but I ain't going to say it were no hell either. An' maybe I's kinder seein' it on de bestest side 'cause I worked in de big house an' ain't never went to de fields like most o' de niggers did. Ma mammy were de big-house cook an' I grewed up right with her in de kitchen an' played with little Miss Jeanne. An' Miss Jeanne taught me to read what little I knowed. An' when she growed up an' I growed up, she kept me with her like her friend all de time. I loved her an' she loved me. Miss Jeanne were de mistress' daughter, but warn't no difference 'tween us 'ceptin' she called me Hager an' I called her Miss Jeanne. But what difference do one word like 'Miss' make in yo' heart? None, chile, none. De words don't make no difference if de love's there.

"I disremembers what year it were de war broke out, but white folks was scared, an' niggers, too. Didn't know what might happen. An' we heard talk o' Abraham Lincoln 'way down yonder in de South. An' de ole marster, ole man Winfield, took his gun an' went to war, an' de young son, too, an' de superintender and de overseer—all of 'em gone to follow Lee. Ain't left nothin' but womens an' niggers on de plantation. De womens was a-cryin' an' de niggers was, too, 'cause they was sorry for de po' grievin' white folks.

"Is I ever told you how Miss Jeanne an' Marster Robert was married in de springtime o' de war, with de magnolias all a-bloomin' like candles for they weddin'? Is I ever told you, Sandy? . . . Well, I must some time. An' then Marster Robert had to go right off with his mens, 'cause he's a high officer in de army an' they heard Sherman were comin'. An' he left her a-standin' with her weddin'-clothes on, leanin' 'gainst a pillar o' de big white porch, with nobody but me to dry her eyes— ole Missis done dead an' de men-folks all gone to war. An' nobody in that big whole mansion but black ole deaf Aunt Granny Jones, what kept de house straight, an' me, what was stayin' with ma mistress.

"O, de white folks needed niggers then mo'n they ever did befo', an' they ain't a colored person what didn't stick by 'em when all they men-folks were gone an' de white womens was a-cryin' an' a-faintin' like they did in them days.

"But lemme tell you 'bout Miss Jeanne. She just set in her room an' cry. A-holdin' Marster Bob's pitcher, she set an' cry, an' she ain't come out o' her room to see 'bout nothin'—house, horses, cotton—nothin'. But de niggers, they ain't cheat her nor steal from her. An' come de news dat her brother done got wounded an' died in Virginia, an' her cousins got de yaller fever. Then come de news that Marster Robert, Miss Jeanne's husband, ain't no mo'! Killed in de battle! An' I thought Miss Jeanne would like to go crazy. De news say he died like a soldier, brave an' fightin'. But when she heard it, she went to de drawer an' got out her weddin'-veil an' took her flowers in her hands like she were goin' to de altar to meet de groom. Then she just sink in de flo' an' cry till I pick her up an' hold her like a chile.

"Well, de freedom come, an' all de niggers scatter like buck-shot, goin' to live in town. An' de yard niggers say I's a ole fool! I's free now—why don't I come with them? But I say no, I's gwine stay with Miss Jeanne—an' I stayed. I 'lowed ain't nary one o' them colored folks needed me like Miss Jeanne did, so I ain't went with 'em.

"An' de time pass; it pass an' it pass, an' de ole house get rusty for lack o' paint, an' de things, they 'gin to fall to pieces. An' Miss Jeanne say: 'Hager, I ain't got nobody in de world but you.' An' I say: 'Miss Jeanne, I ain't got nobody in de world but you neither.'

"And then she'd start talkin' 'bout her young husband what died so handsome an' brave, what ain't even had time that last day fo' to 'scort her to de church for de weddin', nor to hold her in his arms 'fore de orders come to leave. An' we would set on de big high ole porch, with its tall stone pillars, in de eve-nin's twilight till de bats start flyin' overhead an' de sunset glow done gone, she in her wide white skirts a-billowin' round her slender waist, an' me in ma apron an' cap an' this here chain she gimme you see on ma neck all de time an' what's done wore so thin.

"They was a ole stump of a blasted tree in de yard front o' de porch 'bout tall as a man, with two black pieces o' branches raised up like arms in de air. We used to set an' look at it, an' Miss Jeanne could see it from her bedroom winder upstairs, an' sometimes this stump, it look like it were movin' right up de path like a man.

"After she done gone to bed, late one springtime night when de moon were shinin', I hear Miss Jeanne a-cryin': 'He's come! . . . Hager, ma Robert's come back to me!' An' I jumped out o' ma bed in de next room where I were sleepin' an' run in

to her, an' there she was in her long, white night-clothes standin' out in de moonlight on de little balcony, high up in de
middle o' that big stone porch. She was lookin' down into de
yard at this stump of a tree a-holdin' up its arms. An' she
thinks it's Marster Robert a-callin' her. She thinks he's standin' there in his uniform, come back from de war, a-callin'
her. An' she say: 'I'm comin', Bob, dear;' . . . An' 'fore I think
what she's doin', Miss Jeanne done stepped over de little rail o'
de balcony like she were walkin' on moonlight. An' she say:
'I'm comin', Bob!'

"She ain't left no will, so de house an' all went to de State,
an' I been left with nothin'. But I ain't care 'bout that. I followed her to de grave, an' I been with her all de time, 'cause
she's ma friend. An' I were sorry for her, 'cause I knowed that
love were painin' her soul, an' warn't nobody left to help her
but me.

"An' since then I's met many a white lady an' many a white
gentleman, an' some of 'em's been kind to me an' some of 'em
ain't; some of 'em's cussed me an' wouldn't pay me fo' ma
work; an' some of 'em's hurted me awful. But I's been sorry fo'
white folks, fo' I knows something inside must be aggravatin'
de po' souls. An' I's kept a room in ma heart fo' 'em, 'cause
white folks needs us, honey, even if they don't know it. They's
like spoilt chillens what's got too much o' ever'thing—an' they
needs us niggers, what ain't got nothin'.

"I's been livin' a long time in yesterday, Sandy chile, an' I
knows there ain't no room in de world fo' nothin' mo'n love. I
knows, chile! Ever'thing there is but lovin' leaves a rust on yo'
soul. An' to love sho 'nough, you got to have a spot in yo' heart
fo' ever'body—great an' small, white an' black, an' them
what's good an' them what's evil—'cause love ain't got no
crowded-out places where de good ones stays an' de bad ones
can't come in. When it gets that way, then it ain't love.

"White peoples maybe mistreats you an' hates you, but
when you hates 'em back, you's de one what's hurted, 'cause
hate makes yo' heart ugly—that's all it does. It closes up de

sweet door to life an' makes ever'thing small an' mean an' dirty. Honey, there ain't no room in de world fo' hate, white folks hatin' niggers, an' niggers hatin' white folks. There ain't no room in this world fo' nothin' but love, Sandy chile. That's all they's room fo'—nothin' but love."

XVII.

BARBER-SHOP

Mr. Logan, hearing that Aunt Hager had an empty room since all her daughters were gone, sent her one evening a new-comer in town looking for a place to stay. His name was Wim Dogberry and he was a brickmason and hod-carrier, a tall, quiet, stoop-shouldered black man, neither old nor young. He took, for two dollars and a half a week, the room that had been Annjee's, and Hager gave him a key to the front door.

Wim Dogberry was carrying hod then on a new moving-picture theatre that was being built. He rose early and came in late, face, hands, and overalls covered with mortar dust. He washed in a tin basin by the pump and went to bed, and about all he ever said to Aunt Hager and Sandy was "Good-mornin'" and "Good-evenin'," and maybe a stumbling "How is you?" But on Sunday mornings Hager usually asked him to breakfast if he got up on time—for on Saturday nights Wim drank licker and came home mumbling to himself a little later than on week-day evenings, so sometimes he would sleep until noon Sundays.

One Saturday night he wet the bed, and when Hager went to make it up on the Sabbath morning, she found a damp yellow spot in the middle. Of this act Dogberry was so ashamed that he did not even say "Good-mornin'" for several days, and if, from the corner, he saw Aunt Hager and her grandson sitting on the porch in the twilight when he came towards home, he would pass his street and walk until he thought they had gone inside to bed. But he was a quiet roomer, he didn't give anyone any trouble, and he paid regularly. And since Hager was in no position to despise two dollars and a half every week, she rather liked Dogberry.

Now Hager kept the growing Sandy close by her all the time to help her while she washed and ironed and to talk to her while she sat on the porch in the evenings. Of course, he played sometimes in his own yard whenever Willie-Mae or Buster or, on Sundays, Jimmy Lane came to the house. But Jimmy Lane was running wild since his mother died, and Hager didn't like him to visit her grandson any more. He was bad.

When Sandy wanted to go to the vacant lot to play baseball with the neighbor boys, his grandmother would usually not allow him to leave her. "Stay here, sir, with Hager. I needs you to pump ma water fo' me an' fill up these tubs," she would say. Or else she would yell: "Ain't I told you you might get hurt down there with them old rough white boys? Stay here in yo' own yard, where you can keep out o' mischief."

So he grew accustomed to remaining near his grandmother, and at night, when the other children would be playing duck-on-the-rock under the arc-light at the corner, he would be sitting on the front porch listening to Aunt Hager telling her tales of slavery and talking of her own far-off youth. When school opened in the fall, the old woman said: "I don't know what I's gwine do all day without you, Sandy. You sho been company to me, with all my own chillens gone." But Sandy was glad to get back to a roomful of boys and girls again.

One Indian-summer afternoon when Aunt Hager was hanging up clothes in the back yard while the boy held the basket of clothes-pins, old man Logan drove past on his rickety trash-wagon and bowed elaborately to Hager. She went to the back fence to joke and gossip with him as usual, while his white mule switched off persistent flies with her tail.

Before the old beau drove away, he said: "Say, Hager, does you want that there young one o' your'n to work? I knows a little job he can have if you does," pointing to Sandy.

"What'll he got to do?" demanded Hager.

"Well, Pete Scott say he need a boy down yonder at de

barber-shop on Saturdays to kinder clean up where de kinks
fall, an' shine shoes fo' de customers. Ain't nothin' hard 'bout it,
an' I was thinkin' it would just 'bout be Sandy's size. He could
make a few pennies ever' week to kinder help things 'long."

"True, he sho could," said Hager. "I'll have him go see Pete."

So Sandy went to see Mr. Peter Scott at the colored barber-
shop on Pearl Street that evening and was given his first regular job. Every Saturday, which was the barber-shop's only busy
day, when the working-men got paid off, Sandy went on the
job at noon and worked until eight or nine in the evening. His
duties were to keep the place swept clean of the hair that the
three barbers sheared and to shine the shoes of any customer
who might ask for a shine. Only a few customers permitted
themselves that last luxury, for many of them came to the shop
in their working-shoes, covered with mud or lime, and most of
them shined their own boots at home on Sunday mornings before church. But occasionally Cudge Windsor, who owned a
pool hall, or some of the dressed-up bootleggers, might climb
on the stand and permit their shoes to be cleaned by the brown
youngster, who asked shyly: "Shine, mister?"

The barber-shop was a new world to Sandy, who had lived
thus far tied to Aunt Hager's apron-strings. He was a dreamy-
eyed boy who had grown to his present age largely under
the dominant influence of women—Annjee, Harriett, his
grandmother—because Jimboy had been so seldom home. But
the barber-shop then was a man's world, and, on Saturdays,
while a dozen or more big laborers awaited their turns, the
place was filled with loud man-talk and smoke and laughter.
Baseball, Jack Johnson, racehorses, white folks, Teddy Roos-
evelt, local gossip, Booker Washington, women, labor prospects in Topeka, Kansas City, Omaha, religion, politics,
women, God—discussions and arguments all afternoon and
far up into the night, while crisp kinks rolled to the floor, cigarette and cigar-butts were thrown on the hearth of the monkey-
stove, and Sandy called out: "Shine, mister?"

Sometimes the boy earned one or two dollars from shines,
but on damp or snowy days he might not make anything

except the fifty cents Pete Scott paid him for sweeping up. Or perhaps one of the barbers, too busy to go out for supper, would send Sandy for a sandwich and a bottle of milk, and thus he would make an extra nickel or dime.

The patrons liked him and often kidded him about his sandy hair. "Boy, you's too dark to have hair like that. Ain't nobody but white folks s'posed to have sandy-colored hair. An' your'n's nappy at that!" Then Sandy would blush with embarrassment—if the change from a dry chocolate to a damp chocolate can be called a blush, as he grew warm and perspired—because he didn't like to be kidded about his hair. And he hadn't been around uncouth fellows long enough to learn the protective art of turning back a joke. He had discovered already, though, that so-called jokes are often not really jokes at all, but rather unpleasant realities that hurt unless you can think of something equally funny and unpleasant to say in return. But the men who patronized Pete Scott's barber-shop seldom grew angry at the hard pleasantries that passed for humor, and they could play the dozens for hours without anger, unless the parties concerned became serious, when they were invited to take it on the outside. And even at that a fight was fun, too.

After a winter of Saturday nights at Pete's shop Sandy himself became pretty adept at "kidding"; but at first he was timid about it and afraid to joke with grown-up people, or to give smart answers to strangers when they teased him about his crinkly, sand-colored head. One day, however, one of the barbers gave him a tin of Madam Walker's and told him: "Lay that hair down an' stop these niggers from laughin' at you." Sandy took his advice.

Madam Walker's—a thick yellow pomade—and a good wetting with water proved most efficacious to the boy's hair, when aided with a stocking cap—the top of a woman's stocking cut off and tied in a knot at one end so as to fit tightly over one's head, pressing the hair smooth. Thereafter Sandy appeared with his hair slick and shiny. And the salve and water together made it seem a dark brown, just the color of his skin, instead of the peculiar sandy tint it possessed in its natural state. Besides he soon advanced far enough in the art of "kidding" to say: "So's your pa's," to people who informed him that his head was nappy.

During the autumn Harriett had been home once to see her mother and had said that she was working as chambermaid with Maudel at the hotel. But in the barber-shop that winter Sandy often heard his aunt's name mentioned in less proper connections. Sometimes the boy pretended not to hear, and if Pete Scott was there, he always stopped the men from talking.

"Tired o' all this nasty talk 'bout women in ma shop," he said one Saturday night. "Some o' you men better look after your own womenfolks if you got any."

"Aw, all de womens in de world ain't worth two cents to me," said a waiter sitting in the middle chair, his face covered with lather. "I don't respect no woman but my mother."

"An' neither do I," answered Greensbury Jones. "All of 'em's evil, specially if they's black an' got blue gums."

"I's done told you to hush," said Pete Scott behind the first chair, where he was clipping Jap Logan's hair. "Ma wife's black herself, so don't start talkin' 'bout no blue gums! I's tired o' this here female talk anyhow. This is ma shop, an' ma razors sho can cut somethin' else 'sides hair—so now just keep on talkin' 'bout blue gums!"

"I see where Bryant's runnin' for president agin," said Greensbury Jones.

But one Saturday, while the proprietor was out to snatch a bite to eat, a discussion came up as to who was the prettiest colored girl in town. Was she yellow, high-brown, chocolate, or black? Of course, there was no agreement, but names were mentioned and qualities were described. One girl had eyes like Eve herself; another had hips like Miss Cleopatra; one smooth brown-skin had legs like—like—like—

"Aw, man! De Statue of Liberty!" somebody suggested when the name of a famous beauty failed the speaker's memory.

"But, feller, there ain't nothin' in all them rainbow shades," a young teamster argued against Uncle Dan Givens, who preferred high yellows. "Gimme a cool black gal ever' time! They's too dark to fade—and when they are good-looking, I mean they *are* good-looking! I'm talkin' 'bout Harrietta Williams, too! That's who I mean! Now, find a better-looking gal than she is!"

"I admits Harrietta's all right," said the old man; "all right to look at but—sput-t-tsss!" He spat contemptuously at the stove.

"O, I know that!" said the teamster; "but I ain't talkin' 'bout what she is! I'm talkin' 'bout how she looks. An' a song-ster out o' this world don't care if she is a—!"

"S-s-s-sh! Soft-pedal it brother." One of the men nudged the speaker. "There's one o' the Williamses right here—that kid over yonder shinin' shoes's Harriett's nephew or somethin' 'nother."

"You niggers talks too free, anyhow," one of the barbers added. "Somebody gwine cut your lips off some o' these days. De idee o' ole Uncle Dan Givens' arguin' 'bout women and he done got whiskers all round his head like a wore-out cheese."

"That's all right, you young whip-snapper," squeaked Uncle Dan heatedly. "Might have whiskers round ma head, but I ain't wore out!"

Laughter and smoke filled the little shop, while the winter wind blew sleet against the big plate-glass window and whis-tled through the cracks in the doorway, making the gas lights flicker overhead. Sandy smacked his polishing cloth on the toes of a gleaming pair of brown button shoes belonging to a stranger in town, then looked up with a grin and said: "Yes, sir!" as the man handed him a quarter.

"Keep the change," said the new-comer grandly.

"That guy's an actor," one of the barbers said when the man went out. "He's playin' with the *Smart Set* at the Opery House tonight. I bet the top gallery'll be full o' niggers sence it's a jig show, but I ain't goin' anear there myself to be Jim-Crowed, 'cause I don't believe in goin' nowhere I ain't allowed to set with the rest of the folks. If I can't be the table-cloth, I won't be the dish-rag—that's my motto. And if I can't buy the seats I want at a show, I sure God can keep my change!"

"Yes, and miss all the good shows," countered a little red-eyed porter. "Just as well say if you can't eat in a restaurant where white folks eat, you ain't gonna eat."

"Anybody want a shine?" yelled Sandy above the racket. "And if you don't want a shine, stay out of my chair and do your arguing on the floor!"

A brown-skin chorus girl, on her way to the theatre, stepped into the shop and asked if she could buy a *Chicago Defender* there. The barber directed her to the colored restaurant, while all the men immediately stopped talking to stare at her until she went out.

"Whew! . . . Some legs!" the teamster cried as the door closed on a vision of silk stockings. "How'd you like to shine that long, sweet brown-skin mama's shoes, boy?"

"She wouldn't have to pay me!" said Sandy.

"Whoopee! Gallery or no gallery," shouted Jap Logan, "I'm gonna see that show! Don't care if they do Jim-Crow niggers in the white folks' Opery House!"

"Yes," muttered one of the barbers, "that's just what's the matter now—you ain't got no race-pride! You niggers ain't got no shame!"

XVIII.

CHILDREN'S DAY

When Easter came that spring, Sandy had saved enough money to buy himself a suit and a new cap from his earnings at the barber-shop. He was very proud of this accomplishment and so was Aunt Hager.

"You's a 'dustrious chile, sho is! Gwine make a smart man even if yo' daddy warn't nothin'. Gwine get ahead an' do good fo' yo'self an' de race, yes, sir!"

The spring came early and the clear balmy days found Hager's back yard billowing with clean white clothes on lines in the sun. Her roomer had left her when the theatre was built and had gone to work on a dam somewhere up the river, so Annjee's room was empty again. Sandy had slept with his grandmother during the cold weather, but in summer he slept on a pallet.

The boy did not miss his mother. When she had been home, Annjee had worked out all day, and she was quiet at night because she was always tired. Harriett had been the one to keep the fun and laughter going—Harriett and Jimboy, whenever he was in town. Sandy wished Harrie would live at home instead of staying at Maudel's house, but he never said anything about it to his grandmother. He went to school regularly, went to work at the barber-shop on Saturdays and to Sunday-School on Sundays, and remained with Aunt Hager the rest of his time. She was always worried if she didn't know where he was.

"Colored boys, when they gets round twelve an' thirteen, they gets so bad, Sandy," she would say. "I wants you to stay nice an' make something out o' yo'self. If Hager lives, she ain't

gonna see you go down. She's gonna make a fine man out o'
you fo' de glory o' God an' de black race. You gwine to 'mount
to something in this world. You hear me?"

Sandy did hear her, and he knew what she meant. She meant
a man like Booker T. Washington, or Frederick Douglass, or
like Paul Lawrence Dunbar, who did poetry-writing. Or
maybe Jack Johnson. But Hager said Jack Johnson was the
devil's kind of greatness, not God's.

"That's what you get from workin' round that old barber-
shop where all they talks 'bout is prize-fightin' an' hossracin'.
Jack Johnson done married a white woman, anyhow! What he
care 'bout de race?"

The little boy wondered if Jack Johnson's kids looked like
Buster. But maybe he didn't have any kids. He must ask Pete
Scott about that when he went back to work on Saturday.

In the summer a new amusement park opened in Stanton,
the first of its kind in the city, with a merry-go-round, a shoot-
the-shoots, a Ferris wheel, a dance-hall, and a bandstand for
week-end concerts. In order to help popularize the park, which
was far on the north edge of town, the *Daily Leader* announced, under its auspices, what was called a Free Children's
Day Party open to all the readers of that paper who clipped the
coupons published in each issue. On July 26 these coupons,
presented at the gate, would entitle every child in Stanton to
free admittance to the park, free popcorn, free lemonade, and
one ride on each of the amusement attractions—the merry-
go-round, the shoot-the-shoots, and the Ferris wheel. All you
had to do was to be a reader of the *Daily Leader* and present
the coupons cut from that paper.

Aunt Hager and Sister Johnson both took the *Leader* regularly, as did almost everybody else in Stanton, so Sandy and
Willie-Mae started to clip coupons. All the children in the
neighborhood were doing the same thing. The Children's Day
would be a big event for all the little people in town. None of
them had ever seen a shoot-the-shoots before, a contrivance
that pulled little cars full of folks high into the air and then let
them come whizzing down an incline into an artificial pond,

where the cars would float like boats. Sandy and Willie-Mae looked forward to thrill after thrill.

When the afternoon of the great day came at last, Willie-Mae stopped for Sandy, dressed in her whitest white dress and her new patent-leather shoes, which hurt her feet awfully. Sandy's grandmother was making him wash his ears when she came in.

"You gwine out yonder 'mongst all them white chillens, I wants you to at least look clean!" said Hager.

They started out.

"Here!" called Aunt Hager. "Ain't you gwine to take yo' coupons?" In his rush to get away, Sandy had forgotten them.

It was a long walk to the park, and Willie-Mae stopped and took off her shoes and stockings and carried them in her hands until she got near the gate; then she put them on again and limped bravely along, clutching her precious bits of newspaper. They could hear the band playing and children shouting and squealing as the cars on the shoot-the-shoots shot downward with a splash into the pond. They could see the giant Ferris wheel, larger than the one the carnival had had, circling high in the air.

"I'm gonna ride on that first," said Sandy.

There were crowds of children under the bright red and white wooden shelter at the park entrance. They were lining up at the gate—laughing, merry, clean little white children, pushing and yelling and giggling amiably. Sandy let Willie-Mae go first and he got in line behind her. The band was playing gaily inside. . . . They were almost to the entrance now. . . . There were just two boys in front of them. . . . Willie-Mae held out her black little hand clutching the coupons. They moved forward. The man looked down.

"Sorry," he said. "This party's for white kids."

Willie-Mae did not understand. She stood holding out the coupons, waiting for the tall white man to take them.

"Stand back, you two," he said, looking at Sandy as well. "I told you little darkies this wasn't your party. . . . Come on— next little girl." And the line of white children pushed past

Willie-Mae and Sandy, going into the park. Stunned, the two dark ones drew aside. Then they noticed a group of a dozen or more other colored youngsters standing apart in the sun, just without the bright entrance pavilion, and among them was Sadie Butler, Sandy's class-mate. Three or four of the colored children were crying, but most of them looked sullen and angry, and some of them had turned to go home.

"My papa takes the *Leader*," Sadie Butler was saying. "And you see what it says here on the coupons, too—'Free Admittance to Every Child in Stanton.' Can't you read it, Sandy?"

"Sure, I can read it, but I guess they didn't mean colored," he answered, as the boy watched the white children going in the gate. "They wouldn't let us in."

Willie-Mae, between the painful shoes and the hurt of her disappointment, was on the verge of tears. One of the small boys in the crowd, a hard-looking little fellow from Pearl Street, was cursing childishly.

"God damn old sons of biscuit-eaters, that what they are! I wish I was a big man, dog-gone, I'd shoot 'em all, that's what I'd do!"

"I suppose they didn't mean colored kids," said Sandy again.

"Buster went in all right," said Sadie. "I seen him. But they didn't know he was colored, I guess. When I went up to the gate, the man said: 'Whoa! Where you goin'?' just like I was a horse. . . . I'm going home now and tell my papa."

She walked away, followed by five or six other little girls in their Sunday dresses. Willie-Mae was sitting on the ground taking off her shoes again, sweat and tears running down her black cheeks. Sandy saw his white schoolmate, Earl, approaching.

"What's matter, Sandy? Ain't you goin' in?" Earl demanded, looking at his friend's worried face. "Did the little girl hurt her foot?"

"No," said Sandy. "We just ain't going in. . . . Here, Earl, you can have my coupons. If you have extra ones, the papers says you get more lemonade . . . so you take 'em."

The white boy, puzzled, accepted the proffered coupons, stood dumbly for a moment wondering what to say to his brown friend, then went on into the park.

"It's yo' party, white chile!" a little tan-skin girl called after him, mimicking the way the man at the gate had talked. "Whoa! Stay out! You's a nigger!" she said to Sandy.

The other children, in spite of themselves, laughed at the accuracy of her burlesque imitation. Then, with the music of the merry-go-round from beyond the high fence and the laughter of happy children following them, the group of dark-skinned ones started down the dusty road together—and to all the colored boys and girls they met on the way they called out, "Ain't no use, jigaboos! That party's for white folks!"

When Willie-Mae and Sandy got home and told their story, Sister Johnson was angry as a wet hen.

"Crackers is devils," she cried. "I 'spected as much! Dey ain't nary hell hot 'nough to burn ole white folks, 'cause dey's devils deyselves! De dirty hounds!"

But all Hager said was: "They's po' trash owns that park what don't know no better, hurtin' chillens' feelin's, but we'll forgive 'em! Don't fret yo'self, Sister Johnson. What good can frettin' do? Come on here, let's we have a party of our own." She went out in the yard and took a watermelon from a tub of well-water where it had been cooling and cut it into four juicy slices; then they sat down on the grass at the shady side of the house and ate, trying to forget about white folks.

"Don't you mind, Willie-Mae," Hager said to the little black girl, who was still crying. "You's colored, honey, an' you's liable to have a hard time in this life—but don't cry. . . . You, Sandy, run round de house an' see didn't I heard de mail-man blowin'."

"Yes'm," said Sandy when he came back. "Was the mail-man, and I got a letter from mama." The boy sat on the grass to read it, anxious to see what Annjee said. And later, when the company had gone, he read it aloud to Hager.

DEAR LITTLE SON:

How have you all been? how is grandma? I get worried about you when I do not hear. You know Aunt Hager is old and can't write much so you must do it for her because she is not used to adress letters and the last one was two weeks getting here and had went all around everywhere. Your father says tell you hello. I got a job in a boarding house for old white folks what are cranky about how they beds is made. There are white and colored here in the auto business and women to. Tell Madam de Carter I will send my Lodge dues back because I do not want to be transfer as I might come home sometime. I ain't seen you all now for more'n a year. Jimboy he keeps changing jobs from one thing to another but he likes this town pretty well. You know he broke his guitar carrying it in a crowded street car. Ma says you are growing and have bought yourself a new suit last Easter. Mama certainly does right well to keep on washing and ironing at her age and worrying with you besides. Tempy ought to help ma but seem like she don't think so. Do you ever see your Aunt Harrie? I hope she is settling down in her ways. If ma wasn't all by herself maybe I could send for you to come live with us in Detroit but maybe I will be home to see you if I ever get any money ahead. Rent is so high here I never wittnessed so many folks in one house, rooming five and six together, and nobody can save a dime. Are you still working at the barber shop. I heard Sister Johnson was under the weather but I couldn't make out from ma's scribbling what was the matter with her. Did she have a physicianer? You behave yourself with Willie-Mae because you are getting to be a big boy now and she is a girl older then you are. I am going to send you some pants next time I go down town but I get off from work so late I don't have a chance to do nothing and your father eats in the restaurant count of me not home to fix for him and I don't care where you go colored folks has a hard time. I want you to mind your grandma and help her work. She is too old to be straining at the pump drawing water to wash clothes with. Now write to me. Love to you all both and seven kisses XXXXXXX right here on the paper,

> Your loving mother,
> ANNJELICA ROGERS

Sandy laughed at the clumsy cross-mark kisses. He was glad to get a letter from his mother, and word in it about Jimboy.

And he was sorry his father had broken his guitar. But not even watermelon and the long letter could drive away his sick feeling about the park.

"I guess Kansas is getting like the South, isn't it, ma?" Sandy said to his grandmother as they came out on the porch that evening after supper. "They don't like us here either, do they?"

But Aunt Hager gave him no answer. In silence they watched the sunset fade from the sky. Slowly the evening star grew bright, and, looking at the stars, Hager began to sing, very softly at first:

> *From this world o' trouble free,*
> *Stars beyond!*
> *Stars beyond!*

And Sandy, as he stood beside his grandmother on the porch, heard a great chorus out of the black past—singing generations of toil-worn Negroes, echoing Hager's voice as it deepened and grew in volume:

> *There's a star fo' you an' me,*
> *Stars beyond!*

XIX

TEN DOLLARS AND COSTS

In the fall Sandy found a job that occupied him after school hours, as well as on Saturday and Sunday. One afternoon at the barber-shop, Charlie Nutter, a bell-hop who had come to have his hair cut, asked Sandy to step outside a minute. Once out of earshot of the barbers and loafers within, Charlie went on: "Say, kid, I got some dope to buzz to yuh 'bout a job. Joe Willis, the white guy what keeps the hotel where I work, is lookin' for a boy to kinder sweep up around the lobby every day, dust off, and sort o' help the bell-boys out sometimes. Ain't nothin' hard attached to it, and yuh can bring 'long your shine-box and rub up shoes in the lobby, too, if yuh wants to. I though' maybe yuh might like to have the job. Yuh'd make more'n yuh do here. And more'n that, too, when yuh got on to the ropes. Course yuh'd have to fix me up with a couple o' bucks o' so for gettin' yuh the job, but if yuh want it, just lemme know and I'll fix it with the boss. He tole me to start lookin' for somebody and that's what I'm doin'." Charlie Nutter went on talking, without stopping to wait for an answer. "Course a boy like you don't know nothin' 'bout hotel work, but yuh ain't never too young to learn, and that's a nice easy way to start. Yuh might work up to me some time, yuh never can tell—head bell-hop! 'Cause I ain't gonna stay in this burg all my life; I figger if I can hop bells here, I can hop bells in Chicago or some place worth livin' at. But the tips ain't bad down there at the Drummer's though—lots o' sportin' women and folks like that what don't mind givin' yuh a quarter any time. . . . And yuh can get well yourself once in a while. What yuh say? Do yuh want it?"

Sandy thought quick. With Christmas not far off, his shoes about worn out, and the desire to help Aunt Hager, too—"I guess I better take it," he said. "But do I have to pay you now?"

"Hell, naw, not now! I'll keep my eye on yuh, and yuh can just slip me a little change now and then down to the hotel when you start workin.' Other boy ain't quittin' nohow till next week. S'pose yuh come round there Sunday morning and I'll kinder show yuh what to do. And don't pay no mind to Willis when he hollers at yuh. He's all right—just got a hard way about him with the help, that's all—but he ain't a bad boss. I'll see yuh, then! Drop by Sunday and lemme know for sure. So long!"

But Aunt Hager was not much pleased when Sandy came home that night and she heard the news. "I ain't never wanted none o' my chillens to work in no ole hotels," she said. "They's evil, full o' nastiness, an' you don't learn nothin' good in 'em. I don't want you to go there, chile."

"But grandma," Sandy argued, "I want to send mama a Christmas present. And just look at my shoes, all worn out! I don't make much money any more since that new colored barber-shop opened up. It's all white inside and folks don't have to wait so long 'cause there's five barbers. Jimmy Lane's got the porter's job down there . . . and I have to start working regular some time, don't I?"

"I reckons you does, but I hates to see you workin' in hotels, chile, with all them low-down Bottoms niggers, and bad womens comin' an' goin'. But I reckon you does need de job. Yo' mammy ain't sent no money here fo' de Lawd knows when, an' I ain't able to buy you nice clothes an' all like you needs to go to school in. . . . But don't forget, honey, no matter where you works—you be good an' do right. . . . I reckon you'll get along."

So Sandy found Charlie Nutter on Sunday and told him for sure he would take the job. Then he told Pete Scott he was no longer coming to work at his barber-shop, and Pete got mad and told him to go to hell, quitting when business was bad after all he had done for Sandy, besides letting him shine shoes and keep all his earnings. At other shops he couldn't have done that; besides he had intended to teach Sandy to be a barber when he got big enough.

"But go on!" said Pete Scott. "Go on! I don't need you. Plenty other boys I can find to work for me. But I bet you won't stay at that Drummer's Hotel no time, though—I can tell you that!"

The long Indian summer lingered until almost Thanksgiving, and the weather was sunny and warm. The day before Sandy went to work on his new job, he came home from school, brought in the wood for the stove, and delivered a basket of newly ironed clothes to the white folks. When he returned, he found his grandmother standing on the front porch in the sunset, reading the evening paper, which the boy had recently delivered. Sandy stopped in the twilight beside Hager, breathing in the crisp cool air and wondering what they were going to have for supper.

Suddenly his grandmother gave a deep cry and leaned heavily against the door-jamb, letting the paper fall from her hands. "O, ma Lawd!" she moaned. "O, ma Lawd!" and an expression of the uttermost pain made the old woman's eyes widen in horror. "Is I read de name right?"

Sandy, frightened, picked up the paper from the porch and found on the front page the little four-line item that his grandmother had just read:

NEGRESSES ARRESTED

Harrietta Williams and Maudel Smothers, two young negresses, were arrested last night on Pearl Street for street-walking. They were brought before Judge Brinton and fined ten dollars and costs.

"What does that mean, ma—street-walking?" the child asked, but his grandmother raised her apron to her eyes and stumbled into the house. Sandy stopped, perplexed at the meaning of the article, at his aunt's arrest, at his grandmother's horror. Then he followed Hager, the open newspaper still in his hands, and found her standing at the window in the kitchen, crying. Racking sobs were shaking her body and the boy, who had never seen an old person weep like that before, was terribly afraid. He didn't know that grown-up people cried, except at funerals, where it was the proper thing to do. He didn't know they ever cried alone, by themselves in their own houses.

"I'm gonna get Sister Johnson," he said, dropping the paper on the floor. "I'm gonna get Sister Johnson quick!"

"No, honey, don't get her," stammered the old woman. "She can't help us none, chile. Can't nobody help us . . . but de Lawd."

In the dusk Sandy saw that his grandmother was trying hard to make her lips speak plainly and to control her sobs.

"Let's we pray, son, fo' yo' po' lost Aunt Harriett—fo' ma own baby chile, what's done turned from de light an' is walkin' in darkness."

She dropped on her knees near the kitchen-stove with her arms on the seat of a chair and her head bowed. Sandy got on his knees, too, and while his grandmother prayed aloud for the body and soul of her daughter, the boy repeated over and over in his mind: "I wish you'd come home, Aunt Harrie. It's lonesome around here! Gee, I wish you'd come home."

XX.

HEY, BOY!

In the lobby of the Drummer's Hotel there were six large brass spittoons—one in the center of the place, one in each corner, and one near the clerk's desk. It was Sandy's duty to clean these spittoons. Every evening that winter after school he came in the back door of the hotel, put his books in the closet where he kept his brooms and cleaning rags, swept the two short upper halls and the two flights of stairs, swept the lobby and dusted, then took the spittoons, emptied their slimy contents into the alley, rinsed them out, and polished them until they shone as brightly as if they were made of gold. Except for the stench of emptying them, Sandy rather liked this job. He always felt very proud of himself when, about six o'clock, he could look around the dingy old lobby and see the six gleaming brass bowls catching the glow of the electric lamps on their shining surfaces before they were again covered with spit. The thought that he himself had created this brightness with his own hands, aided by a can of brass-polish, never failed to make Sandy happy.

He liked to clean things, to make them beautiful, to make them shine. Aunt Hager did, too. When she wasn't washing clothes, she was always cleaning something about the house, dusting, polishing the range, or scrubbing the kitchen-floor until it was white enough to eat from. To Hager a clean thing was beautiful—also to Sandy, proud every evening of his six unblemished brass spittoons. Yet each day when he came to work, they were covered anew with tobacco juice, cigarette-butts, wads of chewing-gum, and phlegm. But to make them

clean was Sandy's job—and they were beautiful when they
were clean.

Charlie Nutter was right—there was nothing very hard about
the work and he liked it for a while. The new kinds of life which
he saw in the hotel interested and puzzled him, but, being naturally a silent child, he asked no questions, and, beyond the directions for his work, nobody told him anything. Sandy did his
cleaning well and the boss had not yet had occasion to bellow at
him, as he often bellowed at the two bell-boys.

The Drummer's Hotel was not a large hotel, nor a nice one.
A three-story frame structure, dilapidated and run down, it
had not been painted for years. In the lobby two large panes of
plate glass looked on the street, and in front of these were
rows of hard wooden chairs. At the rear of the lobby was the
clerk's desk, a case of cigars and cigarettes, a cooler for water,
and the door to the men's room. It was Sandy's duty to clean
this toilet, too.

Upstairs on the second and third floors were the bedrooms.
Only the poorest of travelling salesmen, transient railroad
workers, occasionally a few show-people, and the ladies of the
streets with their clients rented them. The night trade was always the most brisk at the Drummer's Hotel, but it was only
on Saturdays that Sandy worked after six o'clock. That night
he would not get home until ten or eleven, but Aunt Hager
would always be waiting for him, keeping the fire warm, with
the wash-tub full of water for his weekly bath.

There was no dining-room attached to the hotel, and, aside
from Sandy, there were only five employees. The boss himself,
Joe Willis, was usually at the desk. There were two chamber-
maids who worked in the mornings, an old man who did the
heavy cleaning and scrubbing once or twice a week, and two
bell-boys—one night boy and one day boy supposedly, but
both bellmen had been there so long that they arranged the
hours to suit themselves. Charlie Nutter had started small, like
Sandy, and had grown up there. The other bell-boy, really no
boy at all, but an old man, had been in the hotel ever since it

opened, and Sandy was as much afraid of him as he was of
the boss.

This bellman's name was Mr. George Clark. His uniform
was frayed and greasy, but he wore it with the air of a major,
and he acted as though all the burdens of running the hotel
were on his shoulders. He knew how everything was to be
done, where everything was kept, what every old guest liked.
And he could divine the tastes of each new guest before he had
been there a day. Subservient and grinning to white folks, evil
and tyrannical to the colored help, George was the chief authority, next to Joe Willis, in the Drummer's Hotel. He it was
who found some fault with Sandy's work every day until he
learned to like the child because Sandy never answered back
or tried to be fly, as George said most young niggers were.
After a time the old fellow seldom bothered to inspect Sandy's
spittoons or to look in the corners for dust, but, nevertheless,
he remained a person to be humored and obeyed if one wished
to work at the Drummer's Hotel.

Besides being the boss's right-hand man, George Clark was
the official bootlegger for the house, too. In fact, he kept his
liquor-supply in the hotel cellar. When he was off duty, Charlie, the other bell-hop, sold it for him if there were any calls
from the rooms above. They made no sales other than to guests
of the house, but such sales were frequent. Some of the white
women who used the rooms collected a commission from
George for the sales they helped make to their men visitors.

Sandy was a long time learning the tricks of hotel work.
"Yuh sure a dumb little joker," Charlie was constantly inform-
ing him. "But just stay around awhile and yuh'll get on to it."

Christmas came and Sandy sent his mother in Detroit a big
box of drugstore candy. For Aunt Hager he started to buy a
long pair of green earrings for fifty cents, but he was afraid she
might not like them, so he bought her white handkerchiefs instead. And he sent a pretty card to Harriett, for one snowy
December day his aunt had seen him through the windows
sweeping out the lobby of the hotel and she had called him to

the door to talk to her. She thrust a little piece of paper into his hand with her new address on it.

"Maudel's moved to Kansas City," she said, "so I don't live there any more. You better keep this address yourself and if mama ever needs me, you can know where I am."

Then she went on through the snow, looking very pretty in a cheap fur coat and black, high-heeled slippers, with grey silk stockings. Sandy saw her pass the hotel often with different men. Sometimes she went by with Cudge Windsor, the owner of the pool hall, or Billy Sanderlee. Almost always she was with sporty-looking fellows who wore derbies and had gold teeth. Sandy noticed that she didn't urge him to come to see her at this new house-number she had given him, so he put the paper in his pocket and went back to his sweeping, glad, anyway, to have seen his Aunt Harriett.

One Saturday afternoon several white men were sitting in the lobby smoking and reading the papers. Sandy swept around their chairs, dusted, and then took the spittoons out to clean. This work did not require his attention; while he applied the polish with a handful of soft rags, he could let his mind wander to other things. He thought about Harriett. Then he thought about school and what he would do when he was a man; about Willie-Mae, who had a job washing dinner dishes for a white family; about Jimmy Lane, who had no mama; and Sandy wondered what his own mother and father were doing in another town, and if they wanted him with them. He thought how old and tired and grey-headed Aunt Hager had become; how she puffed and blowed over the wash-tubs now, but never complained; how she waited for him on Saturday nights with the kitchen-stove blazing, so he would be warm after walking so far in the cold; and how she prayed he would be a great man some day. . . . Sitting there in the back room of the hotel, Sandy wondered how people got to be great, as, one by one, he made the spittoons bright and beautiful. He wondered how people made themselves great.

That night he would have to work late picking up papers in the lobby, running errands for the boss, and shining shoes.

After he had put the spittoons around, he would go out and get a hamburger sandwich and a cup of coffee for supper; then he would come back and help Charlie if he could. . . . Charlie was a good old boy. He had taken only a dollar for getting Sandy his job and he often helped him make tips by allowing Sandy to run to the telegraph office or do some other little odd job for a guest upstairs. . . . Sure, Charlie was a nice guy.

Things were pretty busy tonight. Several men had their shoes shined as they sat tipped back in the lobby chairs while Sandy with his boot-black box let them put up a foot at a time to be polished. One tall farmer gave him a quarter tip and a pat on the head.

"Bright little feller, that," he remarked to the boss.

About ten o'clock the blond Miss Marcia McKay's bell rang, and, Charlie being engaged, Joe Willis sent Sandy up to see what she wanted. Miss McKay had just come in out of the snow a short time before with a heavy-set man. Both of them were drunk. Sandy knocked timidly outside her room.

"Come in," growled the man's voice.

Sandy opened the door and saw Miss McKay standing naked in the middle of the floor combing her hair. He stopped on the threshold.

"Aw, come in," said the man. "She won't bite you! Where's that other bell-boy? We want some licker! . . . Damn it! Say, send Charlie up here! He knows what I want!"

Sandy scampered away, and when he found Charlie, he told him about Miss McKay. The child was scared because he had often heard of colored boys' being lynched for looking at white women, even with their clothes on—but the bell-boy only laughed.

"Yuh're a dumb little joker!" he said. "Just stay around here awhile and yuh'll see lots more'n that!" He winked and gave Sandy a nudge in the ribs. "Boy, I done sold ten quarts o' licker tonight," he whispered jubilantly. "And some a it was mine, too!"

Sandy went back to the lobby and the shining of shoes. A big, red-necked stranger smoking and drinking with a crowd of drummers in one corner of the room called to him "Hey, boy! Shine me up here!" So he edged into the center of the group of men with his blacking-box, got down on his knees before the big fellow, took out his cans and his cloths, and went to work.

The white men were telling dirty stories, uglier than any Sandy had heard at the colored barber-shop and not very funny—and some of them made him sick at the stomach.

The big man whose shoes he was shining said: "Now I'm gonna tell one." He talked with a Southern drawl and a soft slurring of word-endings like some old colored folks. He had been drinking, too. "This is 'bout a nigger went to see Aunt Hanner one night. . . ."

A roar of laughter greeted his first effort and he was encouraged to tell another.

"Old darky caught a gal on the levee . . ." he commenced.

Sandy finished polishing the shoes and put the cloths inside his wooden box and stood up waiting for his pay, but the speaker did not notice the colored boy until he had finished his tale and laughed heartily with the other men. Then he looked at Sandy. Suddenly he grinned.

"Say, little coon, let's see you hit a step for the boys! . . . Down where I live, folks, all our niggers can dance! . . . Come on, boy, snap it up!"

"I can't," Sandy said, frowning instead of smiling, and growing warm as he stood there in the smoky circle of grinning white men. "I don't know how to dance."

"O, you're one of them stubborn Kansas coons, heh?" said the red-necked fellow disgustedly, the thickness of whisky on his tongue. "You Northern darkies are dumb as hell, anyhow!" Then, turning to the crowd of amused lobby loungers, he announced: "Now down in Mississippi, whar I come from, if you offer a nigger a dime, he'll dance his can off . . . an' they better dance, what I mean!"

He turned to the men around him for approbation, while Sandy still waited uncomfortably to be paid for the shine. But the man kept him standing there, looking at him drunkenly, then at the amused crowd of Saturday-night loungers.

"Now, a nigger his size down South would no more think o' not dancin' if a white man asked him than he would think o' flyin'. This boy's jest tryin' to be smart, that's all. Up here you-all've got darkies spoilt, belicvin' they're somebody. Now, in my home we keep 'em in their places." He again turned his attention to Sandy. "Boy! I want to see you dance!" he commanded.

But Sandy picked up his blacking-box and had begun to push through the circle of chairs, not caring any longer about his pay, when the Southerner rose and grabbed him roughly by the arm, exhaling alcoholic breath in the boy's face as he jokingly pulled him back.

"Com'ere, you little—" but he got no further, for Sandy, strengthened by the anger that suddenly possessed him at the touch of this white man's hand, uttered a yell that could be heard for blocks.

Everyone in the lobby turned to see what had happened, but before Joe Willis got out from behind the clerk's desk, the boy, wriggling free, had reached the street-door. There Sandy turned, raised his boot-black box furiously above his head, and flung it with all his strength at the group of laughing white men in which the drunken Southerner was standing. From one end of the whizzing box a stream of polish-bottles, brushes, and cans fell clattering across the lobby while Sandy disappeared through the door, running as fast as his legs could carry him in the falling snow.

"Hey! You black bastard!" Joe Willis yelled from the hotel entrance, but his voice was blown away in the darkness. As Sandy ran, he felt the snow-flakes falling in his face.

XXI.

NOTE TO HARRIETT

Several days later, when Sandy took out of his pocket the piece of paper that his Aunt Harriett had given him that day in front of the hotel, he noticed that the address written on it was somewhere in the Bottoms. He felt vaguely worried, so he did not show it to his grandmother, because he had often heard her say that the Bottoms was a bad place. And when he was working at the barber-shop, he had heard the men talking about what went on there—and in a sense he knew what they meant.

It was a gay place—people did what they wanted to, or what they had to do, and didn't care—for in the Bottoms folks ceased to struggle against the boundaries between good and bad, or white and black, and surrendered amiably to immorality. Beyond Pearl Street, across the tracks, people of all colors came together for the sake of joy, the curtains being drawn only between themselves and the opposite side of the railroad, where the churches were and the big white Y.M.C.A.

At night in the Bottoms victrolas moaned and banjos cried ecstatically in the darkness. Summer evenings little yellow and brown and black girls in pink or blue bungalow aprons laughed invitingly in doorways, and dice rattled with the staccato gaiety of jazz music on long tables in rear rooms. Pimps played pool; bootleggers lounged in big red cars; children ran in the streets until midnight, with no voice of parental authority forcing them to an early sleep; young blacks fought like cocks and enjoyed it; white boys walked through the streets winking at colored girls: men came in autos; old women ate pigs' feet and water melon and drank beer; whisky flowed; gin was like water; soft indolent laughter didn't care about anything; and deep nigger-throated voices that had long ago stopped rebelling against the ways of this world rose in song.

To those who lived on the other side of the railroad and never realized the utter stupidity of the word "sin," the Bottoms was vile and wicked. But to the girls who lived there, and the boys who pimped and fought and sold licker there, "sin" was a silly word that did not enter their heads. They had never looked at life through the spectacles of the Sunday-School. The glasses good people wore wouldn't have fitted their eyes, for they hung no curtain of words between themselves and reality. To them, things were—what they were.

"Ma bed is hard, but I'm layin' in it jest de same!"

sang the raucous-throated blues-singer in her song;

"Hey! . . . Hey! Who wants to lay with me?"

It was to one of these streets in the Bottoms that Sandy came breathlessly one bright morning with a note in his hand. He knocked at the door of a big grey house.

"Is this where Harriett Williams lives?" he panted.

"You means Harrietta?" said a large, sleek yellow woman in a blue silk kimono who opened the door. "Come in, baby, and sit down. I'll see if she's up yet." Then the woman left Sandy in the parlor while she went up the stairs calling his aunt in a clear, lazy voice.

There were heavy velvet draperies at the windows and doors in this front room where Sandy sat, and a thick, well-worn rug on the floor. There was a divan, a davenport covered with pillows, a center table, and several chairs. Through the curtains at the double door leading into the next room, Sandy saw a piano, more sofas and chairs, and a cleared oiled floor that might be used for dancing. Both rooms were in great disorder, and the air in the house smelled stale and beerish. Licker-bottles and ginger-ale bottles were underneath the center table, underneath the sofas, and on top of the piano. Ash-trays were everywhere, overflowing with cigar-butts and cigarette-ends—on the floor, under chairs, overturned among the sofa-pillows. A small brass tray under one of the sofas held a half-dozen small glasses, some of them still partly full of whisky or gin.

Sandy sat down to wait for his aunt. It was very quiet in the house, although it was almost ten o'clock. A man came down the stairs with his coat on his arm, blinking sleepily. He passed through the hall and out into the street. Bedroom-slippered feet shuffled to the head of the steps on the second floor, and the lazy woman's voice called: "She'll be down in a minute, darling. Just wait there."

Sandy waited. He heard the splash of water above and the hoarse gurgling of a bath-tub being emptied. Presently Harriett appeared in a little pink wash dress such as a child wears, the skirt striking her just above the knees. She smelled like cashmere-bouquet soap, and her face was not yet powdered, nor her hair done up, but she was smiling broadly, happy to see her nephew, as her arms went round his neck.

"My! I'm glad to see you, honey! How'd you happen to come? How'd you find me?"

"Grandma's sick," said Sandy. "She's awful sick and Aunt Tempy sent you this note."

The girl opened the letter. It read:

Your mother is not expected to live. You better come to see her since she has asked for you. Tempy.

"O! . . . Wait a minute," said Harriett softly. "I'll hurry."

Sandy sat down again in the room full of ash-trays and licker-bottles. Many feet pattered upstairs, and, as doors opened and closed, women's voices were heard: "Can I help you, girlie? Can I lend you anything? Does you need a veil?"

When Harriett came down, she was wearing a tan coat-suit and a white turban, pulled tight on her head. Her face was powdered and her lips rouged ever so slightly. The bag she carried was beaded, blue and gold.

"Come on, Sandy," she said. "I guess I'm ready."

As they went out, they heard a man's voice in a shabby house across the street singing softly to a two-finger piano accompaniment:

> *Sugar babe, I'm leavin'*
> *An' it won't be long. . . .*

While outside, on his front door-step, two nappy-headed little yellow kids were solemnly balling-the-jack.

Two days before, Sandy had come home from school and found his grandmother lying across the bed, the full tubs still standing in the kitchen, her clothes not yet hung out to dry.

"What's the matter?" he asked.

"I's washed down, chile," said the old woman, panting. "I feels kinder tired-like, that's all."

But Sandy knew that there must be something else wrong with Aunt Hager, because he had never seen her lying on the bed in broad daylight, with her clothes still in the tubs.

"Does your back ache?" asked the child.

"I does feel a little misery," sighed Aunt Hager. "But seems to be mo' ma side an' not ma back this time. But 'tain't nothin'. I's just tired."

But Sandy was scared. "You want some soda and water, grandma?"

"No, honey." Then, in her usual tones of assumed anger: "Go on away from here an' let a body rest. Ain't I told you they ain't nothin' the matter 'ceptin' I's all washed out an' just got to lay down a minute? Go on an' fetch in yo' wood . . . an' spin yo' top out yonder with Buster and them. Go on!"

It was nearly five o'clock when the boy came in again. Aunt Hager was sitting in the rocker near the stove then, her face drawn and ashy. She had been trying to finish her washing.

"Chile, go get Sister Johnson an' ask her if she can't wring out ma clothes fo' me—Mis' Dunset ain't sent much washin' this week, an' you can help her hang 'em up. I reckon it ain't gonna rain tonight, so's they can dry befo' mawnin'.'"

Sandy ran towards the door.

"Now, don't butt your brains out!" said the old lady. "Ain't no need o' runnin'.'"

Not only did Sister Johnson come at once and hang out the washing, but she made Hager get in bed, with a hot-water bottle on her paining side. And she gave her a big dose of peppermint and water.

"I 'spects it's from yo' stomick," she said. "I knows you et cabbage fo' dinner!"

"Maybe 'tis," said Hager.

Sister Johnson took Sandy to her house for supper that evening and he and Willie-Mae ate five sweet potatoes each.

"You-all gwine bust!" said Tom Johnson.

About nine o'clock the boy went to bed with his grandmother, and all that night Hager tossed and groaned, in spite of her efforts to lie quiet and not keep Sandy awake. In the morning she said: "Son, I reckon you better stay home from school, 'cause I's feelin' mighty po'ly. Seems like that cabbage ain't digested yet. Feels like I done et a stone. . . . Go see if you can't make de fire up an' heat me a cup o' hot water."

About eleven o'clock Madam de Carter came over. "I thought I didn't perceive you nowhere in the yard this morning and the sun 'luminating so bright and cheerful. You ain't indispensed, are you? Sandy said you was kinder ill." She chattered away. "You know it don't look natural not to see you hanging out clothes long before the noon comes."

"I ain't well a-tall this mawnin'," said Hager when she got a chance to speak. "I's feelin' right bad. I suffers with a pain in ma side; seems like it ain't gettin' no better. Sister Johnson just left here from rubbin' it, but I still suffers terrible an' can't eat nothin'. . . . You can use de phone, can't you, Sister Carter?"

"Why, yes! Yes indeed! I oftens phones from over to Mis' Petit's. You think you needs a physicianer?"

In spite of herself a groan came from the old woman's lips as she tried to turn towards her friend. Aunt Hager, who had never moaned for lesser hurts, did not intend to complain over this one—but the pain!

"It's cuttin' me in two." She gasped. "Send fo' old Doc McDillors an' he'll come."

Madam de Carter, proud and important at the prospect of using her white neighbor's phone, rushed away.

"I didn't know you were so sick, grandma!" Sandy's eyes were wide with fright and sympathy. "I'm gonna get Mis' Johnson to come rub you again."

"O! . . . O, ma Lawd, help!" Alone for a moment with no one to hear her, she couldn't hold back the moans any longer. A cold sweat stood on her forehead.

The doctor came—the kind old white man who had known Hager for years and in whom she had faith.

"Well," he said, "it's quite a surprise to see you in bed, Aunty." Then, looking very serious and professional, he took her pulse.

"Go out and close the door," he said gently to Madam de Carter and Sister Johnson, Willie-Mae and Sandy, all of whom had gathered around the bed in the little room. "Somebody heat some water." He turned back the quilts from the woman's body and unbuttoned her gown.

Ten minutes later he said frankly, but with great kindness in his tones: "You're a sick woman, Hager, a very sick woman."

That afternoon Tempy came, like a stranger to the house, and took charge of things. Sandy felt uncomfortable and shy in her presence. This aunt of his had a hard, cold, correct way of talking that resembled Mrs. Rice's manner of speaking to his mother when Annjee used to work there. But Tempy quickly put the house in order, bathed her mother, and spread the bed with clean sheets and a white counterpane. Before evening, members of Hager's Lodge began to drop in bringing soups and custards. White people of the neighborhood stopped, too, to inquire if there was anything they could do for the old woman who had so often waited on them in their illnesses. About six o'clock old man Logan drove up the alley and tied his white mule to the back fence.

The sun was setting when Tempy called Sandy in from the back yard, where he was chopping wood for the stove. She said: "James"—how queerly his correct name struck his ears as it fell from the lips of this cold aunt!—"James, you had better send this telegram to your mother. Now, here is a dollar bill and you can bring back the change. Look on her last letter and get the correct address."

Sandy took the written sheet of paper and the money that his aunt gave him. Then he looked through the various drawers in the house for his mother's last letter. It had been nearly a month since they had heard from her, but finally the boy found the letter in the cupboard, under a jelly-glass full of small coins that his grandmother kept there. He carried the envelope with him to the telegraph office, and there he paid for a message to Annjee in Detroit:

Mother very sick, come at once. Tempy.

As the boy walked home in the gathering dusk, he felt strangely alone in the world, as though Aunt Hager had already gone away, and when he reached the house, it was full of lodge members who had come to keep watch. Tempy went home, but Sister Johnson remained in the sick-room, changing the hot-water bottles and administering, every three hours, the medicine the doctor had left.

There were so many people in the house that Sandy came out into the back yard and sat down on the edge of the well. It was cool and clear, and a slit of moon rode in a light-blue sky spangled with stars. Soon the apple-trees would bud and the grass would be growing. Sandy was a big boy. When his next birthday came, he would be fourteen, and he had begun to grow tall and heavy. Aunt Hager said she was going to buy him a pair of long pants this coming summer. And his mother would hardly know him when she saw him again, if she ever came home.

Tonight, inside, there were so many old sisters from the lodge

that Sandy couldn't even talk to his grandmother while she lay
in bed. They were constantly going in and out of the sick-room,
drinking coffee in the kitchen, or gossiping in the parlor. He
wished they would all go away. He could take care of his grandmother himself until she got well—he and Sister Johnson. They
didn't even need Tempy, who, he felt, shouldn't be there, because he didn't like her.

"They callin' you inside," Willie-Mae came out to tell him
as he sat by himself in the cold on the edge of the well. She was
taller than Sandy now and had a regular job taking care of a
white lady's baby. She no longer wore her hair in braids. She
did it up, and she had a big leather pocket-book that she carried on her arm like a woman. Boys came to take her to the
movies on Saturday nights. "They want you inside."

Sandy got up, his legs stiff and numb, and went into the
kitchen. An elderly brown woman, dressed in black silk that
swished as she moved, opened the door to Hager's bedroom
and whispered to him loudly: "Be quiet, chile."

Sandy entered between a lane of old women. Hager looked
up at him and smiled—so grave and solemn he appeared.

"Is they takin' care o' you?" she asked weakly. "Ain't it bedtime, honey? Is you had something to eat? Come on an' kiss yo'
old grandma befo' you go to sleep. She'll be better in de mawnin'."

She couldn't seem to lift her head, so Sandy sat down on the
bed and kissed her. All he said was: "I'm all right, grandma,"
because there were so many old women in there that he
couldn't talk. Then he went out into the other room.

The air in the house was close and stuffy and the boy soon became groggy with sleep. He fell across the bed that had been
Annjee's, and later Dogberry's, with all his clothes on. One of
the lodge women in the room said: "You better take off yo'
things, chile, an' go to sleep right." Then she said to the other sisters: "Come on in de kitchen, you-all, an' let this chile go to bed."

In the morning Tempy woke him. "Are you sure you had
Annjee's address correct last night?" she demanded. "The telegraph office says she couldn't be found, so the message was
not delivered. Let me see the letter."

Sandy found the letter again, and the address was verified.

"Well, that's strange," said Tempy. "I suppose, as careless and irresponsible as Jimboy is, they've got it wrong, or else moved. . . . Do you know where Harriett can be? I don't suppose you do, but mother has been calling for her all night. I suppose we'll have to try to get her, wherever she is."

"I got her address," said Sandy. "She wrote it down for me when I was working at the hotel this winter. I can find her."

"Then I'll give you a note," said Tempy. "Take it to her."

So Sandy went to the big grey house in the Bottoms that morning to deliver Tempy's message, before the girls there had risen from their beds.

XXII.

BEYOND THE JORDAN

During the day the lodge members went to their work in the various kitchens and restaurants and laundries of the town. And Madam de Carter was ordered to Tulsa, Oklahoma, where a split in her organization was threatened because of the elections of the grand officers. Hager was resting easy, no pain now, but very weak.

"It's only a matter of time," said the doctor. "Give her the medicine so she won't worry, but it does no good. There's nothing we can do."

"She's going to die!" Sandy thought.

Harriett sat by the bedside holding her mother's hand as the afternoon sunlight fell on the white spread. Hager had been glad to see the girl again, and the old woman held nothing against her daughter for no longer living at home.

"Is you happy, chile?" Hager asked. "You looks so nice. Yo' clothes is right purty. I hopes you's findin' what you wants in life. You's young, honey, an' you needs to be happy. . . . Sandy!" She called so weakly that he could hardly hear her, though he was standing at the head of the bed. "Sandy, look in that drawer, chile, under ma night-gowns an' things, an' hand me that there little box you sees down in de corner."

The child found it and gave it to her, a small, white box from a cheap jeweller's. It was wrapped carefully in a soft handkerchief. The old woman took it eagerly and tried to hold it out towards her daughter. Harriett unwound the handkerchief and opened the lid of the box. Then she saw that it

contained the tiny gold watch that her mother had given her
on her sixteenth birthday, which she had pawned months ago
in order to run away with the carnival. Quick tears came to
the girl's eyes.

"I got it out o' pawn fo' you," Hager said, " 'cause I wanted
you to have it fo' yo'self, chile. You know yo' mammy bought
it fo' you."

It was such a little watch! Old-timy, with a breastpin on it.
Harriett quickly put her handkerchief over her wrist to hide
the flashy new timepiece she was wearing on a gold bracelet.

That night Hager died. The undertakers came at dawn with
their wagon and carried the body away to embalm it. Sandy
stood on the front porch looking at the morning star as the
clatter of the horses' hoofs echoed in the street. A sleepy young
white boy was driving the undertaker's wagon, and the horse
that pulled it was white.

The women who had been sitting up all night began to go
home now to get their husbands' breakfasts and to prepare to
go to work themselves.

"It's Wednesday," Sandy thought. "Today I'm supposed to
go get Mrs. Reinhart's clothes, but grandma's dead. I guess I
won't get them now. There's nobody to wash them."

Sister Johnson called him to the kitchen to drink a cup of coffee. Harriett was there weeping softly. Tempy was inside busily
cleaning the room from which they had removed the body. She
had opened all the windows and was airing the house.

Out in the yard a rooster flapped his wings and crowed
shrilly at the rising sun. The fire crackled, and the coffee boiling sent up a fragrant aroma. Sister Johnson opened a can of
condensed milk by punching it with the butcher-knife. She put
some cups and saucers on the table.

"Tempy, won't you have some?"

"No, thank you, Mrs. Johnson," she called from the dead
woman's bedroom.

When Aunt Hager was brought back to her house, she was
in a long box covered with black plush. They placed it on a

folding stand by the window in the front room. There was a crepe on the door, and the shades were kept lowered, and people whispered in the house as though someone were asleep. Flowers began to be delivered by boys on bicycles, and the lodge members came to sit up again that night. The time was set for burial, and the *Daily Leader* carried this paragraph in small type on its back page:

> Hager Williams, aged colored laundress of 419 Cypress Street, passed away at her home last night. She was known and respected by many white families in the community. Three daughters and a grandson survive.

They tried again to reach Annjee in Detroit by telegram, but without success. On the afternoon of the funeral it was cold and rainy. The little Baptist Church was packed with people. The sisters of the lodge came in full regalia, with banners and insignia, and the brothers turned out with them. Hager's coffin was banked with flowers. There were many fine pieces from the families for whom she had washed and from the white neighbors she had nursed in sickness. There were offerings, too, from Tempy's high-toned friends and from Harriett's girl companions in the house in the Bottoms. Many of the bell-boys, porters, and bootleggers sent wreaths and crosses with golden letters on them: "At Rest in Jesus," "Beyond the Jordan," or simply: "Gone Home." There was a bouquet of violets from Buster's mother and a blanket of roses from Tempy herself. They were all pretty, but, to Sandy, the perfume was sickening in the close little church.

The Baptist minister preached, but Tempy had Father Hill from her church to say a few words, too. The choir sang *Shall We Meet Beyond the River?* People wept and fainted. The services seemed interminable. Then came the long drive to the cemetery in horse-drawn hacks, with a few automobiles in line behind. In at the wide gates and through a vast expanse of tombstones the procession passed, across the graveyard, towards the far, lonesome corner where most of the Negroes rested. There Sandy saw the open grave. Then he saw the casket going down . . . down . . . down, into the earth.

The boy stood quietly between his Aunt Tempy and his Aunt Harriett at the edge of the grave while Tempy stared straight ahead into the drizzling rain, and Harriett cried, streaking the powder on her cheeks.

"That's all right, mama," Harriett sobbed to the body in the long, black box. "You won't get lonesome out here. Harrie'll come back tomorrow. Harrie'll come back every day and bring you flowers. You won't get lonesome, mama."

They were throwing wet dirt on the coffin as the mourners walked away through the sticky clay towards their carriages. Some old sister at the grave began to sing:

> *Dark was the night,*
> *Cold was the ground . . .*

in a high weird monotone. Others took it up, and, as the mourners drove away, the air was filled with the minor wailing of the old women. Harriett was wearing Hager's gift, the little gold watch, pinned beneath her coat.

When they got back to the house where Aunt Hager had lived for so long, Sister Johnson said the mail-man had left a letter under the door that afternoon addressed to the dead woman. Harriett was about to open it when Tempy took it from her. It was from Annjee.

"Dear mama," it began.

We have moved to Toledo because Jimboy thought he would do better here and the reason I haven't written, we have been so long getting settled. I have been out of work but we both got jobs now and maybe I will be able to send you some money soon. I hope you are well, ma, and all right. Kiss Sandy for me and take care of yourself. With love and God's blessings from your daughter,

ANNJEE

Tempy immediately turned the letter over and wrote on the back:

We buried your mother today. I tried to reach you in Detroit, but could not get you, since you were no longer there and neglected to send us your new address. It is too bad you weren't here for the funeral. Your child is going to stay with me until I hear from you.

TEMPY

Then she turned to the boy, who stood dazed beside Sister Johnson in the silent, familiar old house. "You will come home with me, James," she said. "We'll see that this place is locked first. You try all the windows and I'll fasten the doors; then we'll go out the front. . . . Mrs. Johnson, it's been good of you to help us in our troubles. Thank you."

Sister Johnson went home, leaving Harriett in the parlor. When Sandy and Tempy returned from locking the back windows and doors, they found the girl still standing there, and for a moment the two sisters looked at one another in silence. Then Tempy said coldly: "We're going."

Harriett went out alone into the drizzling rain. Tempy tried the parlor windows to be sure they were well fastened; then, stepping outside on the porch, she locked the door and put the key in her bag.

"Come on," she said.

Sandy looked up and down the street, but in the thick twilight of fog and rain Harriett had disappeared, so he followed his aunt into the waiting cab. As the hack clattered off, the boy gave an involuntary shiver.

"Do you want to hold my hand?" Tempy asked, unbending a little.

"No," Sandy said. So they rode in silence.

XXIII.

TEMPY'S HOUSE

"James, you must get up on time in this house. Breakfast has been ready twenty minutes. I can't come upstairs every morning to call you. You are old enough now to wake yourself and you must learn to do so—you've too far to walk to school to lie abed."

Sandy tumbled out. Tempy left the room so that he would be free to dress, and soon he came downstairs to breakfast.

He had never had a room of his own before. He had never even slept in a room alone, but here his aunt had given him a small chamber on the second floor which had a window that looked out into a tidy back yard where there was a brick walk running to the back gate. The room, which was very clean, contained only the bed, one chair, and a dresser. There was, too, a little closet in which to hang clothes, but Sandy did not have many to put in it.

The thing that impressed him most about the second floor was the bathroom. He had never lived where there was running water indoors. And in this room, too, everything was so spotlessly clean that Sandy was afraid to move lest he disturb something or splash water on the wall.

When he came downstairs for breakfast, he found the table set for two. Mr. Siles, being in the railway postal service, was out on a trip. The grapefruit was waiting as Sandy slid shyly into his place opposite the ash-brown woman who had become his guardian since his grandma's death. She bowed her head to say a short grace; then they ate.

"Have you been accustomed to drinking milk in the mornings?" Tempy asked as they were finishing the meal. "If you have, the milkman can leave another bottle. Young people should have plenty of milk."

"Yes'm, I'd like it, but we only had coffee at home."

"You needn't say 'yes'm' in this house. We are not used to slavery talk here. If you like milk, I'll get it for you. . . . Now, how are your clothes? I see your stocking has a hole in it, and one pants-leg is hanging."

"It don't stay fastened."

"It *doesn't*, James! I'll buy you some more pants tomorrow. What else do you need?"

Sandy told her, and in a few days she took him to Wertheimer's, the city's largest store, and outfitted him completely. And, as they shopped, she informed him that she was the only colored woman in town who ran a bill there.

"I want white people to know that Negroes have a little taste; that's why I always trade at good shops. . . . And if you're going to live with me, you'll have to learn to do things right, too."

The tearful letter that came from Annjee when she heard of her mother's death said that Toledo was a very difficult place to get work in, and that she had no money to send railroad fare for Sandy, but that she would try to send for him as soon as she could. Jimboy was working on a lake steamer and was seldom home, and she couldn't have Sandy with her anyway until they got a nicer place to stay; so would Tempy please keep him a little while?

By return post Tempy replied that if Annjee had any sense, she would let Sandy remain in Stanton, where he could get a good education, and not be following after his worthless father all over the country. Mr. Siles and she had no children, and Sandy seemed like a quiet, decent child, smart in his classes. Colored people needed to encourage talent so that the white race would realize Negroes weren't all mere guitar-players and house-maids. And Sandy could be a credit if he were raised right. Of course, Tempy knew he hadn't had the correct environment to begin with—living with Jimboy and

Harriett and going to a Baptist church, but undoubtedly he could be trained. He was young. "And I think it would be only fair to the boy that you let him stay with us, because, Annjee, you are certainly not the person to bring him up as he should be reared." The letter was signed: "Your sister, Tempy," and written properly with pen and ink.

So it happened that Sandy came to live with Mr. and Mrs. Arkins Siles, for that was the name by which his aunt and uncle were known in the Negro society of the town. Mr. Siles was a mail-clerk on the railroad—a position that colored people considered a high one because you were working for "Uncle Sam." He was a paste-colored man of forty-eight who had inherited three houses from his father.

Tempy, when she married, had owned houses too, one of which had been willed her by Mrs. Barr-Grant, for whom she had worked for years as personal maid. She had acquired her job while yet in high school, and Mrs. Barr-Grant, who travelled a great deal in the interest of woman suffrage and prohibition, had taken Tempy east with her. On their return to Stanton she allowed the colored maid to take charge of her home, where she also employed a cook and a parlor girl. Thus was the mistress left free to write pamphlets and prepare lectures on the various evils of the world standing in need of correction.

Tempy pleased Mrs. Barr-Grant by being prompt and exact in obeying orders and by appearing to worship her Puritan intelligence. In truth Tempy did worship her mistress, for the colored girl found that by following Mrs. Barr-Grant's early directions she had become an expert housekeeper; by imitating her manner of speech she had acquired a precise flow of language; and by reading her books she had become interested in things that most Negro girls never thought about. Several times the mistress had remarked to her maid: "You're so smart and such a good, clean, quick little worker, Tempy, that it's too bad you aren't white." And Tempy had taken this to heart, not as an insult, but as a compliment.

When the white lady died, she left one of her small houses to her maid as a token of appreciation for faithful services. By dint of saving, and of having resided with her mistress where there had been no living expenses, Tempy had managed to buy another house, too. When Mr. Siles asked her to be his wife, everybody said it was a fine match, for both owned property, both were old enough to know what they wanted, and both were eminently respectable. . . . Now they prospered together.

Tempy no longer worked out, but stayed home, keeping house, except that she went each month to collect her rents and those of her husband. She had a woman to do the laundry and help with the cleaning, but Tempy herself did the cooking, and all her meals were models of economical preparation. Just enough food was prepared each time for three people. Sandy never had a third helping of dessert in her house. No big pots of black-eyed peas and pigtails scented her front hall, either. She got her recipes from *The Ladies' Home Journal*—and she never bought a watermelon.

White people were for ever picturing colored folks with huge slices of watermelon in their hands. Well, she was one colored woman who did not like them! Her favorite fruits were tangerines and grapefruit, for Mrs. Barr-Grant had always eaten those, and Tempy had admired Mrs. Barr-Grant more than anybody else—more, of course, than she had admired Aunt Hager, who spent her days at the wash-tub, and had loved watermelon.

Colored people certainly needed to come up in the world, Tempy thought, up to the level of white people—dress like white people, talk like white people, think like white people— and then they would no longer be called "niggers."

In Tempy this feeling was an emotional reaction, born of white admiration, but in Mr. Siles, who shared his wife's views, the same attitude was born of practical thought. The whites had the money, and if Negroes wanted any, the quicker they learned to be like the whites, the better. Stop being lazy, stop singing all the time, stop attending revivals, and learn to get the dollar—because money buys everything, even the respect of white people.

Blues and spirituals Tempy and her husband hated because they were too Negro. In their house Sandy dared not sing a word of *Swing Low, Sweet Chariot*, for what had darky slave songs to do with respectable people? And rag-time belonged in the Bottoms with the sinners. (It was ironically strange that the Bottoms should be the only section of Stanton where Negroes and whites mingled freely on equal terms.) That part of town, according to Tempy, was lost to God, and the fact that she had a sister living there burned like a hidden cancer in her breast. She never mentioned Harriett to anyone.

Tempy's friends were all people of standing in the darker world—doctors, school-teachers, a dentist, a lawyer, a hairdresser. And she moved among these friends as importantly as Mrs. Barr-Grant had moved among a similar group in the white race. Many of them had had wash-women for mothers and day-laborers for fathers; but none ever spoke of that. And while Aunt Hager lived, Tempy, after getting her position with Mrs. Barr-Grant, was seldom seen with the old woman. After her marriage she was even more ashamed of her family connections—a little sister running wild, and another sister married for the sake of love—Tempy could never abide Jimboy, or understand why Annjee had taken up with a rounder from the South. One's family as a topic of conversation, however, was not popular in high circles, for too many of Stanton's dark society folks had sprung from humble family trees and low black bottoms.

"But back in Washington, where I was born," said Mrs. Doctor Mitchell once, "we really have blood! All the best people at the capital come from noted ancestry—Senator Bruce, John M. Langston, Governor Pinchback, Frederick Douglass. Why, one of our colored families on their white side can even trace its lineage back to George Washington! . . . O, yes, we have a background! But, of course, we are too refined to boast about it."

Tempy thought of her mother then and wished that black Aunt Hager had not always worn her apron in the streets, uptown and everywhere! Of course, it was clean and white and

seemed to suit the old lady, but aprons weren't worn by the
best people. When Tempy was in the hospital for an operation
shortly after her marriage, they wouldn't let Hager enter by
the front door—and Tempy never knew whether it was on account of her color or the apron! The Presbyterian Hospital
was prejudiced against Negroes and didn't like them to use the
elevator, but certainly her mother should not have come there
in an apron!

Well, Aunt Hager had meant well, Tempy thought, even if
she didn't dress right. And now this child, Sandy—James was
his correct name! At that first breakfast they ate together, she
asked him if he had a comb and brush of his own.

"No'm, I ain't," said Sandy.

"I haven't," she corrected him. "I certainly don't want my
white neighbors to hear you saying 'ain't' . . . You've come to
live with me now and you must talk like a gentleman."

XXIV

A SHELF OF BOOKS

That spring, shortly after Sandy went to stay with Tempy, there was an epidemic of mumps among the school-children in Stanton, and, old as he was, he was among its early victims. With jaws swollen to twice their normal size and a red sign, MUMPS, on the house, he was forced to remain at home for three weeks. It was then that the boy began to read books other than the ones he had had to study for his lessons. At Aunt Hager's house there had been no books, anyway, except the Bible and the few fairytales that he had been given at Christmas; but Tempy had a case full of dusty volumes that were used to give dignity to her sitting-room: a row of English classics bound in red, an *Encyclopedia of World Knowledge* in twelve volumes, a book on household medicine full of queer drawings, and some modern novels—*The Rosary, The Little Shepherd of Kingdom Come*, the newest Harold Bell Wright, and all that had ever been written by Gene Stratton Porter, Tempy's favorite author. The Negro was represented by Chestnut's *House Behind the Cedars*, and the *Complete Poems* of Paul Lawrence Dunbar, whom Tempy tolerated on account of his fame, but condemned because he had written so much in dialect and so often of the lower classes of colored people. Tempy subscribed to *Harper's Magazine*, too, because Mrs. Barr-Grant had taken it. And in her sewing-room closet there was also a pile of *The Crisis*, the thin Negro monthly that she had been taking from the beginning of its publication.

Sandy had heard of that magazine, but he had never seen a copy; so he went through them all, looking at the pictures of prominent Negroes and reading about racial activities all over the country, and about racial wrongs in the South. In every issue he found, too, stirring and beautifully written editorials about the frustrated longings of the black race, and the hidden beauties in the Negro soul. A man named Du Bois wrote them.

"Dr. William Edward Burghardt Du Bois," said Tempy, "and he is a great man."

"Great like Booker T. Washington?" asked Sandy.

"Teaching Negroes to be servants, that's all Washington did!" Tempy snorted in so acid a tone that Sandy was silent. "Du Bois wants our rights. He wants us to be real men and women. He believes in social equality. But Washington—huh!" The fact that he had established an industrial school damned Washington in Tempy's eyes, for there were enough colored workers already. But Du Bois was a doctor of philosophy and had studied in Europe! . . . That's what Negroes needed to do, get smart, study books, go to Europe! "Don't talk to me about Washington," Tempy fumed. "Take Du Bois for your model, not some white folks' nigger."

"Well, Aunt Hager said—" then Sandy stopped. His grandmother had thought that Booker T. was the greatest of men, but maybe she had been wrong. Anyway, this Du Bois could write! Gee, it made you burn all over to read what he said about a lynching. But Sandy did not mention Booker Washington again to Tempy, although, months later, at the library he read his book called *Up from Slavery*, and he was sure that Aunt Hager hadn't been wrong. "I guess they are both great men," he thought.

Sandy's range of reading increased, too, when his aunt found a job for him that winter in Mr. Prentiss's gift-card- and printing-shop, where he kept the place clean and acted as delivery boy. This shop kept a shelf of current novels and some volumes of the new poetry—Sandburg, Lindsay, Masters—which the Young Women's Club of Stanton was then studying, to the shocked horror of the older white ladies of the town. Sandy knew of this because Mr. Prentiss's daughter, a student at Goucher College, used to keep shop and she pointed out volumes for the boy to read and told him who their authors were and what the books meant. She said that none of the colored boys they had employed before had ever been interested in reading; so she often lent him, by way of encouragement, shopworn copies to be taken home at night and returned the next day. Thus Sandy spent much of his first year with Tempy deep in novels too mature for a fourteen-year-old boy. But Tempy was very proud of her studious young nephew. She began to decide that she had made no mistake in keeping him with her, and when he entered the high school, she bought him his first long-trouser suit as a spur towards further application.

Sandy became taller week by week, and it seemed to Tempy as if his shirt-sleeves became too short for him overnight. His voice was changing, too, and he had acquired a liking for football, but his after-school job at Prentiss's kept him from playing much. At night he read, or sometimes went to the movies with Buster—but Tempy kept him home as much as she could. Occasionally he saw Willie-Mae, who was keeping company with the second cook at Wright's Hotel. And sometimes he saw Jimmy Lane, who was a bell-hop now and hung out with a sporty crowd in the rear room of Cudge Windsor's pool hall. But whenever Sandy went into his old neighborhood, he felt sad, remembering Aunt Hager and his mother, and Jimboy, and Harriett—for his young aunt had gone away from Stanton, too, and the last he heard about her rumored that she was on the stage in Kansas City. Now the little house where Sandy had lived with his grandmother belonged to Tempy, who kept it rented to a family of strangers.

In high school Sandy was taking, at his aunt's request, the classical course, which included Latin, ancient history, and English, and which required a great deal of reading. His teacher of English was a large, masculine woman named Martha Fry, who had once been to Europe and who loved to talk about the splendors of old England and to read aloud in a deep, mannish kind of voice, dramatizing the printed words. It was from her that Sandy received an introduction to Shakespeare, for in the spring term they studied *The Merchant of*

Venice. In the spring also, under Miss Fry's direction, the first-year students were required to write an essay for the freshman essay prizes of both money and medals. And in this contest Sandy won the second prize. It was the first time in the history of the school that a colored pupil had ever done anything of the sort, and Tempy was greatly elated. There was a note in the papers about it, and Sandy brought his five dollars home for his aunt to put away. But he gave his bronze medal to a girl named Pansetta Young, who was his class-mate and a new-found friend.

From the first moment in school that he saw Pansetta, he knew that he liked her, and he would sit looking at her for hours in every class that they had together—for she was a little baby-doll kind of girl, with big black eyes and a smooth pinkish-brown skin, and her hair was curly on top of her head. Her widowed mother was a cook at the Goucher College dining-hall; and she was an all-alone little girl, for Pansetta had no brothers or sisters. After Thanksgiving Sandy began to walk part of the way home with her every day. He could not accompany her all the way because he had to go to work at Mr. Prentiss's shop. But on Christmas he bought her a box of candy—and sent it to her by mail. And at Easter-time she gave him a chocolate egg.

"Unh-huh! You got a girl now, ain't you?" teased Buster one April afternoon when he caught Sandy standing in front of the high school waiting for Pansetta to come out.

"Aw, go chase yourself!" said Sandy, for Buster had a way of talking dirty about girls, and Sandy was afraid he would begin that with Pansetta; but today his friend changed the subject instead.

"Say come on round to the pool hall tonight and I'll teach you to play billiards."

"Don't think I'd better, Bus. Aunt Tempy might get sore," Sandy replied, shaking his head. "Besides, I have to study."

"Are you gonna read yourself to death?" Buster demanded indignantly. "You've got to come out some time, man! Tell her you're going to the movies and we'll go down to Cudge's instead."

Sandy thought for a moment.

"All the boys come round there at night."

"Well, I might."

"Little apron-string boy!" teased Buster.

"If I hit you a couple of times, you'll find out I'm not!" Sandy doubled up his fists in pretended anger. "I'll black your blue eyes for you!"

"Ya-a-a-a?" yelled his friend, running up the street. "See you tonight at Cudge's—apron-string boy!"

And that evening Sandy didn't finish reading, as he had planned, *Moby Dick*, which Mr. Prentiss's daughter had lent him. Instead he practised handling a cue-stick under the tutelage of Buster.

XXV.

POOL HALL

There were no community houses in Stanton and no recreation centers for young men except the Y.M.C.A., which was closed to you if you were not a white boy; so, for the Negro youths of the town, Cudge Windsor's pool hall was the evening meeting-place. There one could play billiards, shoot dice in a back room, or sit in summer on the two long benches outside, talking and looking at the girls as they passed. In good weather these benches were crowded all the time.

Next door to the pool hall was Cudge Windsor's lunch-room. Of course, the best colored people did not patronize Cudge's, even though his business was not in the Bottoms. It was located on Pearl Street, some three or four blocks before that thoroughfare plunged across the tracks into the low terrain of tinkling pianos and ladies who loved for cash. But since Cudge catered to what Mr. Siles called "the common element," the best people stayed away.

After months of bookishness and subjection to Tempy's prim plans for his improvement, Sandy found the pool hall an easy and amusing place in which to pass time. It was better than the movies, where people on the screen were only shadows. And it was much better than the Episcopal Church, with its stoop-shouldered rector, for here at Cudge's everybody was alive, and the girls who passed in front swinging their arms and grinning at the men were warm-bodied and gay, while the boys rolling dice in the rear room or playing pool at the tables were loud-mouthed and careless. Life sat easily on their muscular shoulders.

Adventurers and vagabonds who passed through Stanton on the main line would often drop in at Cudge's to play a game or get a bite to eat, and many times on summer nights reckless black boys, a long way from home, kept the natives entertained with tales of the road, or trips on side-door Pullmans, and of far-off cities where things were easy and women generous. They had a song that went:

> O, the gals in Texas,
> They never be's unkind.
> They feeds their men an'
> Buys 'em gin an' wine.
> But these women in Stanton,
> Their hearts is hard an' cold.
> When you's out of a job, they
> Denies you jelly roll.

Then, often, arguments would begin—boastings, proving and fending; or telling of exploits with guns, knives, and razors, with cops and detectives, with evil women and wicked men; out-bragging and out-lying one another, all talking at once. Sometimes they would create a racket that could be heard for blocks. To the uninitiated it would seem that a fight was imminent. But underneath, all was good-natured and friendly—and through and above everything went laughter. No matter how belligerent or lewd their talk was, or how sordid the tales they told—of dangerous pleasures and strange perversities—these black men laughed. That must be the reason, thought Sandy, why poverty-stricken old Negroes like Uncle Dan Givens lived so long— because to them, no matter how hard life might be, it was not without laughter.

Uncle Dan was the world's champion liar, Cudge Windsor said, and the jolly old man's unending flow of fabulous reminiscences were entertaining enough to earn him a frequent meal in Cudge's lunch-room or a drink of licker from the patrons of the pool hall, who liked to start the old fellow talking.

One August evening when Tempy was away attending a

POOL HALL   191

convention of the Midwest Colored Women's Clubs, Sandy
and Buster, Uncle Dan, Jimmy Lane, and Jap Logan sat until
late with a big group of youngsters in front of the pool hall
watching the girls go by. A particularly pretty high yellow
damsel passed in a thin cool dress of flowered voile, trailing
the sweetness of powder and perfume behind her.

"Dog-gone my soul!" yelled Jimmy Lane. "Just gimme a
bone and lemme be your dog—I mean your salty dog!" But
the girl, pretending not to hear, strolled leisurely on, followed
by a train of compliments from the pool-hall benches.

"Sweet mama Venus!" cried a tall raw-bony boy, gazing
after her longingly.

"If angels come like that, lemme go to heaven—and if they
don't, lemme be lost to glory!" Jap exclaimed.

"Shut up, Jap! What you know 'bout women?" asked Uncle
Dan, leaning forward on his cane to interrupt the comments.
"Here you-all is, ain't knee-high to ducks yit, an' talkin' 'bout
womens! Shut up, all o' you! Nary one o' you's past sebenteen,
but when I were yo' age—Hee! Hee! You-all want to know
what dey called me when I were yo' age?" The old man
warmed to his tale. "Dey called me de 'stud nigger'! Yes, dey
did! On 'count o' de kind o' slavery-time work I was doin'—I
were breedin' babies fo' to sell!"

"Another lie!" said Jap.

"No, 'tain't, boy! You listen here to what I's gwine tell you.
I were de onliest real healthy nigger buck ma white folks had
on de plantation, an' dese was ole po' white folks what can't
'ford to buy many slaves, so dey figures to raise a heap o' darky
babies an' sell 'em later on—dat's why dey made me de
breeder. . . . Hee! Hee! . . . An' I sho breeded a gang o' picka-
ninnies, too! But I were young then, jest like you-all is, an' I
ain't had a pint o' sense—laying wid de womens all night,
ever' night."

"Yes, we believe you," drawled Jimmy.

"An' it warn't no time bef o' little yaller chillens an' black
chillens an' red chillens an' all kinds o' chillens was runnin'
round de yard eatin' out o' de hog-pen an' a-callin' me

pappy. . . . An' here I is today gwine on ninety-three year ole an' I done outlived 'em all. Dat is, I done outlived all I ever were able to keep track on after de war, 'cause we darkies sho scattered once we was free! Yes, sah! But befo' de fightin' ended I done been pappy to forty-nine chillens—an' thirty-three of 'em were boys!"

"Aw, I know you're lying now, Uncle Dan," Jimmy laughed.

"No, I ain't, sah! . . . Hee! Hee! . . . I were a great one when I were young! Yes, sah!" The old man went on undaunted. "I went an' snuck off to a dance one night, me an' nudder boy, went 'way ovah in Macon County at ole man Laird's plantation, who been a bitter enemy to our white folks. Did I ever tell you 'bout it? We took one o' ole massa's best hosses out de barn to ride, after he done gone to his bed. . . . Well, sah! It were late when we got started, an' we rid dat hoss lickety-split uphill an' down holler, ovah de crick an' past de mill, me an' ma buddy both on his back, through de cane-brake an' up an' nudder hill, till he wobble an' foam at de mouth like he's 'bout to drap. When we git to de dance, long 'bout midnight, we jump off dis hoss an' ties him to a post an' goes in de cabin whar de music were—an' de function were gwine on big. Man! We grabs ourselves a gal an' dance till de moon riz, kickin' up our heels an' callin' figgers, an' jest havin' a scrumptious time. Ay, Lawd! We sho did dance! . . . Well, come 'long 'bout two o'clock in de mawnin', niggers all leavin', an' we goes out in de yard to git on dis hoss what we had left standin' at de post. . . . An' Lawd have mercy—de hoss were dead! Yes, sah! He done fell down right whar he were tied, eyeballs rolled back, mouth a-foamin', an' were stone-dead! . . . Well, we ain't knowed how we gwine git home ner what we gwine do 'bout massa's hoss—an' we was skeered, Lawdy! 'Cause we know he beat us to death if he find out we done rid his best hoss anyhow—let lone ridin' de crittur to death. . . . An' all de low-down Macon niggers what was at de party was whaw-whawin' fit to kill, laughin' 'cause it were so funny to see us gittin' ready to git on our hoss an' de hoss were dead! . . . Well, sah, me an' ma buddy ain't wasted no time. We took dat animule up by de

hind legs an' we drug him all de way home to massa's plantation befo' day! We sho did! Uphill an' down holler, sixteen
miles! Yes, sah! An' put dat damn hoss back in massa's barn
like he war befo' we left. An' when de sun riz, me an' ma
buddy were in de slavery quarters sleepin' sweet an' lowly-like
as if we ain't been nowhar. . . . De next day old massa 'maze
how dat hoss die all tied up in his stall wid his halter on! An'
we niggers 'maze, too, when we heard dat massa's hoss been
dead, 'cause we ain't knowed a thing 'bout it. No, sah! Ain't
none o' us niggers knowed a thing! Hee! Hee! Not a thing!"

"Weren't you scared?" asked Sandy.

"Sho, we was scared," said Uncle Dan, "but we ain't act like
it. Niggers was smart in them days."

"They're still smart," said Jap Logan, "if they can lie like you."

"I mean!" said Buster.

"Uncle Dan's the world's champeen liar," drawled a tall
lanky boy. "Come on, let's chip in and buy him a sandwich,
'cause he's lied enough fo' one evening."

They soon crowded into the lunch-room and sat on stools at
the counter ordering soda or ice-cream from the fat good-
natured waitress. While they were eating, a gambler bolted in
from the back room of the pool hall with a handful of coins he
had just won.

"Gonna feed ma belly while I got it in ma hand," he shouted.
"Can't tell when I might lose, 'cause de dice is runnin' they own
way tonight. Say, Mattie," he yelled, "tell chef to gimme a beefsteak all beat up like Jim Jeffries, cup o' coffee strong as Jack
Johnson, an' come flyin' like a airship so I can get back in the
game. Tell that kitchen buggar sweet-papa Stingaree's out here!"

"All right, keep yo' collar on," said Mattie. "De steak's got
to be cooked."

"What you want, Uncle Dan?" yelled the gambler to the old
man. "While I's winnin', might as well feed you, too. Take some
ham and cabbage or something. That sandwich ain't 'nough to
fill you up."

Uncle Dan accepted a plate of spareribs, and Stingaree threw
down a pile of nickels on the counter.

"Injuns an' buffaloes," he said loudly. "Two things de white folks done killed, so they puts 'em on de backs o' nickels. . . . Rush up that steak there, gal, I's hongry!"

Sandy finished his drink and bought a copy of the *Chicago Defender*, the World's Greatest Negro Weekly, which was sold at the counter. Across the front in big red letters there was a headline: *Negro Boy Lynched*. There was also an account of a race riot in a Northern industrial city. On the theatrical page a picture of pretty Baby Alice Whitman, the tap-dancer, attracted his attention, and he read a few of the items there concerning colored shows; but as he was about to turn the page, a little article in the bottom corner made him pause and put the paper down on the counter.

ACTRESS MAKES HIT

St. Louis, Mo., Aug. 3: Harrietta Williams, sensational young blues-singer, has been packing the Booker Washington Theatre to the doors here this week. Jones and Jones are the headliners for the all-colored vaudeville bill, but the singing of Miss Williams has been the outstanding drawing card. She is being held over for a continued engagement, with Billy Sanderlee at the piano.

"Billy Sanderlee," said Buster, who was looking over Sandy's shoulder. "That's that freckled-faced yellow guy who used to play for dances around here, isn't it? He could really beat a piano to death, all right!"

"Sure could," replied Sandy. "Gee, they must make a great team together, 'cause my Aunt Harrie can certainly sing and dance!"

"Ain't the only thing she can do!" bellowed the gambler, swallowing a huge chunk of steak. "Yo' Aunt Harrie's a whang, son!"

"Shut yo' mouth!" said Uncle Dan.

XXVI.

THE DOORS OF LIFE

During Sandy's second year at high school Tempy was busy sewing for the local Red Cross and organizing Liberty Bond clubs among the colored population of Stanton. She earnestly believed that the world would really become safe for democracy, even in America, when the war ended, and that colored folks would no longer be snubbed in private and discriminated against in public.

"Colored boys are over there fighting," she said. "Our men are buying hundreds of dollars' worth of bonds, colored women are aiding the Red Cross, our clubs are sending boxes to the camps and to the front. White folks will see that the Negro can be trusted in war as well as peace. Times will be better after this for all of us."

One day a letter came from Annjee, who had moved to Chicago. She said that Sandy's father had not long remained in camp, but had been sent to France almost immediately after he enlisted, and she didn't know what she was going to do, she was so worried and alone! There had been but one letter from Jimboy since he left. And now she needed Sandy with her, but she wasn't able to send for him yet. She said she hoped and prayed that nothing would happen to his father at the front, but every day there were colored soldiers' names on the casualty list.

"Good thing he's gone," grunted Tempy when she read the letter as they were seated at the supper-table. Then, suddenly changing the subject, she asked Sandy: "Did you see Dr. Frank Crane's beautiful article this morning?"

"No, I didn't," said the boy.

"You certainly don't read as much as you did last winter," complained his aunt. "And you're staying out entirely too late to suit me. I'm quite sure you're not at the movies all that time, either. I want these late hours stopped, young man. Every night in the week out somewhere until ten and eleven o'clock!"

"Well, boys do have to get around a little, Tempy," Mr. Siles objected. "It's not like when you and I were coming up."

"I'm raising this boy, Mr. Siles," Tempy snapped. "When do you study, James? That's what I want to know."

"When I come in," said Sandy, which was true. His light was on until after twelve almost every night. And when he did not study late, his old habit of lying awake clung to him and he could not go to sleep early.

"You think too much," Buster once said. "Stop being so smart; then you'll sleep better."

"Yep," added Jimmy Lane. "Better be healthy and dumb than smart and sick like some o' these college darkies I see with goggles on their eyes and breath smellin' bad."

"O, I'm not sick," objected Sandy, "but I just get to thinking about things at night—the war, and white folks, and God, and girls, and—O, I don't know—everything in general."

"Sure, keep on thinking," jeered Buster, "and turn right ashy after while and be all stoop-shouldered like Father Hill." (The Episcopalian rector was said to be the smartest colored man in town.) "But I'm not gonna worry about being smart myself. A few more years, boy, and I'll be in some big town passing for white, making money, and getting along swell. And I won't need to be smart, either—I'll be ofay! So if you see me some time in St. Louis or Chi with a little blond on my arm—don't recognize me, hear! I want my kids to be so yellow-headed they won't have to think about a color line."

And Sandy knew that Buster meant what he said, for his light-skinned friend was one of those people who always go directly towards the things they want, as though the road is straight before them and they can see clearly all the way. But

to Sandy himself nothing ever seemed quite that clear. Why
was his country going stupidly to war? . . . Why were white
people and colored people so far apart? Why was it wrong to
desire the bodies of women? . . . With his mind a maelstrom of
thoughts as he lay in bed night after night unable to go to sleep
quickly, Sandy wondered many things and asked himself many
questions.

Sometimes he would think about Pansetta Young, his class-
mate with the soft brown skin, and the pointed and delicate
breasts of her doll-like body. He had never been alone with
Pansetta, never even kissed her, yet she was "his girl" and he
liked her a great deal. Maybe he loved her! . . . But what did it
mean to love a girl? Were you supposed to marry her then and
live with her for ever? . . . His father had married his mother—
good-natured, guitar-playing Jimboy—but they weren't always together, and Sandy knew that Jimboy was enjoying the
war now, just as he had always enjoyed everything else.

"Gee, he must of married early to be my father and still look
so young!" he thought. "Suppose I marry Pansetta now!" But
what did he really know about marriage other than the dirty
fragments he had picked up from Jimmy and Buster and the
fellows at the pool hall?

On his fifteenth birthday Tempy had given him a book written for young men on the subject of love and living, called *The
Doors of Life*, addressed to all Christian youths in their
teens—but it had been written by a white New England minister of the Presbyterian faith who stood aghast before the flesh;
so its advice consisted almost entirely in how to pray in the or-
thodox manner, and in how *not* to love.

"Avoid evil companions lest they be your undoing (see
Psalms cxix, 115–20); and beware of lewd women, for their
footsteps lead down to hell (see Proverbs vii, 25–7)," said the
book, and that was the extent of its instructions on sex, except
that it urged everyone to marry early and settle down to a
healthy, moral, Christian life. . . . But how could you marry
early when you had no money and no home to which to take a

wife, Sandy wondered. And who were evil companions. Neither Aunt Hager nor Annjee had ever said anything to Sandy
about love in its bodily sense; Jimboy had gone away too soon
to talk with him; and Tempy and her husband were too proper
to discuss such subjects; so the boy's sex knowledge consisted
only in the distorted ideas that youngsters whisper; the dirty
stories heard in the hotel lobby where he had worked; and the
fact that they sold in drugstores articles that weren't mentioned in the company of nice people.

But who were nice people anyway? Sandy hated the word
"nice." His Aunt Tempy was always using it. All of her friends
were nice, she said, respectable and refined. They went around
with their noses in the air and they didn't speak to porters and
wash-women—though they weren't nearly so much fun as the
folks they tried to scorn. Sandy liked Cudge Windsor or Jap
Logan better than he did Dr. Mitchell, who had been to
college—and never forgotten it.

Sandy wondered if Booker T. Washington had been like
Tempy's friends? Or if Dr. Du Bois was a snob just because he
was a college man? He wondered if those two men had a good
time being great. Booker T. was dead, but he had left a living
school in the South. Maybe he could teach in the South, too,
Sandy thought, if he ever learned enough. Did colored folks
need to know the things he was studying in books now? Did
French and Latin and Shakespeare make people wise and
happy? Jap Logan never went beyond the seventh grade and he
was happy. And Jimboy never attended school much either.
Maybe school didn't matter. Yet to get a good job you had to
be smart—and white, too. That was the trouble, you had to
be white!

"But I want to learn!" thought Sandy as he lay awake in the
dark after he had gone to bed at night. "I want to go to college. I want to go to Europe and study. 'Work and make ready
and maybe your chance will come,' it said under the picture of
Lincoln on the calendar given away by the First National
Bank, where Earl, his white friend, already had a job promised
him when he came out of school. . . . It was not nearly so

difficult for white boys. They could work at anything—in stores, on newspapers, in offices. They could become president of the United States if they were clever enough. But a colored boy. . . . No wonder Buster was going to pass for white when he left Stanton.

"I don't blame him," thought Sandy. "Sometimes I hate white people, too, like Aunt Harrie used to say she did. Still, some of them are pretty decent—my English-teacher, and Mr. Prentiss where I work. Yet even Mr. Prentiss wouldn't give me a job clerking in his shop. All I can do there is run errands and scrub the floor when everybody else is gone. There's no advancement for colored fellows. If they start as porters, they stay porters for ever and they can't come up. Being colored is like being born in the basement of life, with the door to the light locked and barred—and the white folks live upstairs. They don't want us up there with them, even when we're respectable like Dr. Mitchell, or smart like Dr. Du Bois. . . . And guys like Jap Logan—well, Jap don't care anyway! Maybe it's best not to care, and stay poor and meek waiting for heaven like Aunt Hager did. . . . But I don't want heaven! I want to live first!" Sandy thought. "I want to live!"

He understood then why many old Negroes said: "Take all this world and give me Jesus!" It was because they couldn't get this world anyway—it belonged to the white folks. They alone had the power to give or withhold at their back doors. Always back doors—even for Tempy and Dr. Mitchell if they chose to go into Wright's Hotel or the New Albert Restaurant. And no door at all for Negroes if they wanted to attend the Rialto Theatre, or join the Stanton Y.M.C.A., or work behind the grilling at the National Bank.

The Doors of Life. . . . God damn that simple-minded book that Tempy had given him! What did an old white minister know about the doors of life for him and Pansetta and Jimmy Lane, for Willie-Mae and Buster and Jap Logan and all the black and brown and yellow youngsters standing on the threshold of the great beginning in a Western town called Stanton? What did an old white minister know about the

doors of life anywhere? And, least of all, the doors to a Negro's life? . . . Black youth. . . . Dark hands knocking, knocking! Pansetta's little brown hands knocking on the doors of
life! Baby-doll hands, tiny autumn-leaf girl-hands! . . . Gee,
Pansetta! . . . The Doors of Life . . . the great big doors. . . .
Sandy was asleep . . . of life.

XXVII.

BEWARE OF WOMEN

"I won't permit it," said Tempy. "I won't stand for it. You'll
have to mend your ways, young man! Spending your evenings
in Windsor's pool parlor and running the streets with a gang
of common boys that have had no raising, that Jimmy Lane
among them. I won't stand for it while you stay in my
house. . . . But that's not the worst of it. Mr. Prentiss tells me
you've been getting to work late after school three times this
week. And what have you been doing? O, don't think I don't
know! I saw you with my own eyes yesterday walking home
with that girl Pansetta Young! . . . Well, I want you to understand that I won't have it!"

"I didn't walk home with her," said Sandy. "I only go part
way with her every day. She's in my class in high school and
we have to talk over our lessons. She's the only colored kid in
my class I have to talk to."

"Lessons! Yes, I know it's lessons," said Tempy sarcasti-
cally. "If she were a girl of our own kind, it would be all right.
I don't see why you don't associate more with the young people of the church. Marie Steward or Grace Mitchell are both
nice girls and you don't notice them. No, you have to take up
with this Pansetta, whose mother works out all day, leaving
her daughter to do as she chooses. Well, she's not going to ruin
you, after all I've done to try to make something out of you."

"Beware of women, son," said Mr. Siles pontifically from
his deep morris-chair. It was one of his few evenings home and
Tempy had asked him to talk to her nephew, who had gotten
beyond her control, for Sandy no longer remained in at night

even when she expressly commanded it; and he no longer attended church regularly, but slept on Sunday mornings instead. He kept up his school-work, it was true, but he seemed
to have lost all interest in acquiring the respectable bearing
and attitude towards life that Tempy thought he should have.
She bought him fine clothes and he went about with ruffians.

"In other words, he has been acting just like a nigger, Mr.
Siles!" she told her husband. "And he's taken up with a girl
who's not of the best, to say the least, even if she does go to the
high school. Mrs. Francis Cannon, who lives near her, tells me
that this Pansetta has boys at her house all the time, and her
mother is never at home until after dark. She's a cook or something somewhere. . . . A fine person for a nephew of ours to associate with, this Pansy daughter of hers!"

"Pansetta's a nice girl," said Sandy. "And she's smart in
school, too. She helps me get my Latin every day, and I might
fail if she didn't."

"Huh! It's little help you need with your Latin, young man!
Bring it here and I'll help you. I had Latin when I was in school.
And certainly you don't need to walk on the streets with her in
order to study Latin, do you? First thing you know you'll be
getting in trouble with her and she'll be having a baby—I see I
have to be plain—and whether it's yours or not, she'll say it is.
Common girls like that always want to marry a boy they think
is going to amount to something—going to college and be
somebody in the world. Besides, you're from the Williams
family and you're good-looking! But I'm going to stop this af-
fair right now. . . . From now on you are to leave that girl
alone, do you understand me? She's dangerous!"

"Yes," grunted Mr. Siles. "She's dangerous."

Angry and confused, Sandy left the room and went upstairs
to bed, but he could not sleep. What right had they to talk that
way about his friends? Besides, what did they mean about her
being dangerous? About his getting in trouble with her? About
her wanting to marry him because her mother was a cook and
he was going to college?

A white boy in Sandy's high-school class had "got in trouble"

with an Italian girl and they had had to go to the juvenile court
to fix it up, but it had been kept quiet. Even now Sandy couldn't
quite give an exact explanation of what getting in trouble with
a girl meant. Did a girl have to have a baby just because a fellow
walked home with her when he didn't even go in? Pansetta had
asked him into her house often, but he always had to go back
uptown to work. He was due at work at four o'clock—besides
he knew it wasn't quite correct to call on a young lady if her
mother was not at home. But it wasn't necessarily bad, was it?
And how could a girl have a baby and say it was his if it wasn't
his? Why couldn't he talk to his Aunt Tempy about such things
and get a clear and simple answer instead of being given an old
book like *The Doors of Life* that didn't explain anything at all?

Pansetta hadn't said a word to him about babies, or anything like that, but she let him kiss her once and hold her on
his lap at Sadie Butler's Christmas party. Gee, but she could
kiss—and such a long time! He wouldn't care if she did make
him marry her, only he wanted to travel first. If his mother
would send for him now, he would like to go to Chicago. His
Aunt Tempy was too cranky, and too proper. She didn't like
any of his friends, and she hated the pool hall. But where else
was there for a fellow to play? Who wanted to go to those
high-toned people's houses, like the Mitchells', and look bored
all the time while they put Caruso's Italian records on their
new victrola? Even if it was the finest victrola owned by a
Negro in Stanton, as they always informed you, Sandy got
tired of listening to records in a language that none of them
understood.

"But this is opera!" they said. Well, maybe it was, but he
thought that his father and Harriett used to sing better. And
they sang nicer songs. One of them was:

> Love, O love, O careless love—
> Goes to your head like wine!

"And maybe I really am in love with Pansetta. . . . But if she
thinks she can fool me into marrying her before I've travelled

all around the world, like my father, she's wrong," Sandy thought. "She can't trick me, not this kid!" Then he was immediately sorry that he had allowed Tempy's insinuations to influence his thoughts.

"Pretty, baby-faced Pansetta! Why, she wouldn't try to trick anybody into anything. If she wanted me to love her, she'd let me, but she wouldn't try to trick a fellow. She wouldn't let me love her that way anyhow—like Tempy meant. Gee, that was ugly of Aunt Tempy to say that! . . . But Buster said she would. . . . Aw, he always talked that way about girls! He said no women were any good—as if he knew! And Jimmy Lane said white women were worse than colored—but all the boys who worked at hotels said that."

Let 'em talk! Sandy liked Pansetta anyhow. . . . But maybe his Aunt Tempy was right! Maybe he had better stop walking home with her. He didn't want to "get in trouble" and not be able to travel to Chicago some time, where his mother was. Maybe he could go to Chicago next summer if he began to save his money now. He wanted to see the big city, where the buildings were like towers, the trains ran overhead, and the lake was like a sea. He didn't want to "get in trouble" with Pansetta even if he did like her. Besides, he had to live with Tempy for awhile yet and he hated to be quarrelling with his aunt all the time. He'd stop going to the pool hall so much and stay home at night and study. . . . But, heck! it was too beautiful out of doors to stay in the house—especially since spring had come!

Through his open window, as he lay in bed after Tempy's tirade about the girl, he could see the stars and the tops of the budding maple-trees. A cool earth-smelling breeze lifted the white curtains, scattering the geometry papers that he had left lying on his study table. He got out of bed to pick up the papers and put them away, and stood for a moment in his pyjamas looking out of the window at the roofs of the houses and the tops of the trees under the night sky.

"I wish I had a brother," Sandy thought as he stood there. "Maybe I could talk to him about things and I wouldn't have to think so much. It's no fun being the only kid in the family, and your father never home either. . . . When I get married, I'm gonna have a lot of children; then they won't have to grow up by themselves."

The next day after school he walked nearly home with Pansetta as usual, although he was still thinking of what Tempy had said, but he hadn't decided to obey his aunt yet. At the corner of the block in which the girl lived, he gave her her books.

"I got to beat it back to the shop now. Old man Prentiss'll have a dozen deliveries waiting for me just because I'm late."

"All right," said Pansetta in her sweet little voice. "I'm sorry you can't come on down to my house awhile. Say, why don't you work at the hotel, anyway? Wouldn't you make more money there?"

"Guess I would," replied the boy. "But my aunt thinks it's better where I am."

"Oh," said Pansetta. "Well, I saw Jimmy Lane last night and he's making lots of money at the hotel. He wanted to meet me around to school this afternoon, but I told him no. I said you took me home."

"I do," said Sandy.

"Yes," laughed Pansetta; "but I didn't tell him you wouldn't ever come in."

During the sunny spring weeks that followed, Sandy did not walk home with her any more after school. Having to go to work earlier was the excuse he gave, but at first Pansetta seemed worried and puzzled. She asked him if he was mad at her, or something, but he said he wasn't. Then in a short time other boys were meeting her on the corner near the school, buying her cones when the ice-cream wagon passed and taking her home in the afternoons. To see other fellows buying her ice-cream and walking home with her made Sandy angry, but it was his own fault, he thought. And he felt lonesome having no one to walk with after classes.

Pansetta, in school, was just as pleasant as before, but in a

kind of impersonal way, as though she hadn't been his girl
once. And now Sandy was worried, because it had been easy
to drop her, but would it be easy to get her back again if he
should want her? The hotel boys had money, and once or twice
he saw her talking with Jimmy Lane. Gee, but she looked
pretty in her thin spring dresses and her wide straw hat.

Why had he listened to Tempy at all? She didn't know Pansetta, and just because her mother worked out in service she
wanted him to snub the girl. What was that to be afraid of—
her mother not being home after school? Even if Pansetta
would let him go in the house with her and put his arms
around her and love her, why shouldn't he? Didn't he have a
right to have a girl like that, as well as the other fellows? Didn't
he have a right to be free with women, too, like all the rest of
the young men? . . . But Pansetta wasn't that kind of girl! . . .
What made his mind run away with him? Because of what
Tempy had said? . . . To hell with Tempy!

"She's just an old-fashioned darky Episcopalian, that's what
Tempy is! And she wanted me to drop Pansetta because her
mother doesn't belong to the Dunbar Whist Club. Gee, but I'm
ashamed of myself. I'm a cad and a snob, that's all I am, and
I'm going to apologize." Subconsciously he was living over a
scene from an English novel he had read at the printing-shop,
in which the Lord dropped the Squire's daughter for a great
Lady, but later returned to his first love. Sandy retained the
words "cad" and "snob" in his vocabulary, but he wasn't thinking of the novel now. He really believed, after three weeks of
seeing Pansetta walking with other boys, that he had done
wrong, and that Tempy was the villainess in the situation. It
was worrying him a great deal; he decided to make up with
Pansetta if he could.

One Friday afternoon she left school with a great armful of
books. They had to write an English composition for Monday
and she had taken some volumes from the school library for
reference. He might have offered to carry them for her, but he
hadn't. Instead he went to work—and there had been no other
colored boys on the corner waiting for her as she went out.

Now he could have kicked himself for his neglect, he thought, as he cleaned the rear room of Mr. Prentiss's gift-card shop. Suddenly he dropped the broom with which he was sweeping, grabbed his cap, and left the place, for the desire to make friends with Pansetta possessed him more fiercely than ever, and he no longer cared about his work.

"I'm going to see her right now," he thought, "before I go home to supper. Gee, but I'm ashamed of the way I've treated her."

On the way to Pansetta's house the lawns looked fresh and green and on some of them tulips were blooming. The late afternoon sky was aglow with sunset. Little boys were out in the streets with marbles and tops, and little girls were jumping rope on the sidewalks. Workmen were coming home, empty dinner-pails in their hands, and a band of Negro laborers passed Sandy, singing softly together.

"I must hurry," the boy thought. "It will soon be our suppertime." He ran until he was at Pansetta's house—then came the indecision: Should he go in? Or not go in? He was ashamed of his treatment of her and embarrassed. Should he go on by as if he had not meant to call? Suppose she shut the door in his face! Or, worse, suppose she asked him to stay awhile! Should he stay? What Tempy had said didn't matter any more. He wanted to be friends with Pansetta again. He wanted her to know he still liked her and wanted to walk home with her. But how could he say it? Had she seen him from the window? Maybe he could turn around and go back, and see her Monday at school.

"No! I'm not a coward," he declared. "Afraid of a girl! I'll walk right up on the front porch and knock!" But the small house looked very quiet and the lace curtains were tightly drawn together at the windows. . . . He knocked again. Maybe there was no one home. . . . Yes, he heard somebody.

Finally Pansetta peeped through the curtains of the glass in the front door. Then she opened the door and smiled surprisingly, her hair mussed and her creamy-brown skin pink from the warm blood pulsing just under the surface. Her eyes were dark and luminous, and her lips were moist and red.

"It's Sandy!" she said, turning to address someone inside the front room.

"O, come in, old man," a boy's voice called in a tone of forced welcome, and Sandy saw Jimmy Lane sitting on the couch adjusting his collar self-consciously. "How's everything, old scout?"

"All right," Sandy stammered. "Say, Pansy, I—I—Do you know—I mean, what is the subject we're supposed to write on for English Monday? I must of forgotten to take it down."

"Why, 'A Trip to Shakespeare's England.' That's easy to remember, silly. You must have been asleep. . . . Won't you sit down?"

"No, thanks, I've—I guess I got to get back to supper."

"Jesus!" cried Jimmy jumping up from the sofa. "Is it that late? I'm due on bells at six o'clock. Wait a minute, Sandy, and I'll walk up with you as far as the hotel. Boy, I'm behind time!" He picked up his coat from the floor, and Pansetta held it for him while he thrust his arms into the sleeves, glancing around meanwhile for his cap, which lay among the sofa-pillows. Then he kissed the girl carelessly on the lips as he slid one arm familiarly around her waist.

"So long, baby," he said, and the two boys went out. On the porch Jimmy lit a cigarette and passed the pack to Sandy.

Jimmy Lane looked and acted as if he were much older than his companion, but Jimmy had been out of school several years, and hopping bells taught a fellow a great deal more about life than books did—and also about women. Besides, he was supporting himself now, which gave him an air of independence that boys who still lived at home didn't have.

When they had walked about a block, the bell-boy said carelessly: "Pansetta can go! Can't she, man?"

"I don't know," said Sandy.

"Aw, boy, you're lying," Jimmy Lane returned.

"Don't try to hand me that kid stuff! You had her for a year, didn't you?"

"Yes," replied Sandy slowly, "but not like you mean."

"Stop kidding," Jimmy insisted.

"No, honest, I never touched her that way," the boy said. "I never was at her house before."

Jimmy opened his mouth astonished. "What!" he exclaimed. "And her old lady out working till eight and nine every night! Say, Sandy, we're friends, but you're either just a big liar—or else a God-damn fool!" He threw his cigarette away and put both hands in his pockets. "Pansetta's easy as hell, man!"

XXVIII.

CHICAGO

CHICAGO, ILL.
May 16, 1918

DEAR SANDY:

Have just come home from work and am very tired but thought
I would write you this letter right now while I had time and
wasn't sleepy. You are a big boy and I think you can be of some
help to me. I don't want you to stay in Stanton any longer as a
burden on your Aunt Tempy. She says in her letters you have
begun to stay out late nights and not pay her any mind. You
ought to be with your mother now because you are all she has
since I do not know what has happened to your father in France.
The war is awful and so many mens are getting killed. Have not
had no word from Jimboy for 7 months from Over There and
am worried till I'm sick. Will try and send you how much money
you need for your fare before the end of the month so when
school is out in June you can come. Let me know how much you
saved and I will send you the rest to come to Chicago because
Mr. Harris where I stay is head elevator man at a big hotel in the
Loop and he says he can put you on there in July. That will be a
good job for you and maybe by saving your money you can go
back to school in Sept. I will help you if I can but you will have
to help me too because I have not been doing so well. Am working for a colored lady in her hair dressing parlor and am learning hairdressing myself, shampoo and straighten and give
massauges on the face and all. But colored folks are hard people
to work for. Madam King is from down south somewhere and

these southern Negroes are not like us in their ways, but she seems to like me. Mr. Harris is from the south too in a place called Baton Rouge. They eat rice all the time. Well I must close hoping to see you soon once more because it has been five years since I have looked at my child. With love to you and Tempy, be a good boy,

Your mother,

ANNJELICA ROGERS.

A week later another letter came to Sandy from his mother. This time it was a registered special-delivery, which said: "If you'll come right away you can get your job at once. Mr. Harris says he will have a vacancy Saturday because one of the elevator boys are quitting." And sufficient bills to cover Sandy's fare tumbled out.

With a tremendous creaking and grinding and steady clacking of wheels the long train went roaring through the night towards Chicago as Sandy, in a day coach, took from his pocket Annjee's two letters and re-read them for the tenth time since leaving Stanton. He could hardly believe himself actually at that moment on the way to Chicago!

In the stuffy coach papers littered the floor and the scent of bananas and human feet filled the car. The lights were dim and most of the passengers slumbered in the straight-backed green-plush seats, but Sandy was still awake. The thrill of his first all-night rail journey and his dream-expectations of the great city were too much to allow a sixteen-year-old boy to go calmly to sleep, although the man next to him had long been snoring.

Annjee's special-delivery letter had come that morning. Sandy had discovered it when he came home for lunch, and upon his return to the high school for the afternoon classes he went at once to the principal to inquire if he might be excused from the remaining days of the spring term.

"Let me see! Your record's pretty good, isn't it, Rogers?" said Professor Perkins looking over his glasses at the young colored fellow standing before him. "Going to Chicago, heh? Well, I guess we can let you transfer and give you full credit for this year's work without your waiting here for the examinations—there are only ten days or so of the term remaining. You are an honor student and would get through your exams all right. Now, if you'll just send us your address when you get to Chicago, we'll see that you get your report. . . . Intending to go to school there, are you? . . . That's right! I like to see your people get ahead. . . . Well, good luck to you, James." The old gentleman rose and held out his hand.

"Good old scout," thought Sandy. "Miss Fry was a good teacher, too! Some white folks *are* nice all right! Not all of them are mean. . . . Gee, old man Prentiss hated to see me quit his place. Said I was the best boy he ever had working there, even if I was late once in awhile. But I don't mind leaving Stanton. Gee, Chicago ought to be great! And I'm sure glad to get away from Tempy's house. She's too tight!"

But Tempy had not been glad to see her nephew leave. She had grown fond of the boy in spite of her almost nightly lectures to him recently on his behavior and in spite of his never having become her model youth. Not that he was bad, but he might have been so much better! She wanted to show her white neighbors a perfect colored boy—and such a boy certainly wouldn't be a user of slang, a lover of pool halls and non-Episcopalian ways. Tempy had given Sandy every opportunity to move in the best colored society and he had not taken advantage of it. Nevertheless, she cried a little as she packed a lunch for him to eat on the train. She had done all she could. He was a good-looking boy, and quite smart. Now, if he wanted to go to his mother, well—"I can only hope Chicago won't ruin you," she said. "It's a wicked city! Good-bye, James. Remember what I've tried to teach you. Stand up straight and look like you're somebody!"

Stanton, Sandy's Kansas home, was back in the darkness, and the train sped towards the great center where all the small-town boys in the whole Middle West wanted to go.

"I'm going now!" thought Sandy. "Chicago now!"

A few weeks past he had gone to see Sister Johnson, who was quite feeble with the rheumatism. As she sat in the corner of her kitchen smoking a corn-cob pipe, no longer able to wash clothes, but still able to keep up a rapid flow of conversation, she told him all the news.

"Tom, he's still at de bank keepin' de furnace goin' an' sort o' handy man. . . . Willie-Mae, I 'spects you knows, is figurin' on gettin' married next month to Mose Jenkins, an' I tells her she better stay single, young as she is, but she ain't payin' me no mind. Umn-unh! Jest let her go on! . . . Did you heerd Sister Whiteside's daughter done brought her third husband home to stay wid her ma—an' five o' her first husband's chillens there too? Gals ain't got no regard for de old folks. Sister Whiteside say if she warn't a Christian in her heart, she don't believe she could stand it! . . . I tells Willie-Mae she better not bring no husbands here to stay wid me—do an' I'll run him out! These mens ought be shame o' demselves comin' livin' on de womenfolks."

As the old woman talked, Sandy, thinking of his grandmother, gazed out of the window towards the house next door, where he had lived with Aunt Hager. Some small children were playing in the back yard, running and yelling. They belonged to the Southern family to whom Tempy had rented the place. . . . Madam de Carter, who still owned the second house, had been made a national grand officer in the women's division of the lodge and many of the members of the order now had on the walls of their homes a large picture of her dressed in full regalia, inscribed: "Yours in His Grace," and signed: "Madam Fannie Rosalie de Carter."

"Used to be just plain old Rose Carter befo' she got so important," said Sister Johnson, explaining her neighbor's lengthy name. "All these womens dey mammy named Jane an' Mary an' Cora, soon's dey gets a little somethin', dey changes dey names to Janette or Mariana or Corina or somethin' mo' flowery then what dey had. Willie-Mae say she gwine change her'n to Willetta-Mayola, an' I tole her if she do, I'll beat her—don't care how old she is!"

Sandy liked to listen to the rambling talk of old colored folks. "I guess there won't be many like that in Chicago," he thought, as he doubled back his long legs under the green-plush seat of the day coach. "I better try to get to sleep—there's a long ways to go until morning."

Although it was not yet June, the heat was terrific when, with the old bags that Tempy had given him, Sandy got out of the dusty train in Chicago and walked the length of the sheds into the station. He caught sight of his mother waiting in the crowd, a fatter and much older woman than he had remembered her to be; and at first she didn't know him among the stream of people coming from the train. Perhaps, unconsciously, she was looking for the little boy she left in Stanton; but Sandy was taller than Annjee now and he looked quite a young man in his blue serge suit with long trousers. His mother threw both plump arms around him and hugged and kissed him for a long time.

They went uptown in the street-cars, Annjee a trifle out of breath from helping with the bags, and both of them perspiring freely from the heat. And they were not very talkative either. A strange and unexpected silence seemed to come between them. Annjee had been away from her son for five growing years and he was no longer her baby boy, small and eager for a kiss. She could see from the little cuts on his face that he had even begun to shave on the chin. And his voice was like a man's, deep and musical as Jimboy's, but not so sure of itself.

But Sandy was not thinking of his mother as they rode uptown on the street-car. He was looking out of the windows at the blocks of dirty grey warehouses lining the streets through which they were passing. He hadn't expected the great city to be monotonous and ugly like this and he was vaguely disappointed. No towers, no dreams come true! Where were the thrilling visions of grandeur he had held? Hidden in the dusty streets? Hidden in the long, hot alleys through which he could see at a distance the tracks of the elevated trains?

"Street-cars are slower, but I ain't got used to them air lines yet," said Annjee, searching her mind for something to say. "I always think maybe them elevated cars'll fall off o' there sometimes. They go so fast!"

"I believe I'd rather ride on them, though," said Sandy, as he looked at the monotonous box-like tenements and dismal alleys on the ground level. No trees, no yards, no grass such as he had known at home, and yet, on the other hand, no bigness or beauty about the bleak warehouses and sorry shops that hugged the sidewalk. Soon, however, the street began to take on a racial aspect and to become more darkly alive. Negroes leaned from windows with heads uncombed, or sat fanning in doorways with legs apart, talking in kimonos and lounging in overalls, and more and more they became a part of the passing panorama.

"This is State Street," said Annjee. "They call it the Black Belt. We have to get off in a minute. You got your suit-case?"

She rang the bell and at Thirty-seventh Street they walked over to Wabash Avenue. The cool shade of the tiny porch that Annjee mounted was more than welcome, and as she took out her key to unlock the front door, Sandy sat on the steps and mopped his forehead with a grimy handkerchief. Inside, there was a dusky gloom in the hallway, that smelled of hair-oil and cabbage steaming.

"Guess Mis' Harris is in the kitchen," said Annjee. "Come on—we'll go upstairs and I'll show you our room. I guess we can both stay together till we can do better. You're still little enough to sleep with your mother, ain't you?"

They went down the completely dark hall on the second floor, and his mother opened a door that led into a rear room with two windows looking out into the alley, giving an extremely near view of the elevated structure on which a downtown train suddenly rushed past with an ear-splitting roar that made the entire house tremble and the window-sashes rattle. There was a wash-stand with a white bowl and pitcher in the room, Annjee's trunk, a chair, and a brass bed, covered with a fresh spread and starched pillow-covers in honor of Sandy's arrival.

"See," said Annjee. "There's room enough for us both, and we'll be saving rent. There's no closet, but we can drive a few extra nails behind the door. And with the two windows we can get plenty of air these hot nights."

"It's nice, mama," Sandy said, but he had to repeat his statement twice, because another L train thundered past so that he couldn't hear his own words as he uttered them. "It's awful nice, mama!"

He took off his coat and sat down on the trunk between the two windows. Annjee came over and kissed him, rubbing her hand across his crinkly brown hair.

"Well, you're a great big boy now. . . . Mama's baby—in long pants. And you're handsome, just like your father!" She had Jimboy's picture stuck in a corner of the wash-stand—a postcard photo in his army uniform, in which he looked very boyish and proud, sent from the training-camp before his company went to France. "But I got no time to be setting here petting you, Sandy, even if you have just come. I got to get on back to the hairdressing-parlor to make some money."

So Annjee went to work again—as she had been off only long enough to meet the train—and Sandy lay down on the bed and slept the hot afternoon away. That evening as a treat they had supper at a restaurant, where Annjee picked carefully from the cheap menu so that their bill wouldn't be high.

"But don't think this is regular. We can't afford it," she said. "I bring things home and fix them on an oil-stove in the room and spread papers on the trunk for a table. A restaurant supper's just in honor of you."

When they came back to the house that evening, Sandy was introduced to Mrs. Harris, their landlady, and to her husband, the elevator-starter, who was to give him the job at the hotel.

"That's a fine-looking boy you got there, Mis' Rogers," he said, appraising Sandy. "He'll do pretty well for one of them main lobby cars, since we don't use nothing but first-class intelligent help down where I am, like I told you. And we has only the best class o' white folks stoppin' there, too. . . . Be up at six in the mornin', buddy, and I'll take you downtown with me."

Annjee was tired, so they went upstairs to the back room and lit the gas over the bed, but the frequent roar of the L trains prevented steady conversation and made Sandy jump each time that the long chain of cars thundered by. He hadn't yet become accustomed to them, or to the vast humming of the city, which was strange to his small-town ears. And he wanted to go out and look around a bit, to walk up and down the streets at night and see what they were like.

"Well, go on if you want to," said his mother, "but don't forget this house number. I'm gonna lie down, but I guess I'll be awake when you come back. Or somebody'll be setting on the porch and the door'll be open."

At the corner Sandy stopped and looked around to be sure of his bearings when he returned. He marked in his mind the sign-board advertising CHESTERFIELDS and the frame-house with the tumbledown stairs on the outside. In the street some kids were playing hopscotch under the arc-light. Somebody stopped beside him.

"Nice evening?" said a small yellow man with a womanish kind of voice, smiling at Sandy.

"Yes," said the boy, starting across the street, but the stranger followed him, offering Pall Malls. He smelled of perfume, and his face looked as though it had been powdered with white talcum as he lit a tiny pocket-lighter.

"Stranger?" murmured the soft voice, lighting Sandy's cigarette.

"I'm from Stanton," he replied, wishing the man had not chosen to walk with him.

"Ah, Kentucky," exclaimed the perfumed fellow. "I been down there. Nice women in that town, heh?"

"But it's not Kentucky," Sandy objected. "It's Kansas."

"Oh, out west where the girls are raring to go! I know! Just like wild horses out there—so passionate, aren't they?"

"I guess so," Sandy ventured. The powdered voice was softly persistent.

"Say, kid," it whispered smoothly, touching the boy's arm, "listen, I got some swell French pictures up in my room—naked women and everything! Want to come up and see them?"

"No," said Sandy quickening his pace. "I got to go somewhere."

"But I room right around the corner," the voice insisted. "Come on by. You're a nice kid, you know it? Listen, don't walk so fast. Stop, let me talk to you."

But Sandy was beginning to understand. A warm sweat broke out on his neck and forehead. Sometimes, at the pool hall in Stanton, he had heard the men talk about queer fellows who stopped boys in the streets and tried to coax them to their rooms.

"He thinks I'm dumb," thought Sandy, "but I'm wise to him!" Yet he wondered what such men did with the boys who accompanied them. Curious, he'd like to find out—but he was afraid; so at the next corner he turned and started rapidly towards State Street, but the queer fellow kept close beside him, begging.

". . . and we'll have a nice time. . . . I got wine in the room, if you want some, and a vic, too."

"Get away, will you!"

They had reached State Street where the lights were bright and people were passing all the time. Sandy could see the fellow's anxious face quite clearly now.

"Listen, kid . . . you . . ."

But suddenly the man was no longer beside him—for Sandy commenced to run. On the brightly lighted avenue panic seized him. He had to escape this powdered face at his shoulder. The whining voice made him sick inside—and, almost without knowing it, his legs began swerving swiftly between the crowds along the curb. When he stopped in front of the Monogram Theatre, two blocks away, he was freed of his companion.

"Gee, that's nice," panted Sandy, grinning as he stood looking at the pictures in front of the vaudeville house, while hundreds of dark people passed up and down on the sidewalk behind him. Lots of folks were going into the theatre, laughing and pushing, for one of the great blues-singing Smiths was appearing there. Sandy walked towards the ticket-booth to see what the prices were.

"Buy me a ticket, will you?" said a feminine voice beside him. This time it was a girl—a very ugly, skinny girl, whose

smile revealed a row of dirty teeth. She sidled up to the startled boy whom she had accosted and took his hand.

"I'm not going in," Sandy said shortly, as he backed away,
wiping the palm of his hand on his coat-sleeve.

"All right then, stingy!" hissed the girl, flouncing her hips
and digging into her own purse for the coins to buy a ticket. "I
got money."

Some men standing on the edge of the sidewalk laughed as
Sandy went up the street. A little black child in front of him tod-
dled along in the crowd, seemingly by itself, licking a big chocolate ice-cream cone that dripped down the front of its dress.

So this was Chicago where the buildings were like towers
and the lake was like a sea . . . State Street, the greatest Negro
street in the world, where people were always happy, lights for
ever bright; and where the prettiest brown-skin women on
earth could be found—so the men in Stanton said.

"I guess I didn't walk the right way. But maybe tomorrow
I'll see other things," Sandy thought, "the Loop and the lake
and the museum and the library. Maybe they'll be better."

He turned into a side street going back towards Wabash Avenue. It was darker there, and near the alley a painted woman
called him, stepping out from among the shadows.

"Say, baby, com'ere!" But the boy went on.

Crossing overhead an L train thundered by, flashing its flow
of yellow light on the pavement beneath.

Sandy turned into Wabash Avenue and cut across the street.
As he approached the colored Y.M.C.A., three boys came out
with swimming suits on their arms, and one of them said:
"Damn, but it's hot!" They went up the street laughing and
talking with friendly voices, and at the corner they turned off.

"I must be nearly home," Sandy thought, as he made out a
group of kids still playing under the street-light. Then he distin-
guished, among the other shabby buildings, the brick house
where he lived. The front porch was still crowded with roomers
trying to keep cool, and as the boy came up to the foot of the
steps, some of the fellows seated there moved to let him pass.

"Good-evenin', Mr. Rogers," Mrs. Harris called, and as Sandy had never been called Mr. Rogers before, it made him feel very manly and a little embarrassed as he threaded his way through the group on the porch.

Upstairs he found his mother sleeping deeply on one side of the bed. He undressed, keeping on his underwear, and crawled in on the other side, but he lay awake a long while because it was suffocatingly hot, and very close in their room. The bedbugs bit him on the legs. Every time he got half asleep, an L train roared by, shrieking outside their open windows, lighting up the room, and shaking the whole house. Each time the train came, he started and trembled as though a sudden dragon were rushing at the bed. But then, after midnight, when the elevated cars passed less frequently, and he became more used to their passing, he went to sleep.

XXIX.

ELEVATOR

The following day Sandy went to work as elevator-boy at the hotel in the Loop where Mr. Harris was head bellman, and during the hot summer months that followed, his life in Chicago gradually settled into a groove of work and home—work, and home to Annjee's stuffy little room against the elevated tracks, where at night his mother read the war news and cried because there had been no letter from Jimboy. Whether Sandy's father was in Brest or Saint-Lazare with the labor battalions, or at the front, she did not know. The *Chicago Defender* said that colored troops were fighting in the Champagne sector with great distinction, but Annjee cried anew when she read that.

"No news is good news," Sandy repeated every night to comfort his mother, for he couldn't imagine Jimboy dead. "Papa's all right!" But Annjee worried and wept, half sick all the time, for ever reading the death lists fearfully for her husband's name.

That summer the heat was unbearable. Uptown in the Black Belt the air was like a steaming blanket around your head. In the Loop the sky was white-hot metal. Even on the lake front there was no relief unless you hurried into the crowded water. And there were long stretches of beach where the whites did not want Negroes to swim; so it was often dangerous to bathe if you were colored.

Sandy sweltered as he stood at the door of his boxlike, mirrored car in the big hotel lobby. He wore a red uniform with brass buttons and a tight coat that had to be kept fastened no matter how warm it was. But he felt very proud of himself holding his first full-time job, helping his mother with the room rent, and trying to save a little money out of each pay in order to return to high school in the fall.

The prospects of returning to school, however, were not bright. Some weeks it was impossible for Sandy to save even a half-dollar. And Annjee said now that she believed he should stay out of school and work to take care of himself, since he was as large as a man and had more education already than she'd had at his age. Aunt Hager would not have felt that way, though, Sandy thought, remembering his grandmother's great ambition for him. But Annjee was different, less far-seeing than her mother had been, less full of hopes for her son, not ambitious about him—caring only for the war and Jimboy.

At the hotel Sandy's hours on duty were long, and his legs and back ached with weariness from standing straight in one spot all the time, opening and closing the bronze door of the elevator. He had been assigned the last car in a row of six, each manned by a colored youth standing inside his metal box in a red uniform, operating the lever that sent the car up from the basement grill to the roof-garden restaurant on the fifteenth floor and then back down again all day. Repeating up-down—up-down—up-down interminably, carrying white guests.

After two months of this there were times when Sandy felt as though he could stand it no longer. The same flow of people week after week—fashionable women, officers, business men; the fetid air of the elevator-shaft, heavy with breath and the perfume of bodies; the same doors opening at the same unchanging levels hundreds of times each innumerable, monotonous day. The L in the morning; the L again at night. The street or the porch for a few minutes of air. Then bed. And the same thing tomorrow.

"I've got to get out of this," Sandy thought. "It's an awful job." Yet some of the fellows had been there for years. Three of the elevator-men on Sandy's shift were more than forty years old—and had never gotten ahead in life. Mr. Harris had been a bell-hop since his boyhood, doing the same thing day after day—and now he was very proud of being head bell-boy in Chicago.

"I've got to get out of this," Sandy kept repeating.

"Or maybe I'll get stuck here, too, like they are, and never get away. I've got to go back to school."

Yet he knew that his mother was making very little money—serving more or less as an apprentice in the hairdressing-shop, trying to learn the trade. And if he quit work, how would he live? Annjee did not favor his returning to school. And could he study if he were hungry? Could he study if he were worried about having no money? Worried about Annjee's displeasure?

"Yes! I can!" he said. "I'm going to study!" He thought about Booker Washington sleeping under the wooden pavements at Richmond—because he had had no place to stay on his way to Hampton in search of an education. He thought about Frederick Douglass—a fugitive slave, owning not even himself, and yet a student. "If they could study, I can, too! When school opens, I'm going to quit this job. Maybe I can get another one at night or in the late afternoon—but it doesn't matter—I'm going back to my classes in September. . . . I'm through with elevators."

Jimboy! Jimboy! Like Jimboy! something inside him warned, quitting work with no money, uncaring.

"Not like Jimboy," Sandy countered against himself. "Not like my father, always wanting to go somewhere. I'd get as tired of travelling all the time, as I do of running this elevator up and down day after day. . . . I'm more like Harriett—not wanting to be a servant at the mercies of white people for ever. . . . I want to do something for myself, by myself. . . . Free. . . . I want a house to live in, too, when I'm older—like Tempy's and Mr. Siles's. . . . But I wouldn't want to be like Tempy's friends—or her husband, dull and colorless, putting all his money away in a white bank, ashamed of colored people."

"A lot of minstrels—that's all niggers are!" Mr. Siles had said once. "Clowns, jazzers, just a band of dancers—that's why they never have anything. Never be anything but servants to the white people."

Clowns! Jazzers! Band of dancers! . . . Harriett! Jimboy! Aunt Hager! . . . A band of dancers! . . . Sandy remembered his grandmother whirling around in front of the altar at revival meetings in the midst of the other sisters, her face shining with light, arms outstretched as though all the cares of the world had been cast away; Harriett in the back yard under the apple-tree, eagle-rocking in the summer evenings to the tunes of the guitar; Jimboy singing. . . . But was that why Negroes were poor, because they were dancers, jazzers, clowns? . . . The other way round would be better: dancers because of their poverty; singers because they suffered; laughing all the time because they must forget. . . . It's more like that, thought Sandy.

A band of dancers. . . . Black dancers—captured in a white world. . . . Dancers of the spirit, too. Each black dreamer a captured dancer of the spirit. . . . Aunt Hager's dreams for Sandy dancing far beyond the limitations of their poverty, of their humble station in life, of their dark skins.

"I wants you to be a great man, son," she often told him, sitting on the porch in the darkness, singing, dreaming, calling up the deep past, creating dreams within the child. "I wants you to be a great man."

"And I won't disappoint you!" Sandy said that hot Chicago summer, just as though Hager were still there, planning for him. "I won't disappoint you!" he said, standing straight in his sweltering red suit in the cage of the hotel elevator. "I won't disappoint you, Aunt Hager," dreaming at night in the stuffy little room in the great Black Belt of Chicago. "I won't disappoint you now," opening his eyes at dawn when Annjee shook him to get up and go to work again.

XXX.

PRINCESS OF THE BLUES

One hot Monday in August Harrietta Williams, billed as "The Princess of the Blues," opened at the Monogram Theatre on State Street. The screen had carried a slide of her act the week previous, so Sandy knew she would be there, and he and his mother were waiting anxiously for her appearance. They were unable to find out before the performance where she would be living, or if she had arrived in town, but early that Monday evening Sandy hurried home from work, and he and Annjee managed to get seats in the theatre, although it was soon crowded to capacity and people stood in the aisles.

It was a typical Black Belt audience, laughing uproariously, stamping its feet to the music, kidding the actors, and joining in the performance, too. Rows of shiny black faces, gay white teeth, bobbing heads. Everybody having a grand time with the vaudeville, swift and amusing. A young tap-dancer rhymed his feet across the stage, grinning from ear to ear, stepping to the tantalizing music, ending with a series of intricate and amazing contortions that brought down the house. Then a sister act came on, with a stock of sentimental ballads offered in a wholly jazzy manner. They sang even a very melancholy mammy song with their hips moving gaily at every beat.

> O, *what would I do*
> *Without dear you,*
> *Sweet mammy?*

they moaned reverently, with their thighs shaking.

"Aw, step it, sweet gals!" the men and boys in the audience called approvingly. "We'll be yo' mammy and yo' pappy, too! Do it, pretty mamas!"

A pair of black-faced comedians tumbled on the stage as the girls went off, and began the usual line of old jokes and razor comedy.

"Gee, I wish Aunt Harriett's act would come on," Sandy said as he and Annjee laughed nervously at the comedians.

Finally the two blacked-up fellows broke into a song called *Walking the Dog*, flopping their long-toed shoes, twirling their middles like egg-beaters, and made their exit to a roar of laughter and applause. Then the canvas street-scene rose, disclosing a gorgeous background of blue velvet, with a piano and a floor-lamp in the center of the stage.

"This is Harriett's part now," Sandy whispered excitedly as a tall, yellow, slick-headed young man came in and immediately began playing the piano. "And, mama, that's Billy Sanderlee!"

"Sure is!" said Annjee.

Suddenly the footlights were lowered and the spotlight flared, steadied itself at the right of the stage, and waited. Then, stepping out from among the blue curtains, Harriett entered in a dress of glowing orange, flame-like against the ebony of her skin, barbaric, yet beautiful as a jungle princess. She swayed towards the footlights, while Billy teased the keys of the piano into a hesitating delicate jazz. Then she began to croon a new song—a popular version of an old Negro melody, refashioned with words from Broadway.

"Gee, Aunt Harrie's prettier than ever!" Sandy exclaimed to his mother.

"Same old Harriett," said Annjee. "But kinder hoarse."

"Sings good, though," Sandy cried when Harriett began to snap her fingers, putting a slow, rocking pep into the chorus, rolling her bright eyes to the tune of the melody as the piano rippled and cried under Billy Sanderlee's swift fingers.

"She's the same Harrie," murmured Annjee.

When she appeared again, in an apron of blue calico, with a bandanna handkerchief knotted about her head, she walked

very slowly. The man at the piano had begun to play blues—
the old familiar folk-blues—and the audience settled into a re-
ceptive silence broken only by a "Lawdy! . . . Good Lawdy!
Lawd!" from some southern lips at the back of the house, as
Harriett sang:

> *Red sun, red sun, why don't you rise today?*
> *Red sun, O sun! Why don't you rise today?*
> *Ma heart is breakin'—ma baby's gone away.*

A few rows ahead of Annjee a woman cried out: "True,
Lawd!" and swayed her body.

> *Little birds, little birds, ain't you gonna sing this morn?*
> *Says, little chirpin' birds, ain't you gonna sing this morn?*
> *I cannot sleep—ma lovin' man is gone.*

"Whee-ee-e! . . . Hab mercy! . . . Moan it, gal!" exclama-
tions and shouts broke loose in the understanding audience.

"Just like when papa used to play for her," said Sandy. But
Annjee was crying, remembering Jimboy, and fumbling in her
bag for a handkerchief. On the stage the singer went on—as
though singing to herself—her voice sinking to a bitter moan
as the listeners rocked and swayed.

> *It's a mighty blue mornin' when yo' daddy leaves yo' bed.*
> *I says a blue, blue mornin' when yo' daddy leaves yo' bed—*
> *'Cause if you lose yo' man, you'd just as well be dead!*

Her final number was a dance-song which she sang in a
sparkling dress of white sequins, ending the act with a mad
collection of steps and a swift sudden whirl across the whole
stage as the orchestra joined Billy's piano in a triumphant arch
of jazz.

The audience yelled and clapped and whistled for more,
stamping their feet and turning to one another with shouted
comments of enjoyment.

"Gee! She's great," said Sandy. When another act finally had the stage after Harriett's encores, he was anxious to get back to the dressing-room to see her.

"Maybe they won't let us in," Annjee objected timidly.

"Let's try," Sandy insisted, pulling his mother up. "We don't want to hear this fat woman with the flag singing *Over There*. You'll start crying, anyhow. Come on, mama."

When they got backstage, they found Harriett standing in the dressing-room door laughing with one of the black-face comedians, a summer fur over her shoulders, ready for the street. Billy Sanderlee and the tap-dancing boy were drinking gin from a bottle that Billy held, and Harriett was holding her glass, when she saw Sandy coming.

Her furs slipped to the floor. "My Lord!" she cried, enveloping them in kisses. "What are you doing in Chicago, Annjee? My, I'm mighty glad to see you, Sandy! . . . I'm certainly surprised—and so happy I could cry. . . . Did you catch our act tonight? Can't Billy play the piano, though? . . . Great heavens! Sandy, you're twice as tall as me! When did you leave home? How's that long-faced sister o' mine, Tempy?"

After repeated huggings the new-comers were introduced to everybody around. Sandy noticed a certain harshness in his aunt's voice. "Smoking so much," she explained later. "Drinking, too, I guess. But a blues-singer's supposed to sing deep and hoarse, so it's all right."

Beyond the drop curtain Sandy could hear the audience laughing in the theatre, and occasionally somebody shouting at the performers.

"Come on! Let's go and get a bite to eat," Harriett suggested when they had finally calmed down enough to decide to move on. "Billy and me are always hungry. . . . Where's Jimboy, Annjee? In the war, I suppose! It'd be just like that big jigaboo to go and enlist first thing, whether he had to or not. Billy here was due to go, too, but licker kept him out. This white folk's war for democracy ain't so hot, nohow! . . . Say, how'd you like to have some chop suey instead of going to a regular restaurant?"

In a Chinese café they found a quiet booth, where the two sisters talked until past midnight—with Sandy and Billy silent for the most part. Harriett told Annjee about Aunt Hager's death and the funeral that chill rainy day, and how Tempy had behaved so coldly when it was all over.

"I left Stanton the week after," Harriett said, "and haven't been back since. Had hard times, too, but we're kinder lucky now, Billy and me—got some dates booked over the Orpheum circuit soon. Liable to get wind of us at the Palace on Broadway one o' these days. Can't tell! Things are breakin' pretty good for spade acts—since Jews are not like the rest of the white folks. They will give you a break if you've got some hot numbers to show 'em, whether you're colored or not. And Jews control the theatres."

But the conversation went back to Stanton, when Hager and Jimboy and all of them had lived together, laughing and quarrelling and playing the guitar—while the tea got cold and the chop suey hardened to a sticky mess as the sisters wept. Billy marked busily on the table-cloth meanwhile with a stubby pencil, explaining to Sandy a new and intricate system he had found for betting on the numbers.

"Harrie and me plays every day. Won a hundred forty dollars last week in Cleveland," he said.

"Gee! I ought to start playing," Sandy exclaimed. "How much do you put on each number?"

"Well, for a nickel you can win . . ."

"No, you oughtn't," checked Harriett, suddenly conscious of Billy's conversation, turning towards Sandy with a handkerchief to her eyes. "Don't you fool with those numbers, honey! . . . What are you trying to do, Billy, start the boy off on your track? . . . You've got to get your education, Sandy, and amount to something. . . . Guess you're in high school now, aren't you, kid?"

"Third year," said Sandy slowly, dreading a new argument with his mother.

"And determined to keep on going here this fall, in spite o' my telling him I don't see how," put in Annjee. "Jimboy's over yonder, Lord knows where, and I certainly can't take care of Sandy and send him to school, too. No need of my trying— since he's big enough and old enough to hold a job and make his own living. He ought to be wanting to help me, anyway. Instead of that, he's determined to go back to school."

"Make his own living!" Harriett exclaimed, looking at Annjee in astonishment. "You mean you want Sandy to stay out of school to help you? What good is his little money to you?"

"Well, he helps with the room rent," his mother said. "And gets his meals where he works. That's better'n we'd be doing with him studying and depending on me to keep things up."

"What do you mean better?" Harriett cried, glaring at her sister excitedly, forgetting they had been weeping together five minutes before. "For crying out loud—better? Why, Aunt Hager'd turn over in her grave if she heard you talking so calmly about Sandy leaving school—the way she wanted to make something out of this kid. . . . How much do you earn a week?" Harriett asked suddenly, looking at her nephew across the table.

"Fourteen dollars."

"Pshaw! Is that all? I can give you that much myself," Harriett said. "We've got straight bookings until Christmas—then cabaret work's good around here. Bill and I can always make the dough—and you go to school."

"I want to, Aunt Harrie," Sandy said, suddenly content.

"Yea, old man," put in Billy. "And I'll shoot you a little change myself—to play the numbers," he added, winking.

"Well," Annjee began, "what about . . ."

But Harriett ignored Billy's interjection as well as her sister's open mouth. "Running an elevator for fourteen dollars a week and losing your education!" she cried. "Good Lord! Annjee, you ought to be ashamed, wanting him to keep that up. This boy's gotta get ahead—all of us niggers are too far back in this white man's country to let any brains go to waste! Don't you realize that? . . . You and me was foolish all right, break-ing mama's heart, leaving school, but Sandy can't do like us. He's gotta be what his grandma Hager wanted him to be—

able to help the black race, Annjee! You hear me? Help the whole race!"

"I want to," Sandy said.

"Then you'll stay in school!" Harriett affirmed, still looking at Annjee. "You surely wouldn't want him stuck in an elevator for ever—just to help you, would you, sister?"

"I reckon I wouldn't," Annjee murmured, shaking her head.

"You know damn well you wouldn't," Harriett concluded. And, before they parted, she slipped a ten-dollar bill into her nephew's hand.

"For your books," she said.

When Sandy and his mother started home, it was very late, but in a little Southern church in a side street, some old black worshippers were still holding their nightly meeting. High and fervently they were singing:

> By an' by when de mawnin' comes,
> Saints an' sinners all are gathered home. . . .

As the deep volume of sound rolled through the open door, Annjee and her son stopped to listen.

"It's like Stanton," Sandy said, "and the tent in the Hickory Woods."

"Sure is!" his mother exclaimed. "Them old folks are still singing—even in Chicago! . . . Funny how old folks like to sing that way, ain't it?"

"It's beautiful!" Sandy cried—for, vibrant and steady like a stream of living faith, their song filled the whole night:

> An' we'll understand it better by an' by!